DARK
&
BEASTLY
FAE

LOLA GLASS

Cover by Aura

Art by Samaiya

To all the fairytales that didn't give me a love story

CHAPTER 1

KIÈRDEN

I paced the elven throne room as foreign, violent magic pulsed on the back of my hand. The brand emanating wicked power glowed crimson, forming shapes and glyphs in the language of the lost gods.

"How do we buy ourselves time?" Vayme asked Alida, the elven leader we'd gone to for help.

The other two fae kings had woken up with the same veil-cursed markings I had. Those damn brands were calling cards for the twisted assassins that plagued our world, Evare, which made them death sentences.

"How do we *remove* the magic?" Ravv growled.

"Making it to the eclipse is the only way we know of to break the connection, but no one makes it to the eclipse," Alida said.

"There must be some solution," Vayme countered

"The only chance you have is to conceal your magic. They'll track you through your power's aura, because your connection to them is entirely magical. But there are women with life magic hidden in the human lands—I can sense them through the forests. Bind them to you as your mates, and their magic will hide yours until the eclipse passes, the bonds vanish, and the monsters are released from their vows."

We all went still.

"She's gone mad," I muttered.

"Absolutely insane," Ravv agreed.

"We didn't survive centuries of wars to be killed by our own people because of *mate bonds*," Vayme said.

"It's the only way. Take the humans, or die." She spun on her heels and strode out of the room.

Chapter 2

Nissa

I watched the thick berry vines grow slowly but steadily, right in front of me. Though I wasn't doing anything to make them grow, I could feel the flow of my magic and energy moving into the ground and plants around me.

I willed it to stop moving, but it didn't.

The fuzzy purple berries were already nearly the size of my fists, but they could still get bigger.

My backside was aching after an hour on the rotting, uneven log that functioned as a bench. My ankles and wrists throbbed too, thanks to the rough rope tying them to said bench.

"Take me back to my prison," I told the man behind me. The sharp tip of his massive steel sword was pressed lightly to the center of my back.

His name was Runo, and his weapon was an attempt at overcompensating for his lacking manhood. I knew from past experience that cracking a joke about it would only lead to him actually cutting me with the damn thing, so I didn't bring it up.

"You stay until Fina gives the word," Runo argued. After a long, long pause, he added, "And your home is not a prison. We've been very generous."

Fina.

My dear, dear mother.

The lovely woman who had shut me in a tower on the day of my thirteenth birthday, after I woke up in a room full of flowers, fruits, and vegetables. It had been nine years since then, and I still hadn't managed to free myself.

"A home you're not allowed to leave is a prison, Runo." I continued staring at the berries, willing them with every ounce of effort to *just stop growing*. It failed, of course. "And if you were really generous, I'd be able to leave this damned town. We both know you're not going to kill me, so put the sword away. Everyone would starve without me at this point."

And I was twisted enough that I'd laugh all the way to their graves if they did. A town that would lock me up to save itself the effort of growing its own plants or creating its own goods didn't deserve my pity.

Of course, that was only one of my controversial opinions. None of which had ever done a single good thing for me.

I was still a prisoner.

At least I had outgrown the nightmares about everything I'd lost when I became that.

Runo put the sword away.

A bell chimed at the edge of town, courtesy of my dearest mother, and Runo grabbed my hands by the rope attached to them. When he led me and my weak, shaking legs toward the next rotting log, I didn't fight him. Fighting had never gotten me anything but a little more pain.

"Try to focus on the melons. My wife loves melons," Runo told me, as he tied my ropes to the next rotting, uneven log.

I fought a snort at his words, moving a little on the log in an attempt to regain feeling in my ass.

The melons in front of me began growing rapidly, through no actual effort on my part.

Time passed slowly, as it always did. My energy trickled away bit by bit, draining into the ground, seeds, and existing plants.

A few more hours passed similarly before I was so completely exhausted that I may as well have been a corpse. Runo finally dragged me back to the tower he considered a generous home.

Fina hadn't come outside to see me.

Neither had anyone else, adult, child, or otherwise. They always hid when I was outside, afraid I might infect them with my magic. It was ironic, really, that they feared my power so completely while relying on it wholly to stay alive.

I itched to develop enough control over it to finally make an escape, but that seemed like an impossibility after so many years.

Runo stopped outside the short door that led into my prison, the same way he always did. He untied the bindings on my wrists and ankles, then unceremoniously pushed my exhausted body onto the stone staircase at the base of my tower.

My legs gave out, and my ribs collided hard with the harsh stone. I groaned at the pain of the impact as I saved my face from yet another bruise with my forearms. My waist-length, dark green hair sprawled over the tanned skin on my arms, and it took a minute to pull it all out of the way. Runo closed and locked the door behind me, as always.

After lifting myself to a seated position with my shaking arms, I slowly used the wall to ease myself up to my feet, tugging my dark, oversized dress out from beneath me.

Every muscle I had trembled with the force of my exhaustion as I made my way up the stairs one by one.

There were so many stairs.

And I was so damn tired.

Still, I climbed.

I'd find a way out that night, I promised myself with every step.

When the moons rose, I'd figure out how to leave the town, I vowed, as I put one foot in front of the other.

Left.

Right.

Left.

Right.

Finally, I reached the top of the stairs.

Relief made my shoulders sag as I stumbled to my bed, ignoring the growl in my stomach.

The town's bellies were full.

Their coffers were, too.

And yet there was never enough food left for me. They kept me hungry, drained, and trapped in a tower, all because it made their lives a little easier.

My back collided with the rough, old mattress, and I winced at the smell of mildew that assaulted my nose in retaliation. As despair began to creep into my mind, making my chest feel tight and my breaths shorten, I forced myself to close my eyes.

When I woke up, I'd figure out a way to get free.

It was a lie, but one I had to force myself to believe if I was going to survive another day.

I cracked my eyes open, rubbing the grit in them. The pit in my stomach was deep and yawning, desperate for food that wouldn't come.

My captors would feed me when they pulled me out at sunrise. They'd give me a bowl of some type of grain with a few chunks of the perfectly-ripe fruits and vegetables I'd grown the day before. I may not have been growing things on purpose, but I was damn good at my job. Or my magic was, I supposed.

The food would only give me enough energy for my magic to drain right back into the earth again, but I still yearned for it.

I eased myself out of bed, wincing in pain at the bruises on my ribs, both new and old. I had to believe that I was going to find a way out; there was no other option.

Slowly, I made my way to the window, and then sat down in the seat below it. The seat was simple and made out of stone like the rest of my tower, but compared to the uneven logs I was forced to occupy outside, it might as well have been a throne.

My gaze moved over the portion of town I could see from my window. Both of Evare's moons were up that night, so everything was illuminated enough for me to see the evidence of my magic. One of the moons rose every second night and the other only rose every third, so most of the time they were only up together once a week. I always looked forward to that night.

Thick, vibrant plants bloomed wildly and covered nearly every building, all of them for the sole purpose of growing food and spices. My mother made sure everyone cut down and burned all of the flowers and purposeless plants that grew.

I could see the two dozen guards walking the streets of the town, and silently went over their names, the way I always did. I knew which guards worked which nights every week, and which routes each of them followed.

Coby.

Kelle.

Ren.

Jor...

Who was that?

My gaze caught on a man I'd never seen before.

Even from my window, I could see that he was built much bigger and stronger than any of the others in town.

Though he strode down the middle of the street, he seemed to be dressed in nothing but a simple pair of shorts. Most men wore thick work pants and long-sleeve tunics to protect themselves from all three of our suns, even though those in my town were rarely forced to work in the heat of the day.

Most of them were rarely forced to work *at all*, thanks to me.

My brow furrowed, and I leaned closer until my forehead and nose met the window.

My gaze flicked between the newcomer and the other men and women walking the streets. He didn't seem to be carrying a weapon of any kind, and the way he moved was strange.

Or maybe not strange. Just different.

He didn't walk, or storm; he prowled, like the jungle cat I'd seen on the border where my town met the Broken Woods as a child. The shifters lived in the Woods, so entry was forbidden to any human who wanted to keep their life.

The prowling man in the streets halted abruptly.

My gaze may as well have been bound to him with rope, for all I could pull it away.

His eyes collided with mine, and even from my tower, I could see his gaze glowing dark blue with magic.

My heartbeat picked up.

Every magical being in Evare had eyes that glowed. It was one of the many things that set us apart from the humans and nonmagical creatures, which I was reminded of as I saw my own eyes glowing bright green every time I looked in the mirror.

The magical man didn't look away, and neither did I.

Something in my chest sort of... thrummed.

Was it hope?

Was it something more?

I didn't know, but I still couldn't take my eyes off him.

His gaze jerked to the side, in the same direction one of the guards was moving. After one last lingering look at the tower, at *me*, he began moving again, faster.

"What are you doing?" I whispered, my eyes following his form until he disappeared from my sight. My heart was still beating fast, and that strange feeling was still thrumming inside me.

Was he there to abduct me?

Veil, I hoped so.

A few other towns had tried to take me for my magic, but with the vast amount of food I grew for them, my mother's people had plenty of time to learn how to fight and plenty of money for weapons. They slaughtered everyone who came for me.

But no one with *magic* had ever tried to abduct me before.

I heard a snap as the metal lock on the door beneath me broke, and then a creak as the door opened.

My heartbeat picked up even faster.

Even if he was just going to kill me, I'd be grateful for the freedom of death.

I faced the top of the stairs head-on when the man cleared them.

His shoulders were back and his dark blue eyes glowed with emotion I couldn't read as they slid up and down my figure, slowly.

My face heated at the judgment that was undoubtedly running through his mind.

I was dirty, and shaking a little.

I'd been starving for years, though my oversized dress may have hidden that.

In contrast, he was absolutely gorgeous. Tall and strong, with lightly-tanned skin that practically shimmered with health. His ears were pointed, marking him as a fae, and inky black tattoos snaked up one of his arms before spreading over part of his chest.

His hair was thick and dark, the length of it curling around his ears. Most human men kept theirs cut close to their heads for ease, and the soft curl of the fae's made my lower belly tighten.

"Veil," I whispered. It was a curse, but also the word for the dividing line between our world and the world of our dead.

"You'll come with me," he said. Though his voice was low, it was flooded with the confidence and certainty of an extremely powerful man.

Then again, he was a fae.

I may as well have been a spider to him, ready to be crushed beneath the heel of his bare foot.

Perhaps if I hadn't wanted the same thing he did, I would've protested. Considering he was offering me the very thing I'd wanted for the past nine years, he wasn't going to hear an argument from me.

I crossed the room. My body felt weak, but I tried to control the shaking.

The fae looked a bit taken aback that I hadn't fought him on it, but turned and made his way back down the steps just as silently as I'd expected him to.

I followed him down, leaning heavily against the wall as I went. He was a lot faster than me, but I didn't call out to him. I was too worried about being caught by the guards outside.

He found me halfway down the stairs, his eyes narrowed as if he was about to lecture me for being slow.

"I haven't eaten much tonight," I whispered to him, not wanting to tell him how malnourished I was in case it would change his mind about taking me.

He grabbed my wrist, and an electric current raced through me. I jerked back, and he released me, looking down at his hand and then at my wrist.

My lips parted in shock as I watched a silver handprint appear where he'd touched me... and the shock became horror when it started to *glow*.

When I looked at the man, I found his entire palm glowing the way my wrist was.

Without further ado, he threw me over his shoulder and ran down the stairs, moving faster than I ever had in my life. He was out of the castle and weaving through the town a heartbeat later, dodging the streets with guards on them easily.

There would be a few guards at the gate, but I assumed the fae was going to avoid them somehow.

"Double moon nights are the best to be on duty," one of them remarked, as we neared.

My rescuer didn't slow down even a little.

"Best visibility," another man agreed. He took a bite of something that made a crisp crunching sound, and my stomach rumbled against the fae's shoulder just as he ran past a group of six guards.

They barely had time to gape at us before my rescuer disappeared around the edge of the gate, and ran right into the Broken Woods.

As their name suggested, the Broken Woods were dark and looked dead, despite the life and magic teeming within. The trees and bushes grew without leaves or color, the dirt beneath them was an eerie reddish-brown, and the bugs and animals that called the place home hunted without cover or fear.

My world was spinning madly, and plants sprouted miraculously in our wake. Tree branches grew thicker, and leaves swelled larger.

"Stop using your magic," the fae barked at me.

I had no control over my magic, but I couldn't say that aloud. What if the fae ditched me because of it? I had to wait until we were somewhere I could stay alive—like a city or town.

Not that a fae city would be much safer than the woods. I'd never seen one, but I assumed they were dangerous.

The sounds of my town rallying help and getting ready to pursue us faded rapidly. They had no chance of catching the fae man. There was a reason we humans stayed away from the many magical beings in Evare, and it wasn't because we had superior strength, speed, or senses.

My abductor slowed.

Fear made me nauseous.

Was he going to drop me because of my magic?

My world tilted, and then my ass landed on something warm and hard.

My entire body shuddered.

I looked down and realized what I was sitting on—then I shuddered again, harder.

It was one of the jungle cats. They were bigger than I'd realized, with sleek black fur that had just a hint of a pattern to it.

A massive, warm chest pinned me against the back of the jungle cat's neck as arms wrapped around me and hands gripped the creature's fur lightly.

The cat took off into the trees, hauling me further from my tower-shaped prison and the town that was the only place I'd ever known. Despite the shock and terror of the situation, only one thought rang through my mind:

I was finally free.

CHAPTER 3

NISSA

As the jungle cat carried us deeper into the forest, flowers bloomed in the dead-looking trees and bushes we passed.

And my energy?

What little I had left drained away steadily.

"By the veil, what is wrong with her?" a masculine voice growled, as my body grew too weak for me to keep holding my head up. It didn't sound like it was in my ear, but where else could it have been?

I had no idea who the voice was talking to, but it sounded like the male fae's.

"She's going to drain herself dry." The gorgeous male voice was getting angrier.

I wondered if I'd started hallucinating, because I honestly thought the voice might've been speaking into my *mind*.

My eyes closed just as the fae behind me jerked my head to the side and said into my ear, "Sillah ovim rett warum."

The words sent tingles down my spine.

I had no idea what they meant, but I could feel them start changing something. Something deep inside me, where my magic was.

Something like... my soul.

That couldn't have been right, though. Could it?

The tingles in my spine turned to pins, and I bit back a scream as the pain grew excruciating. The fae man pressed me against the jungle cat harder, all but *shoving* me against the creature while I bit my cheek.

Something swelled in my middle—something new, hard, dead, and *cold*.

Ice magic, something inside me seemed to whisper. The same icy power I knew all of the fae possessed.

But why could I feel a fae's power inside me?

The fae man swore into my ear, "Veil, what is wrong with your magic?"

I honestly had no idea.

My power was over plants, obviously. But why was it uncontrollable? And why did it drain me so damn fast?

I didn't have answers.

But the ice magic that had appeared in my chest did seem to be slowing the drain of my power, somehow. I was still absolutely exhausted to the point of not functioning, but relief had my body relaxing.

"What did he do?" I wondered, the thought clear and strong.

"Don't speak into my mind, human."

Apparently, I was right about hearing his thoughts.

At least I wasn't going insane.

"I'm not trying to. What did you do to me?" I asked.

"Mated us, temporarily. The next eclipse will remove the bond."

The words made my mind reel and my world spin even more than it was already spinning.

"Mated?" My words sounded faint.

He didn't bother confirming it. We both knew I'd heard him correctly.

I had no idea what it meant to be mated to a fae—I was fairly sure it was their version of marriage—but I also had no energy to figure that out.

So, I just leaned my head against the cat beneath me, closed my eyes, and let myself fall asleep.

The next time I opened my eyes, I found myself staring up at what looked like a chunk of solid ice. If I was surrounded by ice, I logically should've felt cold, but there was no chill in the air.

I sat up slowly, taking stock of my surroundings.

There was... ice.

Just ice.

Everywhere.

I seemed to be in some kind of box made of ice.

My hands lifted to the smooth, hard wall in front of me, and I pressed them against it as I fought my panic.

How was I supposed to get out?

With another look around, I determined that there was no sign of the male fae who captured me.

That wasn't good.

Had he left me for dead in the ice box?

I pushed against the walls, hoping to find the glass thin and easy to shatter. But when I poked, prodded, and smashed it, nothing happened.

I let out a huff as I began running my fingers over the walls and ceiling, trying to find a door of some kind to let me out.

I didn't find anything, though. There was no way out.

My breathing picked up at the thought of being trapped again.

Had I escaped one prison just to be thrown in another?

A moment before my fear turned into panic, the roof of the ice box slid away. The fae from before scowled down at me, then grabbed me by the arms and lifted me out.

He set me down and stepped away, but the weakness in my body had my knees knocking together. My legs gave out, and I stumbled.

Massive hands landed on my waist, catching me before I could fall on my face. My cheeks burned with embarrassment—and then my stomach growled.

Hunger wasn't the most present emotion, though, surprisingly enough.

Something about having his hands on my hips made me feel... calm. Settled, too.

A long moment passed before the fae finally peeled his hands off me and stepped away. Without glancing in my direction, he tossed a huge berry at me.

By some miracle, I caught it without falling again.

My eyes followed him as he walked across a patch of the woods, right over to a pair of jungle cats.

When he sat next to the bigger one and scratched the hair behind its ears, my eyes widened. It started to purr, and they widened even more.

"You're not human at all," the man said, his expression twisted in irritation again.

I looked down at myself.

I mean... I thought I was? Minus the magic and all.

"You have a bonded beast." He gestured toward the second big cat.

I blinked. "That's not mine."

"Don't call her *that*," the man said harshly.

"I'm not a fae. My parents were humans, and I'm pretty sure that makes me human too. I don't know anything about *her*." I gestured toward the creature. "We call them jungle cats."

He went silent for a moment.

I eased myself to the ground, then took a small bite of the berry. I'd never had one that looked like it before, but the black skin was silky and the inside was bursting with flavor.

"They are called esu," he finally said, pronouncing the word *ee-sue*. "Some choose to bond themselves as fae companions."

I gestured to the cat—the esu. "And she thinks I'm a fae, and that we're bonded."

"She does."

I blinked again.

Then I took another bite of my berry, deciding I really didn't have anything to say about that after all.

"No questions?" the man asked me, his expression growing skeptical.

"No." I took another bite.

His skepticism morphed into pure suspicion, but he didn't say anything else.

So I didn't either.

I just needed him to get me to a city. Surely they needed plant-growing magic in icy fae cities. Assuming I got there safely, I could find someone to give me a job and a place to live.

With a job and a place to live, I'd actually be free.

"You're not going to ask why I captured you? Or why I connected us?" His suspicion lowered his voice in a way that made my toes curl and my body warm.

I'd read steamy books before—plenty of them. But none had mentioned someone's voice making me attracted to them.

How unnerving.

I took another bite of my berry, and pointedly did not ask any of those questions.

"You're an assassin," he said, springing to his feet.

The female esu behind him gave a warning growl, and the one next to her joined in.

I eyed them suspiciously, not sure if they were growling at him or me. "If I'm an assassin, I've been very poorly trained."

His glowing blue eyes met my glowing greens.

It was time for a subject change. "Since I'm your captive, you should probably find a place to wash me up. And a new dress for me to wear."

He scoffed. "No."

Very well then.

I took another bite of my fruit.

He stalked back to the esu and sat down.

I found myself staring curiously at the glowing silver mark on his palm and the handprint on my wrist, but didn't ask the fae about it again. He didn't seem like he cared to answer my questions, and I was suspicious about the connection he'd apparently created between us.

A *mate* connection.

I definitely couldn't tell him that he'd saved my life by getting me out of my tower. He might think I owed it to him to be his mate or something.

The fae scowled at me while I finished my fruit. It wasn't anywhere near enough, but I didn't see any other fruit hiding in the trees or bushes nearby.

He rose to his feet while I was looking around, and when I turned my head, I found him climbing on his esu. "We're leaving," he said.

My bonded esu—whatever that meant—prowled over to me.

I eyed her uneasily as she bowed her head toward me.

"You want me to climb on?" I asked.

She bobbed her head.

Guess I was climbing on.

She crouched down, and I slipped onto her back. The moment I touched her fur, my eyes closed and I felt another tingle up my spine.

A soft, warm consciousness met mine before it spoke into my mind. *"Hello, Nissa."*

"Hello." My voice was a lot more tentative than hers. *"Do you have a name?"*

"I do. I am Brightfangs. The king's companion is Deathjaws. Most fae know us only by the first portion of our names."

So Bright, and Death.

Because that wasn't terrifying at all.

She began walking slowly. My eyes slid over to the fae man and his esu as I adjusted my grip on her fur. I didn't want to hurt her, but also didn't want to fall off her back.

"That fae is the king? Do you know his name?" I paused. *"And do esu have magic the way fae do?"*

"Esu have no magic of our own, though we are impervious to all other magics. And yes, Deathjaws' companion is Kierden Jirev, king of the tree fae."

She pronounced his name keer-din jer-ev.

"Tree fae?" I asked.

"There are three branches of fae. Though they all have the same magic, they organize themselves into three kingdoms. Esu know them based on where they live—they have a kingdom in the trees,

one inside the mountains, and a third on an island of ice a ways off the sea's shore."

Damn.

We humans had always been told that the fae just lived in the jungle called the Endless Wilds. I guess we weren't completely wrong, if they did have a city in the trees.

"Is that where we're going?" I asked her. *"To the tree fae city?"*

"Yes. Deathjaws asked me to follow him to Jirev."

"Is he the esu king, since Kierden is the fae king?"

She made a chuffing sound that reminded me a little of a laugh. *"Esu have no rulers. I respect his request because he carries your mate."*

"What does it mean to be a fae's mate?

"There haven't been mated fae for many centuries, but their mate bonds connect their minds and magic."

I grimaced. *"Why did Kierden start a mate bond with me then, even if it's temporary?"*

"I'm uncertain. I'll ask Deathjaws what he knows, but he may not share something if his companion doesn't wish him to. They've been bonded for many, many years."

"That's alright. It's probably better not to make him suspicious. I don't want to cause you any problems with him."

I felt her amusement roll across our connection. *"He'll expect me to inquire for you. Their companion is the top priority for an esu until he or she has taken a mate, and even then, the connection is treasured greatly."*

"Is that why you were in the forest waiting for me? How long were you there?" I asked.

"I felt drawn to you when you were a child, and have kept as close an eye on you as I could since then. The shifters didn't like having me in their woods, so I had to move around continuously and wasn't able to see you often."

"Well, thank you for waiting for me, Bright."

"It was a privilege, Nissa. I rather enjoy watching the plants bloom around you."

"I do too," I admitted. *"I just wish I had some control over it."*

"You will learn." Her simple belief in me was foreign after so many years in that damn tower. It made my throat swell with emotion.

She started to move faster—to jog, then to run, and we both grew quiet. My mind calmed as I felt the plants around me explode with life when we passed them.

I was fairly certain that our mate connection had given me access to Kierden's magic, because the pull of my power was still much slower, as if the ice was chilling it somehow.

That made me appreciate our bond, at least a little bit.

. . .

We ran until the moment my stomach rumbled. When it did, Bright stopped abruptly next to a fruit tree and murmured, *"You need to build your strength. You are very light."*

She was right, so I grabbed a piece of fruit.

Kierden and Death caught up to us a moment later. The king was glaring at me, and Death looked absolutely unsurprised to find me eating. I wondered if he'd spoken mentally to Bright when he realized she wasn't behind him anymore.

"Did you tell them my name?" I asked Bright.

I was coming to like our bond tremendously, already.

"I did not. Neither of them asked me."

Veil, what giant asses.

"Don't tell them, please. If the king decides he cares about my name, he needs to ask for it himself."

She chuffed again, and I took a large, irritated bite of the fruit in my hands.

Kierden scowled at me. "You ate less than an hour ago."

I took another bite.

It felt incredibly good to eat, even if I was still annoyed with the king.

"Deathjaws wants to know why your stomach growled so quickly after eating," Bright said.

"They starved me in the tower," I admitted.

Her rage rolled through me and made my own anger about the years of mistreatment feel justified.

At least I knew I had *someone* on my side.

"I'm sorry, Nissa. If I had known, I would've intervened sooner."

"It's not your fault," I assured her. *"I don't want Kierden to know, since he doesn't care enough to ask my name."*

She didn't seem convinced, but didn't argue. *"I won't tell Deathjaws or the king."*

"Thank you."

I finished the fruit, and then Bright carried me to a river to wash my hands. I ended up splashing my face and arms too, attempting to wash myself, and made her chuff a little more.

Both of us ignored the glaring males beside us.

When I was satisfied that I was as clean as I was going to get without a true bath, I slipped onto Bright's back again, and we took off.

The rest of the day was littered with stops for food. Kierden got angrier with every one of them—and I started to enjoy the power that Bright gave me just by existing even more.

I suppose *freedom* would be a better description than *power*, but freedom felt a lot like power after the life I'd lived.

When Bright stopped and let Death know that I needed to sleep, Kierden slipped off the back of his esu, muttering curses under his breath.

I pretended not to hear him cursing, settling on a fallen log with yet another piece of fruit in my hands.

With a moment of focus, he created another box-shaped shelter that had an opening on one side. If not for his magic tangled with mine, I'd have frozen to death in the structure. Thanks to his power, I didn't seem to feel the cold at all.

"Do you have any questions now?" the man growled at me as I ate.

"Not any you seem willing to answer." Maybe I had a bit of a stubborn streak. Or a lot of one.

He crouched in front of me and grabbed the mass of my hair, which hung to my hips in wild tangles. Before I could push him away, he'd lifted the strands away from my face and was studying my ears.

His expression twisted with some emotion I couldn't read. Probably distaste.

"I told you, I'm human." I pulled my hair out of his grip—or at least tried to. His hands tightened so I let go, shooting him a glare. "Don't touch me."

His eyes flashed with something I couldn't read, and he dug his fingers into my hair so he had complete control over my head's position. With a surprisingly gentle motion, he tilted my face back and exposed my neck.

I was too surprised and confused to bother fighting his hold.

Veil, maybe I was even a little turned on by it.

Bright gave a low, warning growl.

Death started growling with her, too, but neither of the esu made a move to attack either me or Kierden.

"Your magic is draining me dry," he said. "Cut it off, now."

"Give me a reason to."

He glared at me.

I waited.

Finally, he said through gritted teeth, "I started the mate bond because there was no way around it. I was told that I had to ignite the connection between us, or let myself be hunted by the Beast of the Endless Wilds."

It took a moment for the title to set in.

The Beast of the Endless Wilds...

"One of the elves' assassins is looking for you?" I asked, growing alarmed.

Everyone had heard stories about the three monsters the elves had created for protection. According to the legends I'd heard, the creatures had grown too strong and then slaughtered a lot of the elves. Supposedly, they now prowled all of Evare, glutting themselves on the blood and power of any living creatures they could find.

"*Hunting* me." He tilted his head toward a mark I hadn't noticed on the back of his hand—the glowing one that wasn't buried in my hair. "The assassins can only kill those they've been paid to hunt."

My face paled. "And he's coming for you?"

"He was, until I bonded us as mates. Now your magic will conceal mine from him until he manages to track me another way."

Veil.

"Why would being mates change that? What does being mates even mean?" I asked, wanting his definition on top of the vague one Bright had already given me.

"A mate bond is a death sentence among the fae. You'll keep it a secret until the suns' eclipse erases it. Our connection means nothing."

"If you want me to keep it a secret, tell me what it actually *is*. I want concrete answers, Kierden."

He growled, "A sealed bond is a soul-deep connection that lasts through this life and every other that follows after you cross the veil. What I created between us is the start of a connection. It will vanish entirely with the next eclipse unless you seal it by repeating what I said back—which you will not be doing."

Those foreign words ran through my mind as if I'd just heard them. *"Sillah ovim rett warumm."*

"Obviously I have no desire to do that. Why is a mate bond a death sentence? And how does it protect you against a *magical assassin*?"

He scowled, still holding his grip on my hair. "Because your magic is life and mine is death, yours is supposed to hide mine. A mate bond alters the magic of both parties. I'm sure you can feel my ice strengthening you even as your damned plants strangle me slowly. Centuries ago, a cult formed that killed anyone who created a mate bond. Most of the cult was eradicated afterward in revenge, but some of its members slipped through the cracks. All around Evare, they still hunt down mated pairs and slay them mercilessly."

My eyebrows shot upward. "So you're risking *my* life in an attempt to save yourself."

"Yes." He didn't seem apologetic, not even a little.

"Well, at least you can admit that you're a bastard."

He wasn't fazed by the insult. "I gave you the information you wanted. Now cut off the magic."

Guess it was time for honesty. "I can't."

His grip on my hair tightened, and I inhaled sharply at the suddenness of it. Maybe it should've scared me, but for whatever reason, I wasn't afraid of the king in the slightest. "*Now*, human."

A furry, muscular body slammed into the king's side. He released me as the force of the esu rolled both of them. My eyes widened as I watched the king and Bright wrestle, her teeth snapping insanely close to his throat while he only defended himself.

"*Enough.*" A low growl rolled through my mind, and my attention jerked to Death, who was prowling toward the wrestling fae and esu.

Kierden released his hold on Bright. She remained on top of him as she snarled into his face, snapping her teeth at him but not biting him. Fury edged her voice as she said, "*A male esu would sooner skin himself alive than physically hurt his mate. A king should know better, even if your bond is temporary."*

Kierden growled back, "Your companion is *draining me*, and I didn't grip her hair tightly enough to hurt her."

"She's draining you unintentionally, and humans are hurt more easily than fae," Bright snapped. *"You're the one who created the bond, so you have no one to blame but yourself. Apologize."*

"I am a *king*. I apologize to no one."

"No one except your bonded esu—and your bonded mate." She bared her teeth at him, sharp white fangs practically glistening.

"Brightfangs is correct. You bound yourself to the human; she's now your responsibility until the eclipse erases the bond," Death said, still speaking loud enough for me to hear him.

Kierden snarled, but when Bright climbed off him, he covered the distance between me and him in the blink of an eye. His eyes burned with some emotion I couldn't read—probably anger—and he gritted out, "I was not trying to harm you. It won't happen again."

Well, that was a terrible apology.

But something told me it was the best I was going to get, and I really didn't want Bright to kill the fae before he led me to his city.

So, I simply nodded once, and then went back to eating.

CHAPTER 4

NISSA

Kierden's temper calmed as he ate too. We didn't speak to each other, but Bright came over and sat next to me. I found myself stroking her fur and leaning against her.

It had been so long since I felt loved. Or even like I really mattered to someone. And in such a short time she had already made sure I had time to eat and sleep, and defended me too.

Kierden finished his food, then strode to the shelter he'd created. He folded himself inside easily, though he barely fit in the thing.

Not at all interested in snuggling with the big old bastard, I curled up on the ground.

"The shifters could hunt you down if you're not in the shelter," Bright said into my mind. *"You'll need to sleep next to the king."*

"That shelter is tiny," I protested.

"It takes a great amount of magic to keep a small shelter up while a fae sleeps. The king is sacrificing to protect you, even if it doesn't seem like it."

Oh.

"Can't the shifters still smell us, though? Or just follow the trail of my plants?"

"Yes. But when they see me and Deathjaws beside the king's shelter, they will leave. Getting past two esu and through thick ice walls would be no small feat, even for a pack of wolves."

So it was about intimidation on top of physical protection.

Which meant I was going to have to climb into that tiny shelter with Kierden.

I heaved a sigh, then stood up slowly and made my way over on reluctant legs.

The king was taking up the entire space, which meant I was going to have to literally lay on him.

Thanks to all my years in the tower, I had never shared a bed with anyone. Or kissed anyone. Or done anything else resembling sex. I'd read a bunch of books about it though, and overheard a long discussion about it between two adults when I was fifteen, so I had a basic understanding of how everything worked.

I'd tested some things on myself to make sure my body functioned, too. Everyone got lusty when an eclipse happened, so after I'd matured, I had the option of dealing with it or just waiting for the desire to fade. There had been a clear winner.

But that didn't make it any less intimidating to face the fact that I was going to have to literally climb on top of a king.

I walked up to the shelter and peered inside.

Yeah.

Wow.

Not much room.

A sigh escaped me.

The king gave me an annoyed growl but said nothing.

Part of me itched to warn him that I would figure out a way to literally rip him apart with my vines if he trapped me inside it alone again. For obvious reasons, I didn't do well with the thought of being imprisoned again.

But Kierden didn't seem to have realized the purpose of my tower, so I wasn't going to bring it up.

I bit my lip to hide my cringe as I climbed right in on top of the king. My dress tangled around my calves, and I knew I probably smelled terrible, but I ignored those things.

His chest felt insanely good beneath my hands.

I blamed that on the bond.

He gave me a dark look while I tried to get comfortable on top of him, and my cringe grew apologetic. "Sorry."

He muttered something I didn't understand, and I decided not to ask him about it as I finally collapsed on his chest. He was significantly bigger than me, so my forehead nestled against his neck.

"If you're an assassin, I'll make your end incredibly painful," he grumbled to me.

"If I'm an assassin, someone forgot to train me," I mumbled back against his throat. The brush of my lips on his skin made me shiver a little, and one of his hands landed on my lower back.

My toes curled, and I fought hard to ignore the warmth blossoming in my chest.

Something hardened against my belly, and my eyes opened wide.

He was turned on.

I'd turned him on.

"The damn bond is affecting my body," he growled at me.

"Same," I whispered back. I was pretty sure fae senses were good enough that he could probably smell my own growing desire. At least I wasn't the only one who had to deal with that awkwardness.

"You smell terrible," he added.

It sounded like he was trying to convince himself, though.

"So do you," I lied.

The smell on his skin was something deep and wild, and enticed me far, far too much.

I couldn't say that, though.

So we both just went to sleep.

The second day went a lot like the first one.

Kierden only spoke to me to grumble about how many stops I made him take. He didn't ask my name, or about my tower. I didn't ask about his kingdom, or his friends.

We just traveled.

And made an incredible number of stops for food, all of which frustrated the king. They made me happy, though.

We spent the second night the same way we had the first, with both of us denying our growing lust, and then began another day that went exactly the way the first two had gone.

We made it out of the Broken Woods as the last sun set on the third night, and camped near the beginning of a massive strip of desert called the Timeless Sands. It was a no-man's-land of sorts, where humans and magical beings would go to trade or simply coexist. I knew it was full of crime, and had never wanted to see it for myself.

It wasn't safe for the esu to sleep outside alone there, so we all packed together in Kierden's shelter. I ended up trapped between Bright and the king. Her sharp claws and teeth led me to burrow against Kierden, and despite a few grumbles, he didn't tell me to move.

. . .

We all woke up a little more tired the next day, and resumed our journey in grim silence.

Halfway through the morning, we approached a small town. Kierden made me wait a short distance away with the esu while he went in, and a few minutes later, he came back with a big bag of assorted food items for me.

I thanked him profusely, and it seemed to soften him a little. He was much less bitter as we made our way through the desert over the next two and a half days with significantly fewer stops for food. There wasn't much growing anyway, outside of the cacti. My magic made fruits and flowers blossom on the spiky green plants, but we didn't eat them.

Kierden and I didn't become friends, but I had stopped disliking him so much, at least.

He relaxed much more when we finally made it through the desert and into the fiercely-beautiful jungle that was the Endless Wilds. Thick, massive trees packed the space, climbing so far into the sky that they concealed the suns entirely. Their branches and trunks were wrapped in winding vines that brought color everywhere the vibrant human-sized leaves did not.

The esu moved much faster through the jungle, rejuvenated by the thick trees and branches they ran through. The jungle was their home, and it showed.

Kierden and I still didn't talk more than was necessary, or share stories. Despite the hardness I felt against my belly every night when we went to sleep, and the warmth that flooded my body, neither of us acknowledged our physical responses to each other again, or made an effort to become friends.

Both of us knew what our connection was—his selfish attempt to save his own life.

And even though I hadn't admitted it to him, he was saving my life too.

Eight days had gone by when Bright finally warned me that we were approaching the city. Just a little light from one of our moons filtered through the leaves and branches above us, but my eyesight seemed to have gotten better after the connection with Kierden was established, because I could see just fine.

Traveling with a grumpy fae king was a world's improvement from the awful life I'd lived in that tower. My belly was full and there were no ropes on my wrists or ankles. The temporary mate bond was a chain of its own, but for some reason it didn't feel like one.

Hope made my eyes bright and my stomach curl with excitement. Getting closer to a city where I could start fresh with a chance to actually live my life... veil, it was a rush.

Bright and Death moved quickly, climbing higher into the branches, and my eyes widened when I caught my first glimpse of the city.

It was literally built into the trees, with branches and bridges working as pathways, and buildings *carved* into the living giants around us.

The vines thickened as we neared them, slowly crawling further over the branches and trunks. Kierden muttered curses in his mind loudly enough that I could hear him damning my magic, and my lips curved upward.

"Don't destroy my city," he growled into my mind.

"Did you figure out how to control my magic while I wasn't looking?" I shot back.

He didn't answer.

The bastard knew I had no control over it, hadn't attempted to teach me any control, and had failed in every effort to gain control of it himself. He'd decided that he didn't think we would be able to use each other's magic unless we sealed the bond, which we agreed was *not* going to happen.

So yeah, whatever happened to his city was his own fault.

He added, *"Hide the handprint. If anyone asks why I brought you here, tell them the kings have planned an event in their competition that requires humans."*

My forehead knitted. *"An event? I'm not doing an event. What does that even mean?"*

As much as I liked to argue with him, I wasn't taking the risk of getting murdered by some cultist. I wrapped my non-glowing arm over my glowing wrist, so it covered the silver handprint entirely.

"The three fae kingdoms have been at war for centuries. The other kings and I finally settled on a peace treaty a few weeks ago, and had our people put together a bunch of violent events to

*turn the tension into entertainment. That's why there are so
many fae here right now—I was the only one willing to host it."*

My eyes scanned the trees around us with some amount of
interest as we passed group after group of fae, as well as a ton of
trees carved into buildings. There was ice scattered in the trees
too, used as bridges or decorations, though most of it seemed
to be in some stage of melting.

"So there are three cities-worth of fae here?" I asked him.

I had no idea how many fae there usually were to a city, so that
didn't really mean much to me.

*"Three kingdoms'-worth. Each kingdom has only one massive
city, which is always given the surname of its current king. There
used to be more before the war according to the legends, but very
few of us remember those times."*

*"And you left the other kings to run this whole thing so you could
come find me?"* My skepticism was heavy.

*"No. All three of us were targeted by the assassins so we all left to
hunt humans with life magic. There were enough people I
trusted here to run the city while I was gone and the events were
already planned, so it should've gone smoothly."*

I felt like *should've* was the most important word there.

"No one's fighting, so it seems to have worked," Kierden added,
looking past me as we continued.

"I guess that's a good sign..."

"It is. My people are fine."

I nodded, like I believed him. Maybe I did. I supposed that would be determined when I met whoever he trusted.

Assuming he didn't lock me up in his castle.

My body went stiff at the realization that was a possibility. *"Do you think he'll trap me again?"* I asked Bright.

"I don't know," she admitted. *"I can eat him, if he does."*

I tried to smile but failed.

Veil, I hoped he didn't try to lock me up.

If he did, the reluctant peace we had established was going to change drastically. I'd make that bastard regret picking me as his temporary mate, somehow.

The esu carried us through the city for nearly an hour before we reached the largest tree I'd ever seen. It had to be nearly as big as my town, with a house-sized entrance carved into the front. The tree's trunk was dotted with what appeared to be windows, and there were thick vines wrapped around many of its branches, growing toward the tree as if trying to reach out and touch it.

"This is the castle," Bright told me.

Flowers blossomed on the tree and vines as we passed through the open doorway, and Kierden growled a few more curses as we left them behind.

The king had to take at least some of the blame for that. It wasn't my fault he'd combined our magics, making mine work so much better than it usually did, without exhausting me so quickly.

Bright and Death carried us through a maze of hallways before we finally blazed through a door and into a massive room. We'd passed many fae, but none of them bowed at Kierden. They just looked at us both curiously.

The doors to the room closed behind us as I slipped off Bright's back. Kierden dismounted too, and we both gave the esu an affectionate scratch behind the ears while I looked around. The room was made entirely of wood, as was to be expected considering we were in a gigantic tree. The wood was smooth, and sealed with something that made it just a little shiny.

Without saying a word to me about where we were or exactly what we were doing there, Kierden strode toward a large pool of water off to the side of the room. It had to be at least as big as *two* of my tower.

"You're bathing," he told me as he went.

I blinked at him before my gaze moved back to the room. It had to be Kierden's room, based on the way he was making himself at home in it.

It was as big as three homes in my town, with a bed nearly the size of my tower up against one wall, a closet and bathroom up against the second, and the dark stone bathing pool in the corner where the other two met.

There were no windows, but that seemed intentional. It was large, and I could tell everything was made with the utmost luxury. But it seemed... bland.

Even my tower had a few simple decorations.

A pretty blue bowl someone had once sent with my food in it, on the table in the tiny kitchen I'd never had enough food to use.

A small ribbon I'd tied my wild, wavy dark green hair back with as a child.

The many books the town gave me to keep me from going insane.

Kierden's room had none of those things.

My gaze moved back to the pool. If that was his bathtub, perhaps small decorations weren't good enough for him.

My eyes widened when the king pushed his shorts down his thighs, and my cheeks began to burn. Part of me felt like I should jerk my head and look away, but the part of me that warmed every time we shared a bed kept me watching.

I wasn't sure what most men's asses looked like but damn, his was nice. I suddenly understood the appeal of a strong backside.

Self-consciousness had me patting my own.

Nope, it certainly wasn't strong. Or soft.

Guess I'd be leaving my dress on.

"I'll bathe after you," I told the king, finally forcing myself to look away as I turned and began to rub the fur on Bright's head. She leaned toward me as I did.

A chuff escaped her when Death crossed the room rapidly and then dove into the pool in a sleek motion. My gaze followed the esu.

Kierden ignored my words, disappearing beneath the water. Soap bubbled up to the surface as he scrubbed his skin and hair, and I wondered if it took him any effort to stop his ice magic from just leaking out and freezing the water. I couldn't imagine having an ice power that worked the way my own magic did. What a nightmare.

The king broke the surface after a moment and then climbed out of the pool while facing away from me. My eyes followed the water down his back, to his ass, to his thighs, and I found myself wiping at my mouth just to make sure I wasn't drooling.

I wasn't, thankfully.

He grabbed a towel I hadn't noticed hanging nearby and dragged it over his head. I watched as he dried his arms off, and then wrapped the towel around his waist. Before he was done, I made sure to turn myself toward Bright and focused on scratching her ears so he wouldn't realize I'd been staring at him.

But damn, I had really wanted him to turn toward me. I'd never actually seen a cock before, and I was curious.

That was probably a bad thing to admit, but I didn't particularly care if it made me terrible.

As he strode toward the closet, the entry doors burst open and a gorgeous fae woman walked through with a massive esu at her side. All she had on was a black binding around her chest and tiny black shorts. Relief gleamed in the woman's eyes, until they landed on me.

Then, that relief morphed into suspicion.

I knew she couldn't have been his mate, because Bright told me fae didn't take mates. And because of the bond between us, obviously.

But what if she was his lover? No one had told me whether or not fae took companions of the other sex without starting mate bonds.

She and Kierden looked nothing alike. Where he was tan with dark, wavy hair, she was pale with straight white-blonde hair that had streaks of vibrant blue throughout it, matching the electric blue that glowed in her eyes.

"You are a *fool*, Kier," the woman finally said, looking away from me and back at the king. "An utter fool. How could you think this was a good idea? Do you know how many brawls I had to fight to keep the damned Vuuths from tearing our city to shreds?"

"This was the *only* idea. You know it wasn't mine." He disappeared into the closet. "And I'm sure you enjoyed the brawls."

She followed him. Between the nickname and following him in while he got dressed?

Yeah, definitely his lover.

They didn't close the door behind them, so I could see the large gap between them as Kierden faced away from her. He pulled on a pair of tight, small shorts that must've been his undergarments, followed by longer shorts like the ones he'd been wearing since we met.

"My enjoyment doesn't matter because those brawls were unnecessary, and a risk to the peace. I—*veil*, what is on your hand?" She grabbed his wrist as he started to step past her, and there was a long moment's pause before she released it. "Damn. You really are mated."

"Temporarily."

She dragged a hand through the top of her smooth, straight hair. Since she was facing me then, I saw her expression grow considerate. At least until she wrinkled her nose while glancing at me. "You'll need to wash his scent off your skin, along with all that filth. You reek."

I blinked.

Was she talking to me?

She had to be talking to me, right? She hadn't even acknowledged me earlier though, so I was having a hard time believing it.

"She speaks, right?" the fae woman glanced at Kierden.

"Yes, Eisley." He pronounced her name *eyes-lee*. "I already told her to bathe. She didn't listen." The king wound some fabric around his hand, then tied it into place with his teeth. It covered his palm entirely, blocking the glow of our bond and the brand on the back of his hand.

"What's her name?"

My face heated at the way they were talking about me.

"I haven't asked." With that he strode out of the room, abandoning me to the mercy of his lover. Death followed him out, walking confidently at the king's side.

What a damn asshole.

CHAPTER 5

NISSA

The door shut behind them, and Eisley looked at me again. "He didn't even ask for your name? You were traveling for six or seven days, right?"

"Eight," I admitted. "And no, he didn't."

She scoffed. "Bastard."

At least we'd found something to agree on. That would ease the awkwardness of the mate-vs-lover thing. Considering the size of her muscles and the fact that she was a fae, I did *not* want to start a fight with her.

An ache bloomed in my wrist where the glowing handprint was, and I rubbed it absently.

"So, what's your name? You really do have to take a bath, by the way. I don't know how humans are about cleanliness, but you stink badly. And right now, wearing a male's scent on your skin when it's not the eclipse will get you gutted around here."

"I'm Nissa," I said. "I'd rather the king not know my name until he's asked me himself."

"Ohhh, good revenge. I won't tell him." She gave me a wicked grin.

I gave her a small smile in return. "Thank you. Are you guys together, or…" I trailed off, not wanting to come right out and ask if they were lovers.

"Nope." She made a disgusted face. "I'm the bastard's sister."

Ah.

Siblings.

I'd always hoped for one. After I'd lost my family altogether and been locked up, I would've taken just about anything. Sibling, aunt, grandmother, second-cousin-twice-removed…

"Are fae really lax about nudity?" I asked.

Her eyes glittered with amusement. "Yup. Everyone's seen everyone's naked bits a thousand times over. They all look pretty much the same, so no one's worried about it around here."

That made the closet situation more understandable, I supposed.

Since I really did want to take a bath, I headed to the pool. The fae I'd seen so far were extremely muscular, so their naked bits would *not* look like mine. Even as a child, I'd never been particularly skinny or strong. I was decidedly average among humans.

And something told me that I'd never look like the fae, even if I worked hard at it.

"I'll go find you something to wear. Oh, and there's another human woman in the castle with one of the other kings; you can meet her when you don't stink like my brother."

Eisley left the room without waiting for my thanks, and I noticed the gleam of metal on the inside of her thigh, and the back of her arm.

Were those *knives*?

Her bonded esu remained for a moment as he studied me with narrowed eyes. He was just as tall as Death but built even thicker, which made him even more terrifying somehow.

I shivered as he turned around and left the room. The door swung shut behind him, apparently built to allow the esu to come and go as they wished.

"I don't know whether to be nervous or excited about meeting another magical human," I said to Bright as I stripped and then sat down on the ledge of the pool. It had been a long, long time since I last swam. Even as a child, I hadn't been great at it. Something about deep water had always scared me a little.

"I'm sure it'll be nice not to feel so alone," Bright said, and then dove in the same way Death had. She swam around for a minute before climbing out and shaking off. My lips stretched in a grin as water splattered all over Kierden's perfectly-clean floors.

The ache in the marking on my wrist had graduated to a dull throb, which I wasn't a fan of, but I continued to ignore it. I didn't know what was causing it, so there wasn't anything I could do about it.

My thoughts churned a bit. *"I don't know what I'm supposed to do while I'm here. I'd like to find a place to belong, where I can be useful and comfortable. Kierden only brought me so he doesn't get killed before the eclipse, so what does that mean for me after the bond is gone?"* I slipped into the water and found a simple seat below the surface. The temperature was a perfect neutral, and the seat was just deep enough that the top of the water rose a little above my chin.

"The fae still have to grow their food. Make a deal to take over as the farmer and you could live a very comfortable life here or in any of the other fae lands. Kierden's kingdom is known to be the most welcoming as far as the fae go, so this one may be the best choice."

"What if I want to go back to the humans?" I asked. As the words left my lips, I knew that wasn't a possibility. I'd never forget what my own family had done to me, or how my town had starved me to feed and clothe themselves. I hoped they'd all rot without me, even though I knew it was a terrible hope to have.

But some awful feelings were reasonable ones.

"Then we'll find a better town, or a large kingdom."

"He only needs my magic, right?" I asked her. *"Maybe I can leave before the eclipse as long as I stay bonded to him. I don't really want to deal with his grumpiness for the next two and a half months."*

"If he was okay with that, he'd have left you in your town after starting the bond with you."

I wished she wasn't right.

When I found a bar of soap on a ledge near my face, I took it and used it to scrub myself clean. The throbbing in my wrist morphed into a sharp, stabbing pain.

There was nothing to be done about it though, so I did my best to ignore it as I surfaced and started to clean my hair.

After a few minutes, it grew so painful that I had to sit still and squeeze my eyes shut while I waited for it to pass.

"Are you alright?" Bright asked me. She was sitting beside the pool, drying off.

"I don't know. The handprint on my wrist feels like someone's stabbing a knife into it."

She gave a low growl. *"I'll find the king."*

"You don't need to—" I cut myself off as the door shut behind her, leaving me entirely alone.

I leaned the back of my head against the hard stone of the bathing pool and stared up at the wood ceiling.

The pain was bad enough to cloud my mind, and I focused on breathing as I waited for it to abate.

In.

Out.

In.

Out.

I didn't know how much time passed. Five minutes, maybe ten?

The doors to Kierden's room finally opened again, and Eisley came walking back through. She had a bundle of fabric tossed over her arm, and her angry-looking bonded esu at her side.

She frowned when she saw me. "Are you okay?"

I let out a slow breath, not sure I could speak through the pain.

After another minute passed I managed to say, "The handprint is causing me pain."

Her forehead furrowed and she glanced at her esu. He gave me a long glower before slinking away, and she patted his back as he left.

"We'll get Kier back in here."

I closed my eyes. "Sounds like a good way to make him angry."

She laughed. "He's usually angry. It's a requirement when you're a violent fae warrior who's been leading others into battles for hundreds of years. The anger keeps all the other shitty emotions at bay."

I supposed that was decent logic.

Choose anger, and you wouldn't have to acknowledge whatever else you were feeling.

"Sounds like a good way to make yourself miserable," I murmured.

She grinned. "Yup. Come on; let's get you dressed and moving, in case Kier ignores Sharp and we have to hunt him down."

"Sharp?"

"My bonded esu. Sharpclaws. I asked him to try to drag my brother back."

Ohhh.

"Bright went too," I admitted as I eased myself carefully out of the pool. Though I tried not to put pressure on my hand, I mostly failed. "She's my bonded esu, I guess. I'm still trying to wrap my mind around everything."

Eisley looked at my bare body with a deep frown. My face warmed as I quickly wrapped myself in the towel and attempted to wring my hair out with one of the flaps of it.

"Everyone knows Bright," she said.

"Really? Why?"

"She's something of a legend among the fae. She fought fiercely alongside us for centuries but always refused to bond with any of us. None of the fae have even heard her speak before, as far as I know. When there are no battles to fight, she disappears, and no one can find her. Two decades ago, she vanished entirely. No one had seen her since then until today."

Well, that took me aback.

"Why?"

Eisley shrugged. "People would always say that she was waiting for her companion to be born. The assumption was that she must have a soul-deep connection with her companion, one that lasted beyond the veil separating us from the life before and the life after. But fae aren't *born* anymore. We stopped procreating when the last of the mated pairs were murdered, shortly after my birth. Between the horror of that and everyone's focus on the war, there haven't been any new babies, so we didn't know if she'd ever meet her companion."

"People in my town would see an esu in the woods behind our village every now and then while I was growing up," I admitted. "I felt an itch to go out looking for her my entire life, but my father kept me in the village as a kid, and then..." I bit my lip. "Well, it didn't happen."

I didn't want to tell her about my tower.

I didn't even want to *think* about that prison.

"Does Kier know you've been starving?" Eisley asked, abruptly.

My throat swelled.

So much for avoiding that conversation. "I don't think so."

Eisley bobbed her head. "Don't tell him. Mated fae are driven to care for their mates, so he'd make you insane by shoving food in your face constantly until your ribs aren't showing." She handed me the fabric bundle in her hands. "This will probably be too big, but it'll cover more of your skin than anything else I have. We can find you some clothes of your own after tonight's event is over. It already went long, and with Kier there, it's going to go even longer."

I dropped my towel and dressed quickly. The fae undergarments were smaller than human ones, just triangles of fabric that barely covered the important bits, but I wasn't entirely surprised given what Eisley was wearing. She said they called their undergarments "scanties," and according to her, most of Evare did too.

The pain in my wrist was still pretty fierce, but it had faded enough that I could function a little.

"What's the event?"

Eisley grinned. "A wrestling tournament. We started with weapons two weeks ago, and finally graduated to physical fighting without anything but your hands."

Ah.

"It probably doesn't sound interesting to a human since you aren't as violent as us, but picture this—dozens of naked fae males rolling around together as they try to establish dominance."

My cheeks went pink at her description as I tugged the dress into place. It was made up of rich black fabric with a top that arched over my breasts, a voluminous skirt that fell to the middle of my thighs, and two puffy sleeves that wrapped around my biceps and only connected to the dress with tiny strips of fabric.

"You look absolutely killer in black," Eisley said with a grin. Despite what she'd expected, the dress wasn't too big at all. In my starving state, I was about as wide around as a healthy fae woman. I'd definitely be more curvaceous than them when I gained a little of the weight back.

My stomach rumbled as if on cue, and I spread a hand over my abdomen.

Eisley's grin vanished. "Let's find you something fattening to eat, and you can meet the other human."

She handed me a thick metal cuff bracelet to go around my wrist and cover up the handprint as we headed out of the room.

We found the other human woman sitting in a chair in the castle's dining hall when we got there. She was alone at a massive table, with enough plates in front of her to feed the largest family in my town.

She waved when she saw me and Eisley, barely taking her attention off the food in front of her to do so. She wore a dress similar to mine, but hers was tight and the off-shoulder sleeves were long. Her skin was paler than anyone's I'd ever seen, and her hair was somehow both red and orange at the same time.

Eisley gestured for me to sit next to the other human, so I slipped into a chair while she introduced us. "Laeli, this is Nissa. Nissa, this is Laeli."

"You're stuck with a fae bastard too?" Laeli asked me, cutting into something that smelled absolutely incredible.

My stomach rumbled again, louder. "Unfortunately."

She nodded. "It sucks, but at least there's food. I've been locked in a damn cellar since my magic came in, and my town rarely bothered to feed me."

"I was trapped in a tower," I admitted.

She shivered. "I do *not* do well with heights, so I don't envy you. Here." She pushed one of her plates over to me.

Eisley pushed the plate back to Laeli. "I'll have the kitchen make her something." She strode away, leaving me alone with the other human.

"So what's your power?" Laeli asked, pushing the plate back to me.

I didn't hesitate to grab one of the strange-looking pastries off it. "Plants. They grow around me, draining my magic in a few hours. I have no control over it."

Her eyes brightened with interest. "Damn, that's lucky. My magic is uncontrollable too, but it's fire magic. You can feel the heat in the air around me constantly, and if I feel anything too strongly, I burn."

"Really? Have you ever burned yourself?"

She grinned. "I've tried, but the fire dodges me. I'll show you if you're ever around when I light up."

I suddenly found myself hoping she would lose her temper.

The pain in my wrist suddenly flared, and I swore, clutching the pastry so tightly that it balled in my fist. "Veil."

"Do you have a handprint too? These things are miserable."
She tugged the top of her sleeve down, showing a silver
handprint on her bicep and then quickly covering it again. "I
told Ravv that if he keeps walking away from me, I'm going to
melt his ice castle. He's stayed close enough not to ignite the
pain since then. He's a grumpy asshole, but he doesn't seem to
want to start another war."

"Is walking away what triggers it?" I asked, taking a bite of the
crumpled pastry and then setting it on the plate so I could
massage the aching handprint.

"Mmhm. Physical distance seems to do it."

I nodded, considering what she'd said. It had started after
Kierden left me, so I supposed that made sense.

"Does it cause the men pain too?"

"Yep. They like to pretend they don't feel it, though. Makes
them feel better about themselves and those tiny fae cocks."

I snorted, and she flashed me a grin.

I'd never seen a man's cock before, but considering the size of
the fae men, it seemed safe to assume theirs wouldn't be small.

"Alright, here you go." Eisley stepped back up to me with a full
plate in her hands that matched one of Laeli's. I didn't hesitate
to dig into the unfamiliar food. If the plates they'd given us
were any indication, the fae ate a lot more bread, pasta, and
other grains than they did fruits and vegetables. I'd never
complain if there was pasta and bread on the table.

Eisley dropped into the chair next to me. "How's the wrist?"

I didn't want to complain about it, so I took a massive bite of a strange-looking bread instead of answering.

"Bad," Laeli said for me, popping another bite of something in her mouth. "Someone needs to find her king."

"He's helping judge the wrestling tournament, and maybe participating in it," Eisley explained. "We'll have to go to him."

Laeli shrugged. "Ravv must've skipped it."

"She said the men wrestling are all naked," I told her.

Her eyes took on a wicked gleam, and she stood suddenly. "Let's get you out of pain, then."

I laughed.

Eisley rolled her eyes. "Sit down."

"Why? We haven't established whether fae men are as possessive as their bonded animals are with their mates," Laeli pointed out. "This seems like the perfect opportunity to test the theory on someone who can't burn the jungle down." She pointed to me.

"I'm sure they're not possessive of females they're temporarily bonded to," Eisley countered.

"Kierden is disgusted by my ears, let alone the rest of me. Pretty sure possessiveness is off the table," I said.

Even as I said it, I remembered the feel of his hardness against my lower belly as I draped myself over his body.

"Everyone's just called him Kier since he was a kid. He doesn't even introduce himself as Kierden. Did he ask you to call him by his full name?" Eisley asked, her expression a bit curious.

My face warmed. "No. Bright introduced him to me that way, and I guess it stuck. He never actually told me his name himself."

"Hmm." She studied me.

I'd called him that out loud at least once or twice. Why hadn't he corrected me?

"I'm still stuck on the possessiveness, ladies. We need to know, and this is the perfect way to find out," Laeli said with a grin.

I shelved the nickname thing for later, deciding not to worry about it yet. Then I ate as much food as I could possibly handle... until the pain in my wrist grew so bad that I gave in, and off we went.

Chapter 6

Nissa

My pain faded as we approached the stadium that had been carved into a massive tree just for the sake of the violent events the fae had come up with to promote peace.

It was pretty late at night by then, but none of the fae seemed ready to go home. Between the moonlight, my improved eyesight, and some magical lights I didn't have a name for that floated around the forest at random, it was illuminated enough to see without a problem.

And thanks to my pain and the excitement I had about being in a new city, I wasn't anywhere near ready to sleep.

Eisley and I had both asked our bonded esu to come back and carry us to the stadium since they weren't making any progress with Kierden. Because Laeli wasn't bonded to an animal, she rode with Eisley on our way there.

"The wrestling has gotten brutal," Bright murmured to me as she wove through the city. *"Someone convinced Kierden to join, and it grew much bloodier. They do seem to be having a good time though."*

I grimaced at the thought of someone bleeding and *enjoying it*.

Then again, it didn't surprise me at all that the king could find it entertaining. He was technically a warrior, even if his kingdom wasn't at war at the moment.

"Tell me if it makes you nauseous. We don't need you throwing up all that food," she added.

I thanked her, though I was still trying to wrap my head around it. I'd known fae existed my entire life and yet still felt like I'd been dragged into an entirely new world.

Then again, a new world was far preferable to my old one. So, the fresh start was a good thing. Eisley had been kind, and that meant there was a good chance I could convince her to find me a job after the mate connection was gone.

My eyes caught on a clump of vibrantly-colored flowers as we passed them. They were... different. I hadn't seen anything like them in the Endless Wilds or in the Broken Woods before. Flowers seemed hard to come by in the parts of our land full of magical beings.

But around me, they were everywhere. In bright pinks, reds, yellows, and oranges. In deep purples, and vibrant blues.

The vines were thicker and longer, brighter green, too. The leaves on the trees looked even more massive than usual as well.

My magic was still leaking out of me. And maybe out of Kierden too, I realized when we reached the stadium. The outside of the tree that housed it had way more flowers than any of the others we'd passed, and more vines too.

Inside the stadium the fae were roaring wildly, standing on benches that had been carved along the outer edges as they watched someone fighting in the middle. Looking at the enthusiastic group from afar, I never would've guessed there was bad blood between any of them.

Then again, one could never get the full picture from afar. If they could, Kierden would've realized I was a starving prisoner when he found me in my tower. Though there was always a chance he *did* realize I had been a prisoner and simply didn't care.

Bright followed at Eisley's bonded esu's tail. His name was Sharp, if I remembered right.

Sharp maneuvered smoothly to an empty bench right outside the huge metal cage the men were fighting in. We were as close as you could possibly get to the fight, and I—

My thoughts cut off as I slid off off Bright's back and surged toward the thick bars separating us from the fighters.

That was *Kierden's* bare backside. *Kierden's* hair. *His* arm of tattoos, too.

He was wrestling a man who looked just as large as him, and the king seemed to have the upper hand. Or the other man was beneath him, at least.

"By the veil," I breathed as I watched the man buck fiercely against the king's hold. Kierden moved with him a bit, letting the other man fight, but had no problem holding his grip on the guy.

There was blood dripping off both of them in a few different locations, though I couldn't see the wounds that were the source of it. It smeared on the ground as they moved a bit, and finally, the man beneath Kierden slapped his hand on the smooth wooden floor four times.

The king released the other man and rose to his feet smoothly. His lips were stretched in a wicked grin, and the other guy wore a grimace that somehow looked satisfied.

The roaring of the crowd grew deafening as the king wiped blood off his lip, which was definitely swollen. That was the source of some of the blood, but only a little.

My eyes moved slowly over the king's figure and my body heated as I took him in. *All* of him. His cock wasn't hard, but damn, he was still impressive.

He had a few small bleeding cuts on his arms and legs but didn't pay them any mind. The fabric he'd wrapped around his hand still remained, looking a lot bloodier than it had the last time I saw it.

Kierden offered the losing fae a hand, which he accepted. When the king had helped tug him to his feet, he and Kierden clapped each other on the back in a strange hug before he strode off the field.

Kierden turned back to the crowd, opening his arms as he faced them in all his gorgeous, naked glory and roared, "Who will challenge me?"

The words nearly started a frenzy.

"Do it," Laeli whispered to me, nudging me with her shoulder. I had been so lost in looking at Kierden's body that I'd forgotten we were there to test the fae males' possessiveness somehow. "Challenge him. You know you want to roll around with all of that."

My body flushed hotter. "No thanks."

"He would *ravage* her," Eisley tossed out.

Laeli snorted.

I couldn't help but laugh.

Eisley just grinned at me before turning back to watch the fight.

Someone else came out to wrestle Kierden. I didn't see them, because in that moment, his eyes collided with mine.

My breath halted in my lungs, and my body went still.

Kierden's gaze went from bloodthirsty to just plain furious in a heartbeat. His gaze jerked to his sister as his lips twisted in a snarl.

His chest heaved as he turned to face the new challenger.

I couldn't bring myself to look away when he and the man lunged for each other.

They moved so fast it made me dizzy.

Strong arms flexed, thick thighs moved and rolled and swung. Blood spurted, and the fae's back hit the ground so hard I could almost hear the thud over the sound of the fae roaring all around us.

Kierden was back on his feet a moment later, wiping at his nose. He ignored the crowd, his gaze meeting mine once again with even more fury. His mind touched mine—the feeling was foreign and strangely intimate. It had been more than a week since we'd spoken mentally, and that had been an accident.

This was on purpose, and the connection felt thicker and stronger.

"Get out of here now," Kierden snarled into my mind. He was turning toward another challenger as he spoke to me, but he sounded *livid.* I'd never seen or heard him that angry before, and wasn't sure what to think about it.

A thick, furry head bumped lightly against my hip. When I looked beside me I found Bright there, with Death just a short distance away from her. *"Kierden asked Death to remove you from the arena,"* she murmured.

I opened my lips to protest, but noticed that my new friend was gone and looked at Eisley instead. "What happened to Laeli?"

"You didn't hear Ravv show up? He was pissed." She grabbed my arm. "We need to go. Kier looks like he wants to kill me, and I'm usually the one person he *doesn't* want dead."

"I'd rather stay."

"Please? We can find you something new to eat. And some clothes that actually fit." Despite asking politely, she was already tugging me away.

With a sigh, I slipped onto Bright's back. She streaked out of the stadium and then into the trees, once again following Sharp closely.

The marking on my wrist started to ache as we ran. It was still only in the throbbing stage when we stopped in what I assumed was their version of a marketplace. I hadn't been to a market since I was a kid, but I'd always liked walking around to see everything.

The marketplace was a cluster of small shops built into trees and connected by dozens of bridges, ropes, and vines. There were a few icy walkways too. Those were all dripping water, so I wouldn't be going near them. With a little bit of moonlight streaming down on everything through the trees and those small floating lights moving around lazily, it was absolutely beautiful.

My eyes moved over one shop after another. Some had food and others held clothing or jewelry.

Eisley climbed off Sharp's back and led me inside the marketplace. It was flooded with fae and their companions, and I noticed there were three different types of animals. The esu, along with creatures that looked like huge white bears, and some that seemed to be monster-sized wolves with gray fur.

"What kind of animals are those?" I asked Eisley, tilting my head toward one of the busiest shops.

"Oh, the giant wolves are called xuno. Xuno bond with the fae who live in Vayme Vooth's city beneath the mountains." She pronounced xuno like zoo-no. "The bears are called idorr, and they bond with the fae in the ice city on the ocean that Ravv Loire is the king of." She pronounced idorr, eye-door.

Ravv was the one bonded to Laeli, if I remembered right.

My lips curved upward at the irony of a male fae who lived in an ice castle needing a human woman with fire magic to keep him alive.

I didn't have anything to say though, so I just nodded in response to her explanation.

"We'll find clothes first. Hopefully, that'll give some of these fae time to marvel over the sight of a human so they don't obsess over you when we sit down," Eisley added.

I agreed, and then followed her into a building full of dresses and shorts. All of the clothing hung from large wooden racks around the space, which intrigued me. My fingers brushed the rich fabrics, all of them smoother and more luxurious than the clothes humans created.

My town had held me captive for so long to feed them and make money for them, yet they could still never have had the funds to buy the kind of clothing the fae wore. It was a pity for them but gave me a sense of satisfaction.

Perhaps that satisfaction wasn't healthy, but I didn't particularly care.

"What do you like?" Eisley asked, gesturing around the shop. Much of the clothing was brown, black, or dark green. I supposed the fae *were* warriors, and the dark colors would help them hide better.

But my eyes were drawn to the bright colors on a rack in the corner.

"I'm not particular," I told her, pulling my gaze back to the racks nearest to me.

"Nonsense. Everyone is particular, whether they like to admit it or not. Pick what you like, Nissa."

I reluctantly walked to the back of the room.

Having opinions was dangerous when you were a prisoner. And even if I technically wasn't one any longer, it still felt like I was. Not because of Kierden or Eisley, but because of the darkness in my mind.

"Just grab two or three dresses. We're going to get some meat on those bones fast, and then you'll need new clothes again," Eisley said.

I nodded and started looking through the dress options. They were short and fairly scandalous by human standards, but that didn't really matter. I'd get over showing more of my body sooner than I'd get over the years in the tower.

"Which ones are your favorite?" Eisley checked, when I'd gone through all of them.

"I'm not sure," I admitted, rubbing the silky fabric of an extremely pink dress between my fingers. It reminded me of the flowers I'd seen in the jungle—and the ones I'd watched my mother burn so many times from my tower.

She always said they were useless, but they *weren't*. They made me smile, and that meant something. It meant a lot.

Eisley sent me an exasperated look.

My lips curved upward a bit.

She wanted me to have opinions.

Fine; I'd have opinions.

I wanted the dresses that reminded me most of the flowers my village had cut down, the ones that had grown back again, again, and again. The ones that made me happy and brought me hope. I wasn't going to dress like a fae; I was going to dress like a damn *flower*.

"This one," I said, pulling the pink dress off the rack. Two more steps, and I grabbed a vibrant orange one, and a purple one too.

"Perfect. Reo?" Eisley looked toward the corner of the store.

A tall, elegant fae man stood up. He had a mass of curly hair that looked like actual art, brown skin, and eyes that glowed lavender. Unlike the other fae males, he was wearing full-length pants and a fancy shirt. "Ready?"

"Yup. Our little human is trying to gain some weight, so it'd be great if you could leave her some room to grow."

He nodded. "Of course."

They led me into a room, and I tried not to feel weird when the man measured my waist, breasts, and hips with a thin rope, making notes on the wall afterward. My eyes moved over the wood and widened when I saw hundreds of sets of measurements, all written in different places on the wall. Mine was off to the left side, near the middle vertically.

"You keep track of people's sizes?" I asked.

"Of course. I don't want to remeasure when they need new clothing. Take your current dress off; I'll need to alter the clothes while you wear them to make sure everything fits right."

I looked at Eisley for help, and she just nodded.

Guess I was stripping for the stranger.

He stepped back, and I pulled the dress on. He tsked his tongue as it fell into place. "You have a lot of weight to gain, my dear."

"Yeah." I bit my lip, cheeks flushing.

"You'll likely need new dresses in a week or two with more fabric than these have. They'll need to be custom. Do all humans starve?" There was some kind of morbid curiosity in his eyes.

"Reo," Eisley protested.

My cheeks flushed hotter. "It's fine. No, most humans don't starve. The others trapped me because of my magic, so they could use me."

His curiosity was replaced with pity. "Welcome to Jirev then, human. What's your name?"

"Nissa."

He wrote it next to my measurements while I tugged the first dress on.

I watched in fascination as he focused his magic to create needles of ice, threading them in the process. He began tucking some pieces of fabric and untucking others, altering the dress's waistline a bit and adjusting the sleeves so it fit my shorter human body. He left the skirt portion's length where it was when I asked him to, without batting an eye at the request.

A few minutes later, I changed into the next dress and we restarted the process.

After Reo had finished with the final two dresses, Eisley paid the man, and we headed out. Two of my new dresses and the one she'd loaned me were tucked inside a cloth bag that hung over my shoulder. My bright orange dress swayed around my legs with every step I took, and I found myself enjoying the soft motion.

Maybe I liked wearing bright colors and short dresses.

I was feeling much more hopeful about everything after my trip into the dress shop. Something about the way Reo acknowledged me without insulting me made me feel a little more confident in my place with the fae.

My connection with Kierden was... a mess. One I had no idea how to deal with. We were civil most of the time, but friendliness wasn't a thing. All we had was lusty attraction and forced nearness, both of which were useless considering that developing feelings for each other could lead to us getting *murdered*.

But my issues with him didn't mean I couldn't fit in with the fae. My magic was the opposite of theirs, but it was still magic. And I had a bonded esu who already saw me as one of them, so I belonged.

I did.

I just needed to stop letting my fear control me and start acting like it.

So, as we walked to a cute little shop serving food that looked like some type of soup, I lifted my chin and put my shoulders back.

I hadn't escaped the way I hoped, but I *had* escaped. I wasn't a prisoner anymore, and I wasn't hiding either.

We sat down at a table, and I felt eyes on me.

One glance around the room proved it was a *lot* of eyes.

A female fae brought fancy bread and bowls of soup over and set them down in front of us. We thanked her, and she gave me a curious look. "You're the human who's been growing flowers all over the Wilds?"

"Yep." I gave her a small smile, though part of me worried about her reaction.

She smiled. "I love seeing the flowers everywhere. You should stick around after your event with the other humans."

My smile grew at her invitation to stay, even though I wasn't thrilled to hear her mention the competition I was theoretically going to be participating in. "I'll think about it."

"Did you try the berries she already grew over by the falls?" someone asked at the table next to ours. "They were incredible."

Well, that made me feel good.

Hope swelled in my chest.

I was going to find a place. I was going to build a life. A real one, not one trapped in a tower, hoping for everything to change.

And I was going to find it with the fae.

CHAPTER 7

NISSA

As we finished eating, a male fae came and sat down beside me. My face warmed at the short distance between us—and the size of him.

Damn, fae men were huge.

I'd adjusted to Kierden enough that his size didn't affect me other than turning me on sometimes, but the same wasn't true for the rest of the fae. This guy in particular had long, curly dark blue hair gathered in a bun on top of his head, and light brown skin. His cheekbones were insanely chiseled, and he was grinning at me.

Honestly, the grin alone made me like him. I'd never had a man look at me like that.

"Hello," he said.

"Hi." I bit my lip to hide a smile.

He reached over and tugged my lip free from my teeth, his grin widening. Having his hands on my skin made me feel weird, to say the least. But also kind of good. "What's your name, Beautiful?"

Ohh.

He was pulling out the big guns already, calling me *Beautiful*.

"Nissa. What's yours?" I leaned back away from him, just so he didn't get any big ideas.

"Uron. How do you like our city?" He gestured to the forest around us.

"It's kind of magical," I admitted, glancing out the window nearby and looking at the vibrant jungle around us. Everything was even greener than it had been when I arrived, and I could see some of my colorful flowers out there too, bringing it to life even more.

"*Kind of* magical? You haven't seen enough of it, then."

My lips curved upward.

"Stop flirting with her, Uron." Eisley threw a chunk of her bread at him. He caught it easily, his grin stretching wider as he threw it back.

"Why? I'd like to be at the top of her list when she decides who to spend the eclipse with." He winked at me, and my smile grew.

He found me attractive, despite the way I'd been starving and imprisoned and everything else.

"It's two and a half months away. I don't think you need to start now," Eisley drawled back.

"Sure I do. Half the fae in Jirev already want to see what kind of plants Nissa grows when she climaxes."

Heat bloomed on my cheeks, and Eisley scoffed.

"Can I see your ears?" Uron asked, leaning closer to me.

I wasn't sure that I should be encouraging him after his last comment, but it wasn't like my ears were sacred. They were just ears. So, I pulled part of my hair up to let him see one of them.

The look in his eyes morphed to fascination as he reached toward it. My toes curled in anticipation...

But a massive hand grabbed his wrist out of the air, halting the fingers a breath from my ear. I recognized the fabric wrapped around that giant hand just as a low, masculine voice growled, "I didn't bring this little human here for you to bed her, Uron."

"We're a long way from any bed," Uron replied without missing a beat. His grin was back. "And I wasn't doing anything she didn't want."

A long, tense moment passed before Kierden finally forced himself to release Uron's hand. He didn't even look at me before saying flatly, "We're leaving."

I knew he was talking to me based on the complete and utter lack of respect in his voice.

Something inside me wanted to fight back against that lack of respect. To show him that I wasn't a damn object—that he couldn't order me around like I didn't matter.

"Careful, Nissa," Bright murmured into my mind. My intentions must've shown on my face.

"Why don't you guys have sex outside of the eclipse?" I asked Uron, remaining in my chair.

"To make procreating an impossibility," Eisley answered for him as she stood smoothly.

I leaned over the table a little, my fingers splayed wide. "There are herbs to prevent that, though. Humans have them, so I'm sure you do too."

Uron set his hand on mine and opened his mouth to answer.

Kierden ripped the man's hand away from mine, cutting him off with a sharp answer to my question. "We've been at war as long as any of us can remember. Sex was a risk because of the emotions it could inspire. It might create attachments with someone that could be snatched away at any moment."

"But you're not at war now."

The king jerked his head in a nod. "When our peace has been solidified, we'll reconsider our stance against protected sex outside of the eclipse."

"When?" a woman across the room asked.

His gaze lifted to her, and mine did too. We both wanted to hear the answer.

"What day, exactly? A lot of us would like to know," the woman clarified.

Damn, I was impressed with her for standing up to him.

And impressed with him for not seeming surprised or annoyed by her question. If anything, he became slightly less angry after she asked it.

Some of the fae in the shop weren't even from Kierden's city, but they looked curious about his answer too.

"As soon as the other cities have cleared out. I understand the importance of that freedom, and I appreciate the sacrifice all of us have made to prevent distractions and focus on the war. We lost far less fae than we could have."

The mood in the shop grew solemn with his words, and I saw a few of the fae nodding.

"Thank you," the woman said, bowing her head toward him slightly.

Others followed her, until most of the fae in the shop had bowed their heads toward him.

I didn't bow, of course.

The man didn't need any kind of confirmation that he was bigger, better, or more powerful than me. He already acted like I was nothing more than an annoyance.

"Let's go," the king said.

I didn't have to look at him to know he was talking to me.

And something told me it would be a bad idea to protest after everyone had bowed and so clearly offered him their support.

I grabbed my bag of clothes off the floor near my feet and stood. Bright and I followed Kierden, Death, Eisley, and Sharp out of the shop and then we all headed back to the castle.

Kierden and Eisley exchanged a few quiet, angry words before he growled at me to follow him and then strode in the direction I knew his room was.

"Do you think I can convince him to give me my own room?" I asked Bright. *"I'd like some space from the big, angry bastard."*

"I don't see why not." She brushed her side against my leg and I scratched her behind her ears. It was probably early in the morning, but I was still full of arrival-adrenaline, so I didn't feel tired.

Death held the door to Kierden's room open for me with his big, furry body, and I murmured a thank you as I passed him. He surprised me by brushing the side of his head against my thigh. It was the first bit of affection he had ever given me, and I had no idea what I was supposed to think about it.

I stopped abruptly inside the room when I slammed into Kierden's chest. As I stumbled backward, he caught me by the waist. After I was steady I tried to step away, but his grip tightened to stop me.

Bright and Death slipped past us to get into the room. She only brushed up against me, but he made a point of rubbing against both of us.

"What was that?" Kierden glared down at me.

I had to tilt my head back to look him in the eyes, and it made me feel small. That feeling was frustrating, reminding me of the way it had been between me and the men who held me captive in my mother's town. "What was *what*?"

"You and Uron, in the shop."

"He was just being nice." I took a step back, and the king held onto my hips as he stepped with me, ending up even closer to me.

I quickly took another step back, then another, and another, until I was pinned between Kierden and the wall. His body was hard against mine—every inch of him. It made me warmer than I cared to admit.

"You let him touch you," the king said, his voice low and his eyes nearly feral.

"He was being *nice* to me," I repeated, emphasizing the words. "I'm not against being touched by nice men."

The king's lips twisted in a snarl.

His chest was rising and falling faster, his thoughts spilling into my mind.

"She's mine."

"I want her."

"My female."

"My mate."

The thoughts moved rapidly, and so powerfully that it made my mind spin. It made me want him—and I couldn't let myself want him.

"What's my name?" I asked aloud, my attempt at halting his thoughts and my own lust.

The words leaking through our connection stopped abruptly, but he didn't answer.

"You don't get to care who I talk to or touch when you don't know anything about me," I said. "We're not friends or family, Kierden. I don't owe you anything. This mate bond isn't real, and—"

My words cut off when one of his hands lifted to my face. His fingers dug into my hair, his grip firm and unyielding. "A temporary bond is still *real*. Tell me your name."

The command only angered me further. "No."

He stepped closer, pressing his body harder to mine.

I inhaled sharply as his erection pressed against my belly, his muscles pressed close to me.

Maybe I wasn't as impervious to the difference in our sizes as I thought.

"Back up," I breathed.

He didn't back up.

Kierden tilted my head back further instead. "Tell me your name." His fingers started moving slowly on my hip, stroking my skin lightly.

Veil, it felt incredible.

My body grew warmer at the foreign pleasure of his touch. "No."

"I can smell your desire for me in the air, little human. You'll tell me, or I'll make you." His hand dragged down my hip until he found the bare skin on my thigh.

"Go ahead and try." He could do whatever he wanted to me; I wouldn't bend on that. But I was enjoying the way he was touching me far too much to even think about telling him to stop.

Considering what he'd said to his fae in the market, I knew he wouldn't actually have sex with me. And the closest he'd ever gotten to hurting me was gripping my hair, so he could go ahead and do his worst.

His eyes dilated with the challenge, and his erection throbbed against my belly.

Kierden took a small step to the side and then began sliding his hand further up my thigh. My body clenched and my toes curled as I silently urged him higher and higher.

His fingers dragged over the sensitive crease at the top of my thigh, and I took in a sharp breath.

The esu slipped past us again, and the doors swung shut behind them as they left us. I barely even noticed.

"Tell me your name," he said.

"No."

Finally, his fingers brushed the thin fabric covering my core.

My body trembled. My dress hid the view of his hand touching me, but the sight of it disappearing beneath my skirt was still overwhelming in the absolute best way.

"So wet for me already, little human," Kierden growled into my ear, stroking me again through the fabric. "You want my fingers on your bare skin, don't you?"

My chest rose and fell rapidly, his body still holding me in place.

I didn't answer him.

I couldn't admit it.

But we both knew he was right; I wanted more.

He continued touching me, his fingers slow but confident. The pleasure swelled inside me as I neared the edge of my climax.

But then his touch stilled.

"Tell me your name, and I'll let you shatter." His lips brushed my ear as they formed the words.

I clamped my mouth shut, still refusing to give him what he wanted despite my intense need and pleasure.

He wasn't going to break me, or manipulate me through sex.

I was stronger than my desire.

He gave me another slow, long stroke.

A soft cry escaped me and his fingers paused again, halting my pleasure.

I was so close.

So close.

"Tell me, or you'll have no release." His teeth caught my earlobe and dragged slowly, making me shudder.

"No." I clenched my jaw.

Kierden might have been the king, but he wasn't *my* king. He couldn't just give me orders and expect me to follow them.

If he wanted to know something, the bastard would have to earn it, or at the very least ask politely with a sincere apology for not giving a shit about me when we first met.

He released my earlobe, pressing lightly against my core again, making me bite back a groan.

But then he pulled his hand away.

My body cried out for more immediately, but I gritted my teeth against the desire.

Kierden stepped away from me. His eyes were hot as he lifted his fingers to his mouth and licked the wetness of my desire off of them.

"I need my own room," I managed to say without sounding too off balance.

"So you can lock a door behind you and give yourself that release? No. You'll stay with me."

"I'm *not* sleeping with you again."

"Then you'll sleep on the floor."

It was wooden, and obviously very hard. For the sake of my pride, I'd make it work. "Fine."

He strode to his bathroom, but I stepped between him and the escape. His erection was raging and throbbing enough that I knew he was going to take care of it as soon as that door shut between us. "If I don't get to touch myself, neither do you."

His eyes flashed with warning. "How do you intend to enforce that?"

Shit.

He had me.

Veil, this was a terrible idea.

"No closed doors between us."

His gaze turned wicked. "Lovely." With one smooth motion, he turned on his heels and strode to the bathing pool instead.

My throat swelled and my body flushed hotter as he stripped his shorts down his thighs, exposing his perfect ass to me. There was still dried blood on him, I realized, and my eyes narrowed in on one particularly bad cut on his back before he turned.

My mind may as well have frozen altogether when I saw his erection jutting out proudly and straining with the force of his desire.

His desire for *me*.

DARK & BEASTLY FAE

Veil, he was gorgeous.

There was another cut on his thigh, I noticed. It was worse than the one on his back.

"You need to see a healer," I managed to get out.

"No." He slipped into the water. I let out a breath when it covered him entirely so I wasn't staring at his cock anymore.

As much as I enjoyed staring at it, there was always the chance staring might lead to me doing something I shouldn't.

Like licking it.

Or somehow managing to fall on top of it.

"How much faster do fae heal than humans?" I asked. I found myself taking a few steps toward the pool, ignoring the ache of unmet need in my body.

"I don't know." He spread his arms out over the dark brown stone that made up the inside and outer ledge of the pool, leaning back against the wall of the bath and closing his eyes.

"How long will it take your wounds to heal?" I asked him, growing irritated.

"A day or two."

Knowing him, he probably refused to admit any weakness. So, he'd probably underestimated the healing time.

Even if he thought he'd heal twice as fast as he really would, three or four days was incredible for wounds like those. I'd seen a man die from a shallow cut as a kid, and he'd had the wound that killed him for nearly two weeks before the infection took him. My stomach still turned at the memory of how quickly he'd passed after the infection set in.

"At least let me look at them to make sure your life's not at risk," I said.

Kierden didn't argue, which I thought was probably the closest I'd get to an agreement out of him.

I sat down on the edge of the pool. When he didn't move to show me his back immediately, I debated for a few seconds, and then finally put a hand between his shoulder blades and pushed him forward.

The king reluctantly leaned for me and exposed a large wound. There was already a skin-colored patch of some sort covering it, but he'd bled through the fabric. It was stained dark red with blood, not thick enough to stop more from trickling down his back.

"Can I take this off?" I whispered to him, my stomach turning at the sight of the blood.

He grunted, which I decided meant yes.

Carefully, I peeled the bandage away from his skin. The edges were incredibly sticky, but I eventually managed to get it off.

"How did you get this from *wrestling*?" I asked.

He didn't answer right away.

I scooped up some water and used it to rinse the blood off his back, assuming he wasn't going to tell me at all.

After a few minutes, he finally said, "Vayme returned with his human female. He was struggling to control his rage so he challenged me to a match with weapons. First one to draw blood won."

I assumed Vayme was the king who still hadn't gotten back yet when I met Laeli. "You have *two* wounds."

Kierden couldn't have lost twice, could he? He was so damn massive.

"We fought seven rounds. He got the upper hand twice."

Huh.

He hadn't boasted about his strength or about defeating the other man, which seemed out of character.

Then again, all I really knew about him was that he was a king, a warrior, and angry about the fact that we'd bonded. And angry about being hunted by the Beast of the Endless Wilds, though I figured anyone would have the right to be angry about that.

"So you won."

"He was blinded by rage. It made him weak."

Oh, the irony.

When was Kierden not blind with rage when it came to me? And yet, it hadn't made him weak. Not that I could tell.

"Do you have more bandages somewhere?"

"In the bathroom."

I walked over to it. My eyebrows lifted when I found a simple basket full of fresh bandages sitting near the door. I supposed that a centuries-long war meant a lot of wounds, and a lot of wounds meant a lot of bandages.

After returning to Kierden, I kneeled down and splashed his cut again to clean the blood off.

"If the skin's wet, the bandage will stick to it," he said.

It surprised me that he told me before I asked. But I wasn't about to acknowledge any positive feelings for the man, so I changed the subject. "Why did you fight seven rounds if he kept losing?"

"His rage hadn't faded. He lost the first four, then had calmed enough to win the fifth. I took the sixth, and after he won the seventh, his female fainted. He thanked me for my help, then brought her back to the castle to rest."

My eyebrows shot upward as I finished wetting his back and then dried my fingers carefully on my dress. "Why did she faint?"

He grunted again when I pressed the bandage to his wound and held it in place. Part of me expected it to fall off when I let go, but it stayed where I put it as I withdrew my fingers. A quick brush against the edges of the fabric proved that it was stuck tight.

Kierden said, "She's tiny and weak. Not assertive, like you are. Apparently the blood scared her."

My heart went out to the poor girl. If she'd been trapped the way Laeli and I had, I didn't blame her at all for being *tiny*, *weak*, or *not assertive*. Then again, even if she hadn't been trapped, I wouldn't blame her for those things.

Not everyone needed to be strong or stubborn. I didn't even consider myself either of those things, yet apparently Kierden found me attractive. Or at least attractive enough to touch intimately without demanding anything in return except my name.

"I'm not assertive. I just don't let you mistreat me." I tried to change the subject. "Give me your leg. I saw a cut there too."

He grumbled a bit but pulled himself out of the water. I forced myself not to make eye contact with his erection as I studied the cut on his thigh. It was bigger than the last one, so I looked for a bandage to fit it.

"Of course you're assertive. You're wearing an orange dress. Do you know how many fae I've ever seen wear orange?"

My face warmed as I pulled out a bandage. "Only a few?"

He chuckled. "None."

And he was practically ancient, so there must not have been any fae who wore bright colors—at least not in his kingdom.

Whoops.

I leaned over his cut again. It was leaking blood, so I scooped water out of the pool in an attempt to clean it. "Eisley forced me to choose what I liked the most, so it's her fault."

"The fact that you wanted the color in the first place speaks volumes about your personality. You hold back your fire, but it still burns."

"I don't want to *burn* anyone," I countered.

"Does a fire hurt by merely existing?"

The words surprised me.

I didn't have an answer for him.

Kierden added, "Anyone who touches the fire or steps into it burns, but does that put the fire at fault?"

My forehead wrinkled and I forgot about his wound for a moment. "I think you're telling me not to hide my feelings and emotions, in a roundabout way."

He made a noise of amusement. "I'm telling you that you can't hurt anyone by existing, little human. If someone is hurt by opinions that don't belong to them, they are responsible for their own perceived pain."

"That sounds like a perspective only a fae can live by. Humans try not to hurt each other... or at least the good ones do." I finally looked back at his wound and washed it off again.

"Perhaps. Fae do not live our lives with an intent to please anyone; we simply exist. No one is responsible for someone else's peace of mind."

That sounded kind of nice, honestly.

I'd like to be able to see the world that way, even though I didn't know how I'd ever get to that point.

"You said you're always at war, though, and you guys are pretty violent. That's the opposite of peace of mind."

He chuckled. "No one remembers the purpose of our war. We didn't fight over offenses or glory; we fought because it was a tradition, and it's hard to break tradition after that many centuries. Now that we've broken it, we fight for fun."

I supposed I wasn't going to win that argument. Surprisingly enough, I didn't mind.

"So do you hate my orange dress?" I tried to lighten the mood. "I feel like you insulted it."

As soon as the words slipped out, I wondered why I cared what his opinions about my dress were. Maybe I was just trying to stir the pot or stoke the flames.

He grunted as I pressed the bandage over the cut on his leg and held it in place for a moment. "The color doesn't bother me, though I'd prefer you wear nothing at all."

My eyes widened, and then caught on the thick length of his erection.

I couldn't ignore it any longer.

My hand lingered on his thigh, though the bandage had to have been secured for ages already.

"There's curiosity in your eyes," Kierden said.

"I've never seen a cock before," I admitted, immediately biting my lip and regretting the admission.

"Then this is quite the treat for you," he drawled.

The sarcasm relaxed my shoulders, and I bit back a laugh as my face heated "Oh, yes."

He chuckled. The sound surprised me so much that I looked up at him, and found his lips curved upward slightly.

My gaze dipped back to his erection, and I wondered if the romance books had lied to me about the way cocks felt. Steel and silk, they always claimed.

The king said, "Your forehead is creased. You're welcome to throw a towel over me if I'm bothering you."

I warred with my conscience for a moment before deciding not to hide what I wanted. "Can I touch you?"

His gaze was scorching. "You don't ever need to ask to give me pleasure. The answer is always yes."

My face flushed. "I'm not going to get you off. You left me all frustrated."

"Tell me your name and I can fix that."

I blushed hotter. "No."

He chuckled. "You don't have to make me climax to touch me, little human. Any touch would be a pleasure."

I wanted to turn him down and walk away...

But I was too curious.

So I lifted my hand off his thigh and carefully wrapped it around his erection. He throbbed in my grip, just as hard and soft as the books had promised me. "Damn, Kierden," I whispered, trying to ignore the wetness between my thighs.

"You approve?" Kierden was trying to make a joke, I thought, but his voice was too low and intense for it to hit right.

"You feel incredible." I slowly slid my hand down the length of him, and then back up again.

He growled at me, catching one of my knees and using it to open my thighs for him. His fingers dragged over my core again through the fabric that covered them, and I bit back a moan.

I wanted more.

But I couldn't let him manipulate me.

Still... I could brush the edge a little. I could tease him, and let him tease me.

I stroked his cock again.

Kierden found my clit despite the fabric covering me, and teased me there.

I continued touching him lightly, careful not to take him too close to his release.

His fingers worked me harder and faster until they froze on my clit, leaving me right on the edge of my climax. I could've moved my hips and used him to get myself off...

But I wasn't ready to let him win, or to push him into taking our little standoff to further heights by claiming the pleasure I wanted so desperately.

So, I let go of him and stood up quickly. "I'm going to go to bed. On the floor, as promised."

His voice was strained when he growled back, "Don't take any of my pillows."

He would go back to being an asshole, I supposed. Not that he'd ever really stopped. I'd just... adjusted.

Yet as I walked to the empty corner of the room across from the bed, I found myself realizing that I didn't hate Kierden. Not even a little.

...Of course, that didn't mean I *liked* him. That would've been simply ridiculous.

CHAPTER 8

KIERDEN

My female was tossing and turning on the ground, making soft, adorable huffing noises. I was drying off slowly in my closet, fighting the urge to hang my little human's clothing up with my own.

Of course, I needed to stop thinking of her as mine.

And I needed to convince her to share the bed with me without giving away how fiercely I wanted her.

I wasn't sure how to make either of those things happen, though. I couldn't let myself truly pursue her the way my instincts were driving me to.

For a male like me, there was no uncertainty. She was either mine in every damn way, or she was nothing.

I wanted everything—yet claiming her the way I wanted to would be the end for both of us.

So I couldn't acknowledge my desire.

I had to keep pushing her away as much as I could manage.

Our bond would disappear when the eclipse came around, along with the itch of the wicked magic pulsing beneath my skin.

The urge to study the silver glow of our connection struck me hard. I gritted my teeth and grabbed a pair of shorts, tugging them up my thighs and then tucking my erection below the tight waistband. The fabric would hide nothing, but I didn't want to hide from my human.

Even more than I itched to be free of the Beast's wicked magic, I wanted to know her. I wanted to ask her questions and hear her perspective. I wanted to see her smile and make her laugh.

And I wanted to know her damn *name*.

But knowing any of that would only take me closer to the one thing I truly desired, yet could never have:

A mate.

It irritated me that she had refused to give me her name, though pride swelled in my chest for the same reason.

She wouldn't let me control her.

It was perhaps the most infuriating thing about her, as well as one of the sexiest.

Even in the Broken Woods, she had refused my control. She had dodged my every attempt to assert dominance over her, sometimes simply by meeting my eyes and saying nothing at all.

I crossed the room and slipped beneath the luxurious blankets on my bed. Though I had no real need for the luxury, it eased the nightmares that plagued me at times.

My human continued tossing and turning.

Even if I'd closed my eyes, I wouldn't have been able to sleep. Not while she was on the floor. I hadn't managed to fall asleep before her while we slept together yet, my mind constantly struggling with the driving need to touch her.

Her scent and skin had been difficult to resist in the forest, even with the dirt and sweat clouding it.

Now, resistance was growing impossible.

I ached badly for her. I'd never had urges intense enough to feel like *needs* before. The need to taste her. To touch her. To watch her unravel on my fingers, tongue, and cock, repeatedly.

My cock throbbed as I remembered the soft noises she'd made, and the way she'd reacted to my touch.

Veil, I'd wanted her.

I still did.

There was nothing to be done about it, so I tried to settle myself.

I was failing.

"Did the bond cause you pain when I was fighting?" I asked her, unable to stay silent while she continued tossing and turning. I could nearly *smell* the woman's frustration.

"Yes. Bright and Sharp tried to bring you back to me." She didn't bother acting like she was asleep—or hiding the frustration in her voice.

She had every right to be exactly that, too. I hadn't even thanked her for tending my wounds, something only a sibling or healer would normally do.

I had treated her terribly in my attempt to prevent myself from falling in love with her. As much as I despised hurting her, my intention had been to keep her alive.

But she would hate me if I didn't find another way to maintain that distance, and some part of me couldn't stand the idea of her hatred.

"Death didn't tell me until after the fights had ended. I'll stay closer from now on."

There was a long pause, as if she was debating what to say. She finally settled on, "Thank you." After another pause, she asked, "Did it hurt you too?"

The pain had melded with the twisted magic of the Beast's tracking rune on my skin. It was brutal, but I couldn't tell her that. Not while I still felt like a monster for leaving her hurting for so long.

"Some," I said.

"The fighting probably distracted you."

She was right, though she didn't sound happy about it.

The doors swung open, and both of our bonded esu came walking back into the room.

"That ended quickly," Death drawled into my mind.

My lips curved wickedly at his sarcasm. *"Asshole."*

"Likewise. I assume your female fought back when you pinned her?"

"She enjoyed it, actually."

He leapt onto the bed smoothly and silently, settling in the spot he always claimed as his. *"Not enough to sleep beside you again."*

"She wanted her own room. I said no. This was her revenge."

He chuffed, showing his amusement. *"I like her."*

"I noticed."

"You know how I feel about fae not taking mates. Perhaps you should reconsider your stance." He settled his head on top of his paws.

"You find it unnatural," I agreed. *"And yet you lack a mate of your own."*

"I've pursued Brightfangs multiple times, as you know. I only lack a mate because I have yet to persuade her to see things as they really are."

"And how are things really?"

"She belongs at my side, as I belong at hers. Our souls were meant to be one. The fact that our bonded companions are in the same position is merely a push from someone on the other side of the veil."

Death rarely waxed romantic, but when he did, he did it fiercely.

"So you want me to believe that my human and I are merely side characters in your love story?" I asked.

"Of course. And the fact that you just called her yours only emphasizes my point."

"I know. It's a problem I haven't gotten under control yet."

"Technically, the marking on both of you does declare her yours. So you're not wrong."

I let out a long breath. *"You are terrible backup, my friend."*

"As are you." He adjusted the position of his head. *"Figure out a way to tell Brightfangs that she's meant to be mine without angering her. She still refuses to believe me when I say it."*

"You'd be better off convincing her human."

"I intend to."

Off in my human's corner, I heard a cute, frustrated huffing noise.

She cleared her throat and said, "I'm not sure if you're aware, Kierden, but Death is trying to convince Bright that you want me in your bed."

I jerked my gaze back to the esu.

He batted his eyes, completely unrepentant.

"Death wants Bright in the bed and has resorted to underhanded methods to make it happen, then," I said.

Death stared at me for a moment before letting out a huff.

There was a long pause before my human finally said, "Oh."

She stood slowly, still wearing the same orange dress she'd had on earlier. Most female fae slept in their scanties, but I wasn't about to ask her to strip. The last thing I needed was more temptation where she was concerned.

She crossed the room, sat down on the edge of the bed, and gave Death a quick smile. "Can I talk to Kierden for a second?"

He pretended to consider it. Finally, he licked her on the nose and slipped past her, heading straight for Bright. The female esu made a noise of amusement as he plopped down beside her.

My human leaned closer and whispered, "We could share the bed for their sake. Bright insists she's not interested in him as a mate, but it sounds like she's been alone for a long time, so it could be a good thing."

I murmured back, "They can both hear you from here."

Her head whipped around, and her cheeks blushed a gorgeous crimson color that made me itch to run my fingers over them. I ignored the itch.

She turned back to me, glared, and announced loudly, "I'm sleeping over here."

Her feet slipped under the blankets, and both esu joined us on the bed.

Just as I turned toward my female, Bright stepped between us and plopped down on her belly in Death's usual spot. Her eyes narrowed suspiciously at me, but she said nothing. Esu could only broadcast their thoughts directly to their bonded fae or to everyone nearby, which meant she and I couldn't have a private conversation then and there.

Something told me that if we could, she would've threatened me.

"Get her name if you can," I told Death quietly.

"Mmhm." His eyes remained open and fixed on Bright as he settled on the other side of me and dropped his head on my abdomen so he could watch Bright.

My human's eyes shut. She snuggled up against her bonded esu, and her breathing leveled out almost immediately.

As I watched her chest rise and fall evenly, I was forced to admit the truth.

I *did* want my human to be my mate... even if I couldn't act on it without getting us both killed.

CHAPTER 9

NISSA

I expected Kierden to be gone when I woke up, but he wasn't.

When I silently studied him from between my cracked eyelids, I was surprised to find him awake *and* still there.

He was sitting up in bed with his back to the wall and a book open in his hands. The quick way his eyes moved over the paper told me he must've been enjoying whatever he was reading.

I assumed that meant he was reading fiction, and some part of me softened.

Something about the possibility that he liked fictional stories too made him seem more like a real person to me and less like a mystical fae warrior-king.

His dark hair was messy, and his eyes were a bit sleepy. Something about the complete and utter relaxation in his posture made me feel strangely comfortable waking up in bed with him. I could still hear both of the esu snoring softly, so we may as well have been completely alone.

Minus the large, warm, furry bodies in bed with us, of course.

Kierden's eyes flicked to me and lingered. He lifted a hand off his book and pressed a finger to his lips in the universal sign to be quiet.

"Did their snoring keep you up?" he asked me.

Feeling his words in my mind was soft, comfortable, and intimate.

I wasn't entirely sure I liked that.

Then again, some other part of me was absolutely certain I loved it.

"No."

"Yesterday was a long day, so I'm not surprised. At least we're not traveling today."

I felt like I'd woken up in an alternate universe, with an alternate man. Had a good night's sleep in his own bed really been all he needed to remember how to be kind? If so, we should've moved faster on our way back to his kingdom.

My stomach rumbled softly, and the esu didn't budge. They were the ones who had been running while we traveled, so I wasn't surprised that they were exhausted. I'd need weeks to recover if I did what they had.

I stretched quietly, then eased myself out of the bed and padded to the bathroom, using the facilities and then changing.

When I emerged, I stared for a long moment at the bed. It held a gorgeous, mostly-naked fae king who was reading quietly while snuggling with both of our bonded esu.

Nope, I could *not* get back in there without developing some kind of positive feelings about our situation.

Not wanting to stop and chat, I slipped out of the room as silently as possible. I was pretty sure I knew where to find the dining hall, and didn't think it was far enough away to cause either of us any pain.

My stomach rumbled again as I maneuvered through the halls.

"Where are you going?" the king asked, falling into step beside me.

Damn, I'd hoped for a little space from him. Guess that wasn't happening.

"The dining hall."

"Always so hungry," he said, his voice almost... playful.

That joke did *not* hit right.

If he'd been starving for as many years as me, he'd be hungry all the time too.

But I didn't want to explain anything about my past to him, so I didn't say anything.

We stepped into the dining hall and only found one other couple inside. I didn't recognize either of them, though that wasn't a surprise.

The woman's skin was as pale as Laeli's, and she was wearing a long human-style dress that looked supremely uncomfortable, though not dirty. Her vibrant blue hair was gathered up in a bun on top of her head. A few of the strands had escaped, and seemed to be blowing in a breeze that had absolutely no place in the castle.

I looked around the room, trying to find the source of the breeze, but found nothing.

Guess I knew what her magic was.

"That's Vayme and his human," Kierden murmured into my mind.

I nodded, and the king motioned to someone in the kitchen as he walked beside me to the table.

Like Kierden, Vayme had his hand wrapped in fabric. Unlike my king, Vayme wore a pair of thick-looking pants instead of loose shorts, and his brown hair was long and thick, falling to his shoulders. He had a beard too, but it was trimmed fairly short.

"Hi," I said, as we approached the table.

Vayme shot me a dark look, and Kierden's hand lifted to my lower back as he stepped closer to me. When I glanced sideways at him, I found his eyes narrowed and his body tensed.

Vayme finally lifted two fingers in a tiny wave and grunted before returning to his food.

"Hello," his human whispered, and my attention went to her. Veil, she looked even skinnier than me and Laeli. I itched to ask for her story, but didn't want to share mine while Kierden was right there. "I'm Kaelle," she said, pronouncing it kay-elle. "I think Laeli told me about you. You have plant magic, right?"

"Yep." I gave her a quick smile, and she returned it, though hers was faint.

My heart ached for her.

"He hasn't hurt you, right?" I sat down beside her, gesturing toward Vayme.

The king's glare snapped up to me.

Kierden murmured into my mind, *"Careful."*

"No, he's fine. Thanks for asking, though." She carefully took my hand and squeezed it lightly. I felt the breeze blowing off her skin, and it caught me off-guard a little, but I nodded.

Someone brought out plates of food for me and Kierden, and the tension dissipated as he pulled a chair up to sit next to me. Kaelle released my hand so I could eat, and silence reigned as all of us focused on our meal.

"Were you glad to leave your city?" Kaelle asked me softly, as she set her fork down next to her plate.

"I was," I said simply.

She nodded, and the empathy in her eyes as she looked between me and Kierden told me she understood the space I was trying to put between us. "Has he hurt you?" Her voice was barely above a whisper.

Kierden growled in response .

I put a hand to his chest, stopping him before he could rise to his feet. "No. He hasn't."

She nodded, eyeing the food that remained on Vayme's plate. He wordlessly moved some of it to hers.

I removed my hand from Kierden's chest and went back to my own food. "Do *you* miss your city?" I asked her. Though I'd been from a small town, it wasn't surprising that she'd come from a larger one. There were a lot in the human lands, and some of the biggest considered themselves their own kingdom. If any of those places had learned about my magic, they would likely have slaughtered my town to take me.

I'd wished for that to happen more times than I wanted to admit.

"Oh, I'm from a teeny, tiny town." She bit her lip, as if to stop herself from saying something, and then added a moment later, "Laeli was from a big city though, so I assumed you were too."

"My town was small, too. They would kill anyone who got close enough to try to take me."

Her eyes widened. "So they protected you?"

I wasn't sure how to explain without giving away things I didn't want Kierden to know. "In a way, yes."

"What does that mean?" His voice was low in my mind, making me shiver.

Kaelle nodded, her expression growing empathetic. She started eating the food Vayme had put on her plate, and all of us grew silent again. It hadn't passed my notice that the kings didn't really acknowledge each other, but the last thing I wanted to do was start another fight between them. Since they'd been at war for a long time, it wasn't surprising they didn't like each other much.

"Have you seen any sign of the Monster?" Kierden asked Vayme, finally addressing the other king as we all finished our food.

"Not yet." The man's forehead wrinkled, his gaze disturbed. "The ache in the rune has gotten worse, though."

"Mine as well," Kierden admitted. "I assume they'll search the human lands after losing the trail of our magic there, and then return here."

Vayme nodded slowly. "Should you need a place to hide, my castle is open to you and the female. They won't expect us to rely on each other."

"Thank you." Kierden's expression was grim, but his words did seem genuine.

"The Monster is hunting you?" I asked Vayme as my curiosity grew. He was another of the elves' assassins, who had all been created from other beings in Evare.

The twisted wolf shifter hunting Kierden was called the Beast of the Endless Wilds.

The dragon shifter assassin was called the Demon of the Weeping Skies. Everyone despised dragons for their harshness and cruelty, so he was the one I'd be most afraid of.

The Monster of the Aching Chasm had been a gargoyle before he was transformed.

At least, that was what the stories I'd heard as a kid said.

"Yes." Vayme dipped his head in a nod, though his face twisted in a scowl.

"Does he really drink *blood*?" Kaelle shivered a little as she asked.

"I don't know. Pray we don't find out."

Kierden grabbed his empty plate as well as mine. "The events will start in a few hours." He left me where I was as he went to return the plates to the kitchen.

Kaelle sighed.

I figured that was my cue to leave, so I gave the other woman a quick smile and fell into step beside Kierden as he strode out of the dining hall.

When we'd turned down another hallway, Kierden opened a door I didn't recognize and gestured for me to go inside. I stepped in, and he shut the door behind himself.

A quick glance around showed that we'd found an empty bedroom.

Hope beat in my chest.

Was he going to give it to me?

"About what happened in the forest," Kierden said, slipping his hands in the pockets of his shorts.

Oh.

This wasn't about the room at all.

"When you grabbed my hair?" I frowned.

"Yes. I don't apologize often, but..." He let out a long breath.

Was he actually going to apologize?

He hadn't even hurt me.

"It wasn't my intention to cause pain. I *am* sorry." His words seemed genuine, though unnecessary. And I believed him when he said he didn't apologize often, so I wasn't going to tell him not to.

"You didn't really hurt me, but thanks for apologizing."

Relief crossed his face, and he changed the subject abruptly. I figured he was glad to be done talking about it. "I plan to spend all day at the event. You're coming, to avoid the pain of our separation."

Guess he was back to giving me orders. I didn't mind it as much as I had the day before, for some reason. "Alright. Does everyone always fight naked?"

He scowled. "At the events, yes."

I flashed him a smile. "Then it's my lucky day."

His scowl deepened.

I hoped he was remembering the way I'd touched him the night before, because I was.

He opened the door for me, still looking unhappy about my question.

My lips curved upward at his discomfort, though. At least I could bother him as much as he bothered me.

We headed out shortly after that, taking a walking path through the city so our bonded esu could continue catching up on sleep. There were fae with their companion animals everywhere, and a lot of their eyes lit up when they saw me and Kierden. Many of them were picking fruit, and some even had flowers tucked behind their ears. I wasn't sure which of us they were smiling at, but considering the silent, respectful nods they gave him, I assumed it was me.

Walking through the trees and over bridge after bridge connecting them was fascinating. I looked at everything, unable to decide what to focus on. It really was an entirely different world than the one I'd grown up in.

"My farmers have already asked that you be assigned to their fields in the hours since you've been here," Kierden told me, after we'd walked for a while in silence. It wasn't a short distance, but I appreciated the chance to get out and move.

"Really? That would be perfect." I smiled, waving back at a fae woman who waved at me.

Kierden said into my mind. *"It would not be perfect. If you focus your magic on our fields, you'll drain us both faster."*

"I have no control over my magic. Focusing it doesn't do anything, remember? It drains consistently into whatever is around me, so if I lived on a field, I could grow food. Then your people wouldn't want me to leave."

His scowl deepened. *"You could learn control."*

"How? I had nothing but time to learn it in my town. My magic flooded out of me in just a few hours, leaving me exhausted constantly. If I couldn't figure it out then, how would I figure it out now?"

There was a long pause.

The king finally heaved a great big sigh and said, *"I'll try to teach you."*

"We'd just end up arguing. And besides, I don't think your magic works the same way mine does. It feels really different."

"Perhaps if you learn how to stop draining my magic, we'll get along better."

"Maybe if you stop being an asshole to me, we'll get along better," I shot back.

The look he shot me was a weary one.

I changed the subject. *"How many more days until the fighting is over? I'm thinking this place will be a sex fest as soon as you give the word."*

The king's expression turned disgruntled. *"You think correctly."*

"You'll have to give me my own room, then. I'm not sharing the bed you sleep with other women in."

He scowled. *"So you can invite the likes of Uron into your room? No."*

My anger rose quickly, along with something that felt like... jealousy.

I wasn't calling it that though. And I'd never admit it. *"It wouldn't be wrong for me to have sex with an attractive man who's been kind to me,"* I argued. *"I bet you've hooked up with dozens of these fae secretly, even while your ridiculous anti-sex law was in place."*

"I have kept every one of my laws, and that one wasn't my idea to begin with."

"Because you'd rather have a new woman in your bed every night. Maybe even two," I spat.

My anger had been rising steadily, and I didn't know why. Not jealousy; definitely not jealousy.

Probably because he was trying to tell me what to do, and I wanted freedom.

"Because I have no taste for casual sex," he snarled back. *"I grew up with mated parents. I saw how they loved each other. Sex with no emotion behind it is deadening for me."*

His words shocked me right into silence.

My mind went back to the way he'd touched me, in his room. And the way he'd let me touch him.

If he had no taste for it, he had only agreed to it to get what he wanted... and because he knew it was what *I* wanted.

New anger hit me hard, but I kept it silent.

I was done with him. Absolutely done. When our bond broke, I'd be thrilled if I never saw the bastard again.

He didn't say anything else to me as our walk continued, and I didn't say anything else to him.

The event started an hour or two after we arrived. I remained on the bench in the area that seemed to be reserved for Kierden, the one Eisley had brought me to the night before. He left me there to go figure out the logistics of something when someone asked him for help, and I stayed where I was, entirely alone.

My anger cooled as I sat there, and I settled into a calm state of trying to determine how I was going to act with Kierden. It sounded like he was going to force me to continue sleeping in his room, to prevent me from having casual sex while we were bonded. I could survive another two months or so of that; it wasn't the end of the world. I hadn't had sex before, anyway, so I wasn't entirely sure what I was missing out on.

Then again, I could always spend a bunch of time out at the shops meeting new people. If more of them were as friendly as Uron, I might eventually develop feelings for one of them enough to trust them to take my virginity.

Or perhaps I'd just get tired of holding out and ask someone to show me how it worked.

There were many options, regardless of where I slept.

As I considered my options, I decided to show Kierden the same quiet indifference I gave him in the forest after he rescued me, rather than allowing myself to fight with him again. The fighting only made us both feel things more strongly, which wasn't good for us.

Eisley joined me after a while, her gaze a bit bleary. She didn't say much to me at first, but sniffed the air and gave me a weird look.

"What?" I frowned at her.

She leaned closer and sniffed me, then made a face. "You smell like Kier again."

Oh.

I hadn't bathed after he... well, touched me. Against the wall and by the pool. *Intimately.*

"There's only one bed in the room, and he's too paranoid to let me sleep anywhere else."

Understanding dawned in her gaze. "Veil."

"Yeah."

She rubbed her eyes. "It's fine. You don't smell that strong right now. Just don't get too close to anyone so they don't pick up on it. And start bathing every morning."

I nodded, and she leaned against me a bit as we both stared out at the empty cage.

Shortly after that, Kierden joined us on the bench, and the fighting began. They were doing some kind of specialized hand-to-hand combat, with smooth, graceful motions. It was fascinating to watch, honestly.

And the nudity made it even more fascinating.

Hours and hours passed, and it was dark again by the time we left. Despite the lunch we'd been fed in the middle of the day, and the part of hers that Eisley gave me, I was starving.

Our esu had joined us partway through the day, so they carried us back to the castle, and we poured into the dining hall with a group of other fae.

As I ate, I learned that no one except the king and his sister technically lived in the castle, but that it was always open for anyone who needed a break or wanted an escape for a few days. There was a massive pool inside it somewhere, as well as a bunch of space for training, and a huge library.

Since everyone was welcome, there were constantly people coming in and out. There were usually only a few fae staying there, but everyone had done so at one point or another.

It fascinated me that they could rely on each other like that and surprised me to hear that Kierden was so welcoming.

But then again, I supposed I didn't really know him. It had been less than two weeks since he saved me from my tower, after all.

After we finished eating, Kierden and I went to his room and collapsed in bed. We didn't talk—he still seemed frustrated about our conversation earlier, and I was still absolutely not interested in being his friend.

Both of us fell asleep snuggled with our bonded esu, and despite the tension between us, I still slept so much better than I ever had in my tower.

CHAPTER 10

NISSA

The following two weeks passed quickly.

I was quiet, but observed the fae and tried to learn as much as I could about their land.

Kierden was still grumpy, but surprisingly enough, not angry or cruel.

I still didn't give him my name, and he only asked once a day or so. He didn't try to persuade me to give it to him with his hands or body again, either.

By some miracle, we also didn't fight. It still felt like a few steps back after the way we'd talked and touched each other while I cleaned his wounds, but that was my goal. What he'd said in the forest about not being interested in casual sex made it pretty damn clear that he had been trying to manipulate me even more than I'd realized, and I wasn't involving myself with someone like that.

Even when I patched his wounds again after he fought a few more times, we only exchanged surface-level pleasantries about the many flowers and fruits I was accidentally growing, our favorite foods, and other similar topics.

We spent our days at the friendly fighting events, and then started training for the *human fight* the kings had used as a cover when they brought us to Kierden's city. Me and the other girls were absolutely terrible with weapons of every kind, so they decided they were just going to have to give us all swords and see what happened.

On the fifteenth day since we'd arrived, my stomach clenched as Bright approached the arena.

Kierden didn't seem worried for me, but Bright was still trying to give me strategies to help me win the fight.

I really didn't care about winning. I was just concerned with the surviving part, considering that Laeli had fire magic and Kaelle had wind. They could wreck me, and the worst I could possibly do was wrap them in vines. It was more likely that I'd just end up growing them a damn snack.

Kierden had also tried to teach me to control my magic, but we hadn't gotten anywhere. He wouldn't admit it, but I was pretty sure he had adjusted to my magic draining him slowly. He didn't seem worse for wear, despite his moodiness.

The drain on my power would get worse again after the eclipse. I'd need to convince someone else to bond with me when that came around just so I could live a normal life. I still had two more months to worry about that, luckily.

"I have a bad feeling about this fight," I said quietly to Bright as she wove through the benches, toward a room behind the fighting cage. We would get ready inside the room.

There were already a few fae in the stands, and they wished me luck when they saw us. I waved a little but couldn't manage a smile.

"You've never fought before," she reminded me. *"All of us have bad feelings about new things."*

I sighed softly. *"Laeli and Kaelle's magic is unpredictable."*

"So is yours."

"Not in the same way theirs is, though."

"Believe in yourself," she said simply. *"And know that if anything goes wrong, we will get you out quickly."*

"You and who else? Kierden obviously doesn't care that my life's going to be at risk."

"Have you seen the other women with their swords? They're just as bad as you. No one accidentally dies in a fight."

I didn't think that was true. Maybe none of the fae, who were all badass fighters with centuries of experience, died *accidentally* in a fight. But a couple of human women with uncontrollable magic and no experience? We were a very different story.

What guarantee was there that Kaelle wouldn't accidentally throw a gust of wind that impaled me with her sword? What guarantee was there that Laeli wouldn't get stressed and catch on fire, then light *me* on fire?

"I hope you're right," I said to Bright, as she slipped into the room behind Death.

Kierden and I were the first ones there, so he went over and picked the first sword off a rack near the wall for me.

Bright licked my knee and prowled over to the corner of the room, where she plopped down on her belly and set her head on her paws so she could watch me.

Eisley arrived just after us, carrying three sets of clothing hidden by thick bags and wearing a massive grin. I heard metal clanging inside the clothing bags and fought a groan.

"I don't like that face," I warned her, waving my finger toward her expression. "You look downright wicked."

She laughed. Honestly, it was almost a cackle. "You're going to hate it."

I groaned.

Vayme and Kaelle arrived then, distracting me from Eisley, her evil smile, and whatever she had in those clothing bags. Ravv and Laeli were just behind them, and I could hear the crowd outside getting louder.

My nerves churned my stomach, but I tried hard to ignore them. After a few weeks of regular meals, I had filled out a lot more. My stomach was starting to get a little softer and my thighs were filling out a bit, although I could still see my ribs when I looked at myself in the mirror. If I ate more, I could have filled out faster, but Kierden's playfulness about how often I ate meant I was careful not to act as hungry as I was.

Unlike me, Laeli and Kaelle were gaining weight and growing curves rapidly. I'd noticed Vayme silently loading Kaelle's plate with his own food on multiple occasions and Laeli stealing food from Ravv's, who usually looked grumpy about it. I didn't think Kierden had noticed it; I knew him well enough to be nearly confident that he would have fed me more than I could ever eat if he knew why I was so hungry.

"You can't look partial to any of the women. As far as anyone knows, you only captured them for this and have no real connection to them," Eisley told the kings, waving them out of the room. The kings glowered and glared at her but all made their way out. Their companions stayed in the room: Death, Gleam (Ravv's bonded idorr), and Strong (Vayme's bonded xuno).

Kaelle and Laeli hadn't bonded with any animals yet, but the other kings' companions were a lot more protective of them than Death was of me. He was mostly focused on trying to convince Bright to be his mate, which I thought was kind of adorable.

And though Death wasn't protective of me, he was always affectionate, brushing up against my side and licking me whenever he passed me. He'd even started taking Bright's place between me and Kierden at night.

When the kings were gone, Eisley said cheerfully, "I brought your outfits for the fight. I'm sure it won't be super exciting, considering how terrible you all are, so the outfits are meant to distract everyone with your soft, bouncy bodies."

Compared to Laeli's and Kaelle's, my body wasn't soft or bouncy, but I understood the concept. If I'd been eating five huge meals a day like they were, I would've grown just as fast.

I didn't think that had occurred to Eisley any more than it had occurred to Kierden, though. She would've done something about it if it had. She just didn't understand humans well.

And yeah... Kierden was going to be *furious* if he found out that my town had starved me. I didn't plan on him finding out, though.

At least, I didn't plan on it until Eisley unzipped the bag.

I groaned at the sight of the outfit. I couldn't even call it a dress. It was just a pair of fancy scanties. The top portion was made with thin strips of metal that curved and would barely cover my nipples. The bottom portion had three strips—one over each hip, and one that would cover my lower bits, for the most part.

"Oh, that's terrible," Laeli said with a grin. "The kings are going to lose it."

Kaelle shivered. "I can already imagine the look of utter shame and disappointment on Vayme's face."

Laeli snorted. "Veil, not a chance. Barely-contained lust, sure."

"He isn't attracted to me," Kaelle said.

"Of course he is. You'll see."

They both looked at me to see my reaction.

I was still grimacing, trying hard to think my way out of the situation I'd just landed myself in.

There was no way, other than refusing to wear the outfit. And Eisley would literally wrestle me into it if I refused when she was that excited.

"Hello?" Eisley waved a hand at me.

I wordlessly lifted my short orange dress to my breasts and pointed to my ribs.

All of the girls went silent.

"You haven't gained much weight yet?" Eisley frowned, deeply.

"Kierden doesn't know the truth about the tower. I'm pretty sure he thinks it was to protect me because of my magic. If I suggest an extra meal, he'll make jokes about it or ask questions. And he's never seen me naked, so..." I shrugged helplessly, letting my dress fall back into place.

Death prowled over to me, his chest rumbling with a warning growl. He brushed the hem of my dress with his nose, and I sighed, lifting it.

He bumped my ribs, asking for an explanation without using words.

"I was starving," I told him. "For a really long time."

His eyes widened with what was clearly horror.

"Don't tell him. I didn't want him to know." I dropped my dress again.

With a low, angry rumble, he stepped up closer and leaned against me. It was the closest thing he could offer to a hug, and I reluctantly wrapped my arms around him. His chest was still rumbling with unhappiness as I did.

"We can just fight in our normal dresses," Kaelle said. "Kier doesn't need to know."

"Actually, I think this would be the perfect opportunity to show him how much of an asshole he is," Laeli said, a wicked glint in her eyes. "All of his people will be able to see how humans look when we're being fed properly—even if we aren't quite there yet. Everyone will know that Kier hasn't been feeding you enough."

Well, when she put it like that, it sounded downright vicious.

And... I kind of loved it.

Eisley's forehead wrinkled with alarm.

Kaelle moved between her and the door, blocking her path out. Eisley probably could've killed the small blue-haired human with her little finger alone, but she wouldn't. We all knew that.

"Fighting in your dresses is a *great* idea," Eisley said quickly.

Laeli looked at me, and I nodded.

She plucked the metal outfits out of the fae woman's hands, and Eisley sighed. "He's going to kill me."

Laeli snorted. "In your dreams, maybe." She handed me and Kaelle our outfits.

I released Death, but he just snuggled up closer to me. The poor guy probably felt bad. I didn't blame him for not knowing; if he had, he would've made Kierden do something about it a long time ago.

When I started changing, Death gave me space. He went back to Bright and sat down next to her. The way her eyes narrowed told me he was talking to her, possibly saying something she didn't like.

"Thank you for letting me have my secrets," I murmured to her. *"I know keeping them wasn't the smartest decision, but it was important to me."*

"You couldn't make your own choices for too much of your life, Nissa," Bright replied, her voice smooth and sure. *"I couldn't make that one for you. It was for the sake of your pride, and I understood that, even if I didn't always agree."*

"This is going to be terrible," Eisley muttered, as she took all our original dresses from us and then tied strips of glittering fabric over our glowing handprints to hide them from the rest of the fae.

"This was *your* idea," Laeli said, flashing Eisley a grin while she adjusted the metal outfit to cover her nipples better.

"Oh, I'm not going down for this. I will pin it on you, because I *know* your king will protect you." She pointed at Laeli, who was honestly the most plausible one of us to pin it on, if we weren't blaming Eisley.

And Ravv would definitely defend her. He was the only king who had shown any sign of the possessiveness that was apparently supposed to be expected.

"Did you hear that?" Kaelle's face jerked toward the caged area we would be fighting in.

"Did we hear what?" I asked her.

"I don't know. It sounded... strange." She frowned.

"I'm sure it's just the crowd. They get really rowdy."

A female fae rapped on the door and called out, "Ready?"

We all looked at each other.

"I guess," Laeli called back.

Eisley grimaced deeply as we grabbed our swords. The fact that I was going to get some sort of revenge on Kierden during the fight made me forget the bad feeling I'd had about it.

The male fae at the door stepped in and took one look at us before his face went red. His eyes were glued to Laeli. The fae were all used to being nearly naked, but with their constant warring, they were all muscular and thin. And that was a direct contrast to the natural softness of humans.

Eisley cleared her throat, and he jerked his gaze to her.

Coughing a bit, he nodded respectfully at us all, and then stepped through the door that led out into the cage. A deafening roar went through the crowd, making my stomach roll.

He gave a quick introduction about the humans the kings had abducted for them, and then Eisley pushed us all out together.

We didn't stumble, by some miracle.

We also didn't jog or move with any other kind of enthusiasm. But the crowd didn't care—their yelling and roaring and stomping had me fighting back a small smile.

When we reached the middle of the cage I turned, and my eyes met Kierden's. He was up against the bars of the cage, his eyes burning as he gripped the metal.

Good.

He'd noticed.

Kaelle said something, but I didn't hear it. Her wind was blowing harder than I'd ever felt it though, which didn't seem like a great omen.

The fae man set us up across from each other, so we formed a triangle, and then he announced the start of the fight with a booming yell.

None of us moved as he crossed the cage, and then closed the door.

Only one of Kaelle's hands was on her sword. The other one was pressed to her temple, and she grimaced like she was in pain.

The crowd's roaring started to die down.

I looked at Laeli.

She shrugged, lifting her sword.

Guess we were still doing it.

I lifted mine too, and then Kaelle's eyes flew open, her wind whipping through the area. "He's here," she whispered.

The crowd had gone quiet enough for us to hear.

"Who?" Laeli asked, frowning.

"One of the assassins. I can feel him."

My eyes widened. "How can you feel him? How do you know?"

"I see and feel auras," she said quietly. "My wind comes from them. And his is *terrible*."

"What are you waiting for?" Ravv shouted from beside Kierden.

They couldn't hear us.

They didn't know what she was saying.

"What do we do?" I asked.

Kaelle's eyes darted around the cage. "I don't know."

"We need to get everyone out," Laeli said. Steam was coming off her arms and hands, a good sign that she was close to catching on fire.

"Oh, it's far too late for that," a low, masculine voice purred. The voice's owner appeared beside us, and we all stumbled backward. "Which one of you is connected to Kier Jirev?"

The man was absolutely gorgeous, with tan skin, wavy black hair, and even bigger muscles than the fae kings. He looked more like a god than a monster. His eyes glowed red, and his lips lifted in a feral grin that spoke of sex and sin.

"The Beast of the Endless Wilds," Laeli whispered.

The crowd in the stands was deadly silent.

His grin widened, and I saw his fangs. Was he a vampire somehow, too? "Hello, sweetheart. Is Kier using your magic to hide his?"

She said nothing, her eyes wide with panic. Flames danced just off her skin, not burning her but getting close.

As if on cue, yells and shouts erupted above us, and the fae started to *move*. The door we'd come through to get into the cage rattled as if someone was trying to get through it, but the Beast must've locked it from the inside. I heard snarling and roaring from fae around us—maybe the kings—but assumed that if they hadn't left yet, they would soon.

Kierden certainly needed to.

They were all warriors, but a smart warrior knew when to run. And clearly, that moment had come.

The wind blew against us as if we were in a ferocious storm. Laeli had caught fire, and was burning brightly.

Kaelle started to open her mouth, and I had the feeling she was going to lie for me. I couldn't let that happen.

"I'm mated to Kier," I blurted. "It's me."

His lips curved upward wickedly. "See how easy that was?" I blinked, and he was gone.

A massive hand closed over my shoulder, and another covered my mouth to muffle my scream. "You smell absolutely delicious, don't you?"

My head was wrenched to the side a moment later, and I felt a sharp pain in my shoulder before a feeling of bliss overwhelmed me.

The pain vanished for a moment, but the bliss remained. Something rumbled against me as a male voice mused, "Surely a fae king of any worth would at least attempt to defend the female he's claimed as his. Come out and fight, Kier."

Another sharp pain stung my shoulder, and then my eyes closed as even more bliss followed.

Some part of me wondered if I was really going to die before Kierden even learned my name.

CHAPTER 11

KIERDEN

The blood pounding in my ears and the fear burning my lungs were unlike anything I'd ever felt before. There was a record of every battle I'd ever fought on my arm, in ink, and yet I had never been afraid of a loss the way I was in the moment the Beast appeared beside my mate.

My concern had nothing to do with my life, and *everything* to do with hers.

Death was snarling in my mind, him and the rest of our bonded animals already ramming the gate to the cage, trying to get through.

But it was made of gargoyle steel. When locked from the inside it was impenetrable, created to protect its occupants during the vulnerable moments of their fight.

The other kings and I charged the door. For once, we were preparing to fight together instead of against one another.

"He's here for you," Vayme snarled, as we ran. "You need to go."

"I won't leave her," I snarled back.

"Then we fight."

"We can't break it," Death growled to everyone as we reached the door, finding the animals' sides bloody and their chests heaving. Eisley and a few of the other kings' allies were there too, each of them holding weapons. *"Tell your females to get it open."*

I gave the command to my human as I lunged for the walls of the room, gripping the bars while I tried to see into the cage.

She didn't respond, and I couldn't see through the other humans' magic.

Ravv's female was burning brightly enough to take up half the space. Vayme's female had her wind blowing so fiercely that it worked with the fire to conceal everything.

Veil, I hoped she wasn't on fire or in the arms of the Beast. He would play with his food before consuming my magic, and there was no better way to break the mind of a male than to torture his female.

"Come on, little human," I demanded. *"Open the door."*

Still, I received no response.

A small form ran through the wind and fire. A moment later, the little human with blue hair burst through it. Vayme caught her in his arms, and hugged her fiercely.

"Nissa told him she was bonded to you, and he bit her. He's drinking her blood," the girl said, lifting her watering eyes to mine. "We didn't know he was a vampire. I didn't know. I should've warned everyone."

Her wind blew more fiercely, and the cage started to rattle around us.

Nissa.

My human.

She was talking about my mate.

"Laeli's on fire," Vayme's human added, her voice starting to shake as the wind grew even fiercer. "She can't stop it. I—"

We couldn't fight in that wind. Not against the Beast.

"Get her out of here. Go to the elves," I said to Vayme, my voice cold as the calm of battle began to seep into my mind, body, and blood. "Tell them if their assassins kill any of our people, *including* our mates, we will consider it an act of war and will come for them as one."

Our magic wasn't as strong as theirs, but they were soft. They didn't know how to fight.

And we were weapons, down to our very souls.

Together, no group of creatures could stand against us.

He jerked his head in a nod, then threw his female onto the back of his bonded xuno.

"We destroy the Beast, and then tame my female's flames," Ravv said, as we sprinted into the cage. Both of us threw ice out to protect ourselves against his human's flames.

I tapped into my magic to create both long, icy blades I preferred to fight with. Though Ravv and I had never fought *together*, we had fought each other enough times to know one another's strengths and weaknesses. He was ferocious; he would take the offense, without a shred of defense.

So he would distract the Beast, and I would free my female.

My sister was behind me, with all of our bonded animals. They were the only ones I would trust with my human.

My *Nissa*.

Ravv roared as he lunged for the Beast, massive claws of ice over his fingers, knuckles, knees, and forehead. More were blossoming; the man used his entire body as a weapon.

I saw the Beast through the crowd, and my vision went red when I saw the bastard's teeth buried in my unconscious female's shoulder. The elves' assassins had been made with some variation of the curse that could turn humans into vampires, so they all relied on blood for sustenance.

Him feeding on Nissa only heightened my rage.

The Beast saw Ravv coming and dropped my female, moving in the blink of an eye. Fae were much faster than humans, but the assassins were even faster than fae.

Eisley caught my female as the Beast appeared behind Ravv, grabbing the king by his throat. The Beast snarled, and the smell of his tainted blood flooded the air as Ravv's ice tore into his hands and arms.

The Beast threw himself backward, ice still lodged in his limbs as he moved. Death and Gleam launched at him, and he vanished just in time to dodge them.

I sensed him behind me just before his hands landed on my shoulders. The ice of one sword sliced through his abdomen as I spun, slashing at his throat with the other.

The bastard barely had time to duck away.

He charged toward Eisley, who had a knife out and wore a face that said she'd make the Beast regret his vow to hunt me down.

A screaming, flaming human woman threw herself between Eisley and the Beast before he could reach her.

Ravv roared and tried to grab his female, but wasn't fast enough. She collided with the Beast, and an unearthly scream escaped him.

A moment later, he was gone.

Ravv caught his human, gripping her to his chest as he dragged her further from the rest of us. Her magic wouldn't hurt him, because their bond had knitted it with his like mine with Nissa's.

I covered the distance between me and my female in a heartbeat, dropping to my knees beside her and taking her from Eisley's arms. With her fragile body pressed to mine, I slowly inhaled her scent. The way it had mixed with the Beast's was nearly enough to drive me mad, but I couldn't allow myself to lose control.

Not when the Beast could still be in my city.

I had no idea how quickly he could heal, or how soon he would return.

Nissa was breathing steadily. Her skin was ashen, but her heartbeat was normal.

My body trembled slightly as I slowly lowered my forehead to hers, simply closing my eyes and holding her close for a long, long moment.

I had nearly lost her.

The assassins technically couldn't kill anyone they hadn't vowed to end, but they worked around it by *nearly* killing anyone they wanted to and then letting nature do the rest of the work.

"Please take Nissa to my room," I asked Bright in a low voice.

She dipped her head, and I looked at Eisley. "I need you to get Dirue while I secure the perimeter." Dirue was the healer, and the oldest fae in our city. Though she had no healing magic, she knew more about herbs and wounds than anyone else.

"I can secure it so you can get her and stay with Nissa," Eisley said, unshaken despite the insanity that had just gone down. She was a damn good warrior, and that was the reason she was my second-hand, not because of our shared blood.

"I need you with my mate. The Beast could very well still be here, and I won't risk letting him near her for a second time," I said.

"Alright. I'll do it." Eisley jerked her head in a nod.

It killed me not to be at Nissa's side while she was in pain, but there was no alternative. I couldn't risk her life again for my own desires.

"I'll follow the Beast's scent trail to make sure he's gone," Ravv said, his jaw tight as he gripped a shaking Laeli even tighter.

I agreed.

He asked one of his most trusted fae, Elwynne, to stay with Laeli. After she agreed, he whispered something to his mate, and her flames slowly receded. When they were gone completely, her eyes looked haunted and she was still shaking badly, clearly traumatized.

I lifted my female carefully up to Bright's back, and Bright slipped out with Eisley and Sharp.

Ravv handed his mate to Elwynne, and both women left on the back of her bonded idorr.

A long, slow breath escaped me.

The other king looked at me and nodded.

I nodded back.

It was all the acknowledgement either of us were ready to give at the moment. Merely fighting together was a difficult task, considering all of the pain we'd caused each other over the centuries. But in this situation, we were all united in being completely at the mercy of our bonds.

Both the bonds we despised that connected us to the assassins... and the ones we were still trying to figure out with the humans.

Death and I ran two circles around our city's perimeter, then snaked our way through the bridges and paths. We were both quiet, though there was no anger between us, only solemn contemplation.

Ultimately, I had allowed my little human to be in that cage. I had gone with the lie that we brought the humans back for that event alone, and there was no one to blame but me.

The weight of responsibility for that choice was heavy on my shoulders. As was the weight of her health, which I'd never questioned until the truth of it was before my eyes.

"You saw her ribs?" Death asked me as we began another loop.

"I did."

I'd never seen her bare before, or in anything that showed her abdomen. And she was the same size as Eisley, so I'd assumed she was healthy.

I'd been trying to keep my distance to avoid getting her murdered... and I'd hurt her in doing so.

Veil, I'd *starved* her.

"You didn't starve her. She's eaten every meal with you," Death said as if reading my mind. *"She chose not to tell you because she wanted you to ask. The female wants to be chased, but you've kept her at an arm's length for her safety."* We'd known each other long enough that he didn't need to hear my thoughts to know what I was thinking most of the time.

"She needed more food. I should've realized there was a reason for her hunger," I said bitterly.

My father would've noticed immediately if my mother wasn't eating enough or if she had seemed hungrier than normal. He had noticed everything about her.

Then again, they had been mated for a long time before they had me.

Regardless, I was at fault.

Completely and utterly at fault.

"You were trying not to let yourself feel anything for her. A useless feat, as I said from the beginning. All creatures are meant to take mates," Death said.

"She'll never forgive me for this."

"Perhaps not. But if you had known, you would've fed her. A fact she is doubtlessly aware of. She was waiting for you to pay attention to her."

I grimaced. *"After this, she's going to beg me to ignore her again."*

Death chuffed. *"Perhaps. But she's a stubborn enough female to appreciate your strong will, even if it takes her time to admit it."*

Ravv found us soon after that, and we exchanged reports. The Beast was still bleeding badly when he disappeared into the Wilds, and Ravv had followed his scent trail for an hour before heading back when there was no sign of it turning around. I hadn't found evidence of the Monster or the Demon, either.

Both of us itched to check on our mates, so we headed back to the castle to set up an assload of patrols.

When we approached, we found Eisley standing outside the castle, arguing vocally with a massive group of my fae. Ravv headed in another direction, but Death went down there without a second thought.

"What's going on?" I asked, raising my voice as I slid off Death's back and stepped up beside Eisley.

"We want to know what the Beast was doing here," a woman at the front of the group said. Her name was Tal, and she had been a pain in my ass since I turned down her invitation to spend the eclipse with her two centuries earlier.

They deserved the truth, even if it made them angry. And I doubted they would take the risk of selecting a new king so soon after the war ended, regardless of any anger they felt.

"Someone made a bargain with the Beast to kill me," I said bluntly, as I unwound the fabric from my hand and then lifted it up to show them both the brand and my glowing palm.

Their gasps were audible at the sight of it.

I added, "Someone made bargains with *all* of the elves' assassins, one to kill each of the kings. Apparently a few fae in the other kingdoms were willing to sacrifice their lives for the sake of our deaths."

The responding silence was so thick and heavy, it may as well have been alive.

None of my fae had gone missing or been found drained of life, so I knew none of them had made the deadly bargain.

"After we woke up with the brands, we went to the elf Alida and asked her for a way to buy time. She directed us to the humans with life magic. Their power neutralizes the death of the ice in our veins to hide us from the assassins when combined with ours as mates."

A long pause followed the explanation, and I added, "I have bonded with the human female Nissa, under the advice of Alida, and it is protecting me from the Beast. When the eclipse comes, it will erase both the Beast's brand, and our temporary bond."

Some eyes were narrowed in anger.

Some were wide with shock.

No one was afraid; we'd faced far too many battles for that.

"Have you had sex with her?" someone demanded.

"I have not and will not, unless we all agree to remove the law against it," I said firmly. "You know I am a male of honor. I gave you my word, and I have kept it."

A few murmured agreements sounded.

"Let's remove the law," a male voice called out. "If the Beast is hunting you, he's hunting all of us. And if I'm going to die at the hands of an assassin, I'd like to do so after spending the night in someone's bed."

A few chuckles followed his request.

"Get me proof of everyone's agreement, and we'll remove it," I said.

"I've got it," someone else called out. The crowd parted and Weva slipped through, then handed me a thick roll of paper. "Everyone signed it, except you."

"Even Eisley?" I lifted an eyebrow.

"She was the first one." She gave me an impish grin, and I chuckled.

"Alright." I didn't bother opening it. There weren't any of my people who would be unwilling to sign it; I knew that without a doubt. "The law is removed. Have at it."

A few people whooped, though it was half-hearted after the drama of all that had just happened.

Eisley leaned closer to me, her expression anxious as she whispered, "Nissa isn't doing well. I was coming to find you."

My heart dropped into my abdomen.

"I can run a rotation of patrols through the jungle to keep an eye out for the assassins," Jor said from behind a few of the other males. "See if you can help her. We heard the Beast drank from her."

Murmurs of agreement sounded.

I dipped my head toward him. "Thank you. And yes, she decided to tell the Beast that she was bonded to me. Probably saved the other humans' lives."

"Then she could've very well prevented another war, too," a female I couldn't see murmured.

"Plus, she grows the most delicious fruit. You've got to convince her to stay here, even after your bond breaks," someone added.

A few people chuckled. I didn't let myself react, afraid I'd make an admission that would let them know just how large my aversion was to the thought of letting her go.

"I'll see what I can do." With that, I headed into the castle to find my female.

I moved quickly through the hallways with Eisley, Sharp, and Death as we headed to my room.

"Dirue can't get her to respond to anything," Eisley said as we went. "When I told her you two had bonded, she said your blood can heal Nissa. Something about the magic of mate bonds."

Dirue knew mate bonds better than the rest of us, since she was one of the only fae old enough to remember the details about them.

"What about Ravv's human?" I asked.

"She's not hurt in any way, just shaken up."

"Good."

I pushed the door to my room open.

My eyes landed on my female, and fear struck me hard.

She looked like death itself had come for her.

Her tan skin was grayish, and she was so damn still in my bed that it terrified me.

"Veil," I snarled. "Someone should've come for me *hours* ago."

Dirue had no bonded esu anymore; she had lost hers in a battle centuries earlier, so there was no beast to growl at me for getting angry with her.

"Her heart is still beating, but you'll need to give her your blood; it will heal her much faster than anyone or anything else can. In the past, mates would share blood every month or two to strengthen each other," Dirue said much more calmly than I felt.

"How do I feed it to her?" I growled at the healer as I sat beside Nissa on the bed. Bright was already next to her, with her head resting on my human's shoulder.

"If she were conscious, it would be better for her to drink from here." She tapped the place where her neck met her shoulder.

The place where Nissa had been bitten by the Beast.

"She's obviously not conscious," I gritted out.

"You'll need to cut yourself and hold the wound to her mouth. It will be rather intimate, but she does need a lot of blood. When she wakes, lift her up and have her drink from here." She tapped her neck again.

"Fine. Get out," I barked.

Conjuring a blade of ice took less than a heartbeat, and slicing through my wrist with it was just as fast.

My fingers were gentle on Nissa's soft, fragile lips as I parted them and then pressed my weeping wound to her mouth. My blood dripped down her chin, but onto her tongue, too.

She stirred a little as soon as she tasted me. After a few moments, she started to drink.

There was a thick, satisfying pleasure in the way the color slowly returned to her face as she swallowed my blood.

A few minutes passed, and then her eyes flew open. She gripped my wrist, holding it tighter to her mouth.

My cock hardened as she sucked, her eyes dazed but hot.

When I was sure she was conscious enough, I pulled my wrist from her grip and lifted her onto my lap. "Bite me, female." My chest rumbled with the thickness of my desire as I spoke.

I felt the tug of magic in our connection as she sank her teeth into my skin. The magic must've lengthened them because her small, human teeth weren't made for biting the way most magical beings' were.

My eyes caught on something near the door. It took a moment to recognize that Dirue was standing near the entrance to my room, watching us.

Death and Bright had already slipped out, and I could hear one or both of them growling from outside the room.

Possessive rage crashed into me when I realized the healer was witnessing my female and I in a vulnerable, intimate moment.

"Get out," I roared at her, nearly shaking the bed with my fury.

My human didn't so much as flinch at my anger. Dirue dipped her head in a small bow and then slipped away. It made me proud that Nissa didn't fear me—that she knew I wasn't going to hurt her.

I clutched her tightly to my chest as she continued drinking, my cock throbbing against her core where she straddled me. I wouldn't acknowledge my desire while she was hurting, but there would be no hiding it.

She pulled away, sucking in a deep breath of air. Her eyes were mostly clear when she looked at me.

"Take more," I growled at her.

She started to hesitate, but when I tugged her head back to my shoulder, she bit me again.

There was fierce pleasure in providing something for my mate that no one else could. Fiercer than the thrill of any battle won or enemy defeated. Perhaps the fiercest joy I had ever felt.

I held her tight and didn't plan to let go until she forced me to.

CHAPTER 12

NISSA

When I lifted my face from Kierden's shoulder the second time, I felt alive again. My body was still shaking from trauma and blood loss, but I could move. I could breathe unobstructed. I could *feel*.

At least, I could feel enough that drinking his blood was turning me on. That was annoying to say the least, since I was still trying to hate the bastard.

"More," he ordered me as I sucked in air. I could feel blood dripping down my chin, and was still trembling.

"I need a few minutes," I said, reaching a shaking hand toward my mouth.

Kierden's fingers beat mine, my body going still as he slowly wiped the blood from my face then slid his finger into my mouth.

I fought a groan.

Why did his blood taste so damn good?

Even his skin tasted good.

I found myself sucking on his finger, and decided I'd deny it if he ever brought it up again.

When I'd finally developed the strength to release him, I leaned back a bit. My head started to tilt, but Kierden caught it with his gigantic hand and held it up for me.

"I guess I probably have to tell you my name, since you just saved my life," I murmured.

"You do."

"It's Nissa. Not long or complicated. Just Nissa."

"It suits you," he said.

I wasn't sure if that was an insult or a compliment.

His voice lowered. "And I must admit that Kaelle gave it to me when the Beast had you."

"That was pretty bad, huh?" I whispered. "I didn't know he would drink my blood. Telling him I'm bonded to you was a risk."

"Not a measured one," he growled.

"Of course it was measured. He would've grabbed one of the other women if I hadn't, and I couldn't risk their lives." My voice was growing softer as my exhaustion set in.

When Kierden pulled my face gently to his neck, on the side I hadn't bitten, I rested it against him without a fight.

There was no reason to fight when his skin felt so good on mine.

It probably wasn't the answer he wanted to hear, but I was too exhausted to be thinking clearly.

"I would prefer you risk *everyone's* lives before yours," he said. I felt something on my cheek that reminded me of the way my father used to kiss my forehead as a child, strangely enough. Perhaps I imagined it.

"Well, you're the only one who feels that way," I whispered back.

"And the only one whose opinion matters when it comes to your life, Nissa."

The words would've stunned me if I'd been more conscious. I wasn't, so I didn't fully understand them.

I felt him move, and supposed he had climbed out of bed. The world spun a bit. My body wasn't recovered enough for the motion to feel natural. "Where are you going?"

"I'm bathing you. If you want me to leave your scanties on, I will." His voice grew grumpier when he said the last bit.

My lips turned downward. "You say that like you're actually interested in me being naked."

He moved my thigh just slightly, so his erection pressed against my leg as he walked. "I can assure you that I am."

"You don't do casual sex. You only pinned me to that wall to control me," I mumbled.

He scoffed. "We're halfway *mated*, Nissa. There would be nothing casual about us having sex. It would electrify our bond, and probably strengthen it too."

Oh.

I hadn't thought of it like that.

And damn, I liked the way he said my name. Like it wasn't just a word but was something important. Something that *mattered*.

He stripped his shorts off with one hand, then sat down on the ledge of the bathing pool with me on his lap.

Trying to ignore the feel of his bare thighs against my legs, I asked, "So you actually liked touching me?"

"I've hardly thought of anything else since," he growled. "Having you beside me constantly is the only thing that's kept me from stroking myself to the memory of it day in and day out."

Damn, I loved that.

And as much as I didn't want it to, it erased the bitterness I'd felt toward him when I thought he'd feigned interest in touching me. The same bitterness I'd been using to keep myself from growing too fond of him or starting to like him in any way.

"Maybe you can stroke yourself to the memory of it sometime while I watch," I mumbled.

My exhaustion was making things come out of my mouth that I wouldn't have said otherwise.

"Any day and any time, little human." I felt that feeling again —the feeling of his lips on my cheek. "Am I removing your scanties, or not?"

He dragged my mind back to the bathing pool. We were still sitting on the ledge.

"I can take them off. They're too uncomfortable to leave on." I started to pull my head away, but he tugged it back and tucked it against his neck again.

"No." His hands were gentle as they slid down my back to the metal over my lower bits.

I shivered slightly, and his cock responded to my movement. The throb of it made me warmer. I was too exhausted for anything steamy to happen, but I still liked feeling his body's reaction to me.

"Stay still. I'm going to break it with ice." He smoothed a hand over my lower back again and made me shiver once more.

"Ice can break metal?"

"Ice can break just about anything if you try hard enough. A few flimsy strips of metal aren't a problem." His knuckles brushed my skin with a little pressure, and then I felt a gentle snap near my hip. He moved to the other side and repeated the motion.

Then his hand slid between our bodies.

I clenched at his nearness to my core.

"Stay still, Nissa."

He snapped the metal there, and then carefully eased it down and under me. The backs of his fingers brushed my clit, making me feel all hot and fluttery.

"You smell divine," he said as he tossed the metal away. My backside landed on his thighs, and I inhaled unevenly at the pressure of his bare cock against my core.

Veil, that was blissful.

"I'm sure I smell like blood and the Beast."

"You did." Kierden found the latch at the back of the piece that wrapped around my breasts. He snapped the thin bands that went over my shoulders, and then eased me away from his chest so he could pull the metal away. "Now, all I can smell is your desire."

He pulled me back against his chest, then slipped into the water. My throat closed at the intense feeling of my breasts pressed against his warm, hard, bare chest.

I tried to clear my throat, and failed, so I distracted myself from my desire by asking, "Can the Beast hurt you or find you through me?"

"No. He can only hunt his target, just as he can only purposefully kill that person or creature. The elves thought that little rule would protect them from their assassins. As you saw, there are ways around it."

Veil.

"He was terrifying," I admitted. "But strangely attractive. I always assumed monsters were ugly."

"What good is an ugly monster? The more attractive it is, the more efficiently it can lure its pray or lull it into comfort."

"Well, that's a scary thought," I murmured.

"Aren't fae beautiful? And elves, demons, and dragons? The beauty of a creature distracts others from seeing the truth."

"I don't know if *that's* the case. I thought you were beautiful when we first met, but I still knew you were a bastard when you opened your mouth," I murmured.

He chuckled. "Perhaps you're a monster too, then." His finger trailed up my tailbone. I shivered against him, making his cock throb again.

"I don't think I'm beautiful enough to be a monster," I admitted. "I'll never look like you guys. And I have the ugly round ears, which I obviously can't change."

"If you knew how many times I've imagined tracing those round ears with my tongue, I doubt you'd find them ugly."

"You're the one who told me they were ugly!" I exclaimed.

He scoffed. "I did *not*."

"Yes, you did. You pulled my hair away from them on the first day and gave me this look of complete and utter disgust. I thought you might vomit."

He snorted. "Because of your *ears*? How weak did you think I was?"

"I didn't think you were weak. I thought you were an asshole, disgusted by my ears, and a fae elitist," I said matter-of-factly. "I still believe two of those things."

"I don't even want to know which ones," he grumbled. "If I made a disgusted face, it's because I was disgusted by how badly I wanted to taste them."

"You did not want to *taste* my *ears*."

He leaned his head down and slowly dragged the tip of his tongue over the curve of my ear. I shivered, hard. With my bare body literally in his hands, the moment was very, very intimate.

And I wasn't entirely certain I didn't like it.

I fought to keep my voice even. "I bet it tastes like an ear."

"Want to try it?" He pulled my face away from his neck.

When I opened my mouth to ask how he thought I would taste my own ear, he slid his tongue between my lips... and licked the length of mine.

Then he withdrew and pulled my head back to rest against his throat.

My mind spun again at the sudden increase in intimacy. "You just *licked* my *tongue*."

"After I licked your ear."

"You're supposed to hate me," I whispered against his neck.

"Tomorrow, perhaps."

Panic swelled in my chest. "No. You can't be nice to me today and then go back to being an asshole tomorrow. I won't know what to think or how to feel."

"I don't value kindness the way humans do, Nissa. If someone deserves my respect, I give it to them, but I'm not going to walk around smiling and asking people how their day is. I'll probably always be an asshole."

He misunderstood me. "I know *that*. I just meant you can't go back to being an asshole *to me*. I don't like the push and pull of it; it doesn't make me feel safe."

"I apologize for making you feel unsafe. That was never my intention, and it won't happen again." His voice was quiet, but I didn't question him. Kierden had never been a liar. "What else did your people do to you?"

Well, that was a dangerous question.

"What do you mean, what else?" I asked. If he wanted vulnerable answers from me at that point, he was going to have to ask directly and share vulnerable answers of his own.

"I know they starved you, little human. I saw the evidence on your body. It infuriates me that I didn't put the pieces together sooner—and frustrates me that you didn't attack me for the first comment I made about your hunger."

Hurt curled in my abdomen at the reminder, but I didn't move away from him. His body still felt too damn good against mine to move away. "Why *did* you make those comments?"

He let out a long breath. "I am immensely attracted to you. I was trying to make you hate me, because your hate made it easier to stay away."

"It didn't make me *hate* you, it frustrated me. I knew that if I told you the truth, you'd start loading my plate with your food. I just didn't want you to find out unless you cared about me enough to ask."

"If you knew I would've fed you, doesn't that imply that I would've cared?" he countered.

"Maybe? I don't know. I was just hurt, and I didn't understand the way you were treating me."

A moment passed before he admitted, "I've told you before that those who seal mate bonds in my kingdom are murdered. Despite the danger, some couples choose to create a bond secretly. No matter what they do to hide it, we always find them dead in their bed within a few days, with glowing golden handprints confirming their connection."

Sadness flooded me for their sake.

Though I couldn't imagine a love strong enough to make me risk my life for it, I still ached for them.

Kierden admitted, "Sometimes they tell me after they create the bond, in hopes that I can help protect them. Even when I guard them myself, they still die. We've never found the cultist who must be hiding among our people. It's the greatest shame of my life."

"Do you think they use poison?"

"They must, though I haven't figured out what kind, or how they use it. Even when I watch them cook for themselves and no one else knows about their bond, they always end up dead."

If he'd seen that many couples die because of a mate bond, I had to think he was probably afraid for our lives because of ours. And that kind of fear would change a person; I knew, because I'd looked it in the face when I was alone, starving, and locked in that damn tower.

"So you were an ass to me to protect me," I said.

"Yes."

"That's a shitty way to protect someone, Kierden." I closed my eyes, but my lips curved upward just slightly with his low chuckle. The rumble of it against my bare breasts felt incredible.

"I know. It won't happen again."

I bit my lip. "It might have to, though. If anyone finds out we're together..."

"I had to tell my people about the bond. There was no way around it. As far as they know, we have no feelings for each other and plan to separate when the eclipse comes. No one is killed over silver bonds, only golden ones."

Damn.

"*Do* we have feelings for each other?" I asked, after a long moment.

He didn't answer immediately, so I waited.

Kierden finally said, "I suppose we're still figuring that out." He added, "Don't think I didn't notice you avoid telling me about your town."

Damn.

"Can we talk about it tomorrow? Or after I sleep? I don't know what time it is, but I'm too exhausted for that conversation."

"I suppose. Let me clean you and get you to bed, little human."

"I need something to sleep in," I mumbled to him, as he started slowly washing my back with soap and water. "I'm tired of sleeping in my dresses."

"Most fae sleep in their scanties."

My eyes closed at the blissful peace of him touching me like that. "Too uncomfortable."

He considered it as he continued washing the wound where my shoulder met my neck very carefully. It didn't hurt as much as I had expected it to. "I have a few old shirts. I haven't worn them in a long, long time, but they might work."

"That sounds nice."

He chuckled. "You are absolutely stunning."

My lips curved upward. "Ears and all?"

"Mmhm." He licked the curve of my ear again, making me laugh softly.

When he was done washing me, he dried me off and then carried me to the closet.

He pulled a shirt out of the back of his closet, then set me down on my feet just long enough to dry my hair with a towel and tug the shirt into place. The fabric was loose and soft, exactly what I'd wanted. It barely fell to the middle of my thighs, but I didn't mind showing skin thanks to the dresses I'd been wearing.

"You're going to need to drink more of my blood before you go to sleep," he told me as he set me down again in the bathroom. I was only on my feet long enough for him to get out a bandage, wet my skin, and then cover the puncture wounds on my neck with it.

"Am I? I feel fine."

"It's supposed to help you heal faster. Unless you'd rather eat?"

I made a face. "I don't think I can choke anything down."

His eyes gleamed wickedly, and I got the feeling he was holding back a sex joke as he said, "Blood it is, then."

Kierden carried me back to the bed, setting me on his lap and tilting his head to the side. I frowned at the wounds I'd left on him. They were already partway healed, but still looked terrible.

"I don't want to hurt you again," I said.

His hands skimmed my bare thighs, sliding toward my ass and making me warmer. "Think of it as revenge for the times I treated you poorly."

"Going out in the metal outfit was revenge, and look where that got me."

He stroked my ass, his hands just below the hem of my shirt. "That was *brilliant* revenge. The Beast's interference wasn't your fault."

I made a noise of agreement. "Did it bother you?"

"Learning about my own errors alongside the rest of my kingdom? Immensely." He squeezed my ass lightly in his hands.

"I expected you to yell at me."

"Why would I yell when I can think of far better punishments?" He squeezed my ass again, harder.

The tight grip made me hotter. "In the Woods when we first met, you didn't correct me when I called you by your full name. Why?"

"The way it sounded on your lips was too perfect for me to ask you to shorten it."

"I can call you Kier. Or at least, I can try."

"Don't. It makes me hard when you say my name." He used his grip on my ass to drag me against his erection just a little harder.

"You must be hard a lot around me, then," I said.

"Constantly. Now, stop changing the subject and bite me, Nissa."

My face flushed bright red, but I finally followed the command.

The taste of his blood was even better than I remembered. It calmed me and made me hot for him at the same time, and I found myself rocking against his erection as I drank from him.

He never pulled away from me or pushed me to stop, letting me take as much as I wanted.

My mind spun when I finally released his neck, my body flushed but full and relaxed.

He pulled me to his chest, lowering us to the bed on our sides. His front was pressed tightly to my back and his erection nestled between my thighs as he pulled the blankets over us.

"Veil, you want me," he rumbled.

My face flushed. "I don't."

We both knew it was a lie.

"My shorts are drenched with your desire, little human." His lips brushed my ear, and I shivered against him. He was right; I wanted him fiercely. "I owe you a climax. Let me give it to you."

My heart skipped a beat. "I don't know if I'm ready to reciprocate."

"I didn't ask you to."

There was no way I could deny that I wanted what he was offering. His touch and a release, nothing more. I whispered, "Okay."

His chest rumbled again. He pulled one of my legs over his hip, opening me up. The blankets still covered me, and his hand slid down the front of my thigh before stopping a breath away from my core.

"Tell me I can touch you, Nissa." He dragged his tongue over the curve of my ear again. "Tell me your body is mine to relax and relieve. Tell me you want to feel my fingers inside you when I bring you to climax."

My body flushed hotter. "I already gave you permission."

His fingers brushed my clit lightly—so lightly. "I want to hear you say it again."

I inhaled sharply as he brushed my clit once more with that same soft, teasing touch. My body was tense, every damn part of me clenched and waiting and *desperate*.

So I gave him what he'd asked for. "I want you to touch me, Kierden. I want you to make me climax. I want you to bury your fingers inside me and prove that you like the way I feel."

He gave me a satisfied growl and *finally* lowered his fingers to my center.

I sucked in a breath when he stroked my clit lightly. The feel of his huge, warm fingers on my folds was unreal, and my pleasure swelled almost instantly.

His cock throbbed between my thighs as he stroked me again and again, murmuring, "You're so damn wet for me, little human."

I couldn't form a single word to reply. The pleasure built so fast I couldn't believe it.

He rumbled, "So hot and slick. Veil, I can't wait to have you wrapped around my cock." He teased my slit with a thick digit while he continued stroking me, and it was just too much.

I cried out, my hips jerking against his hand as I climaxed harder than I'd ever dreamed was possible.

My chest heaved as I came down from the high, my world spinning again. I had never felt so damn relaxed before, though there was enough desire still curling in my abdomen that I wanted to urge Kierden to keep going.

He slid his fingers out from between my thighs and returned my leg to its original positon. "Sleep now, Nissa."

I sighed but nodded and then started drifting off to sleep.

The bed dipped a few minutes later, when Death and Bright slipped into the room. Both of them snuggled up against me instead of taking their own sides, and my lips curved upward slowly.

I'd nearly been killed by the Beast of the Endless Wilds... and yet I would risk myself again if I knew it would bring me back to everything that had happened afterward.

CHAPTER 13

NISSA

I woke up in the same position I'd fallen asleep in, with my back pressed to Kierden's front. His erection was still tucked between my legs, and his hands had started moving slowly over my thighs again at some point.

I couldn't remember ever feeling so content when I woke before.

Foreign words crossed my mind, and I felt a soft urge to speak them.

Sillah ovim rett warum.

I didn't voice them, but there was a light pressure of some sort pushing me to.

It took a moment, but I realized where I'd heard them before —when Kierden started the bond between us. If I spoke them, it would seal our connection.

And theoretically also send murderers after us, on top of the Beast that was already hunting us.

So obviously, I couldn't say the words.

Kierden murmured into my ear, "Eisley brought food."

Apparently he'd realized I was awake.

"Okay." I made no move to get up. For once, I wasn't very hungry. I felt good, honestly. Really good. Better than I had in a long time.

He rolled away from me and lifted me to a sitting position.

Guess I was eating after all.

Kierden left me on the bed while he crossed the room and opened the door, angling his body so no one could see past him when he did.

"How is she?" Eisley asked quietly.

"Fine, now." He didn't budge.

"Please let me see her. I know I should've sent someone for you sooner, but Dirue said not to. It was a moment of poor judgment for both of us. We didn't realize how fragile humans are."

"A moment of poor judgment that could've cost Nissa her *life*," the king growled.

Maybe I'd been closer to death than I realized.

But Eisley had helped keep me sane since I'd been in Kierden's kingdom, so I couldn't leave her to deal with him on her own. I slipped out of bed and padded toward the door.

"You knew she had been starved too," Kierden said flatly.

His sister didn't answer immediately.

I pulled the door away from the king and stepped out in front of him, flashing Eisley a small smile. There was a rolling cart next to her, and the food on it looked absolutely incredible. My stomach rumbled, unsurprisingly. "I'm fine, Eisley. And I'm sure you had a good reason for everything you did or didn't do. No one here knows how to deal with humans."

Her gaze moved to me, grateful.

Kierden's hand landed on my hip, his grip tight as he pulled me back two steps until I collided with his chest.

"Thank you for the food." I caught Eisley's hand long enough to squeeze it, then grabbed the handle of the cart. "I really am fine. I'm sure he'll get tired of me and let me out of here soon." With that, I stepped backward.

Kierden didn't move, though, so all I managed to do was press my ass to the erection waiting for me.

"We'll talk later," Kierden warned her.

I looked up at him long enough to flash him a glare, and he met my eyes for the briefest moment before looking back to Eisley. "And..." He paused for a moment. "Thank you."

Her expression softened, and she dipped her head in a nod.

He set a hand on the cart's handle too and then took a few steps back, pulling me and the food inside with him before closing the door unceremoniously.

"You're not shaking anymore," he said, picking me up easily and carrying me toward the bed.

"Which means I can walk on my own feet."

He set me down on the mattress—next to the snoring esu, who had ended up snuggling together at some point. When he sat down on the other side, he pulled the food cart closer. His gaze moved over it like he was cataloguing everything.

I started to reach for a bowl of fruit on the side closest to me, but before I could grab it, he plucked a plate off the cart and set it in my hands.

I blinked down at the food.

It was some kind of breakfast cake, with thick chocolate sauce drizzled over it and nuts sprinkled over that.

"Why?" I asked him, not bothering to explain what I was questioning. We both knew I was asking why he'd picked that.

"Your diet will mainly consist of things to help you gain weight until you've recovered from the trauma you don't want to tell me about." He grabbed a bowl of some strange gel-like substance and set it next to me, then plucked another three plates off the cart and added it to the others he'd given me.

"I already feel better than I have in ages," I told him. "I think your blood might have healed the effects of that *trauma I don't want to tell you about*. Or at least made a dent in it."

When I looked down at my thigh, I honestly thought it looked a little thicker.

He leaned closer to me, grabbed the hem of my shirt, and lifted it up.

Some part of me wanted to shrink at the sudden intensity of his stare. But he had bathed with me the night before, and given me a climax too, so there wasn't really anything to hide from.

"You do look healthier," he said, with approval in his voice. "Your ribs are nearly hidden. But the other humans had more curve, so you still need to eat a lot."

With that, he dropped my dress.

My face burned. "So you looked at the other women and then decided I wasn't good enough?"

His eyes narrowed at me. "No. I saw your ribs, and then looked at the other women to see if theirs were visible. My attention was purely scientific. I felt no desire for them."

My responding gaze was skeptical.

"I was standing right next to the other kings. Either of them would've attacked me if they thought I was looking at their mate with interest. Take the fact that they didn't as your evidence."

"Kaelle doesn't think Vayme is even attracted to her," I countered.

"She's wrong," he said bluntly.

The look I gave him said I didn't believe him.

"Even if he isn't, fae are territorial. Having a mate makes that worse." Kierden added another plate to the crowd of them he'd already put in front of me.

"Are you saying you feel territorial of me?"

"Of course." He looked at me like the question was ludicrous.

I looked at him the same way.

Neither of us gave in for a long, long moment.

I was waiting for him to clarify vocally. The fact that I was still sleeping in his room at his insistence seemed like evidence enough of him being territorial, but I wanted him to say that.

He was waiting for... me to call him out, maybe?

For me to say I didn't believe he was territorial?

When another minute passed without either of us giving in, he finally looked away from me just long enough to cut into my chocolate-covered cake and lift the bite to my mouth.

I narrowed my eyes at him.

He narrowed his back.

Reluctantly, I took the bite.

"You're mine," he finally said. "The feelings and emotions behind that knowledge are complex, but the certainty remains. You belong to me. All else seems inconsequential, unless it puts your life at risk."

"And that's why you've been an asshole to me?"

"Moreso than I typically am," he agreed. "My kindness could be your end, and that made the distance between us a necessity."

Damn.

Death started to stir beside me, but I stroked his head, and he fell back asleep with a rumble of contentment.

"If we were to be together, we'd either have to let our bond break with the eclipse or seal it and keep it a secret," I said.

"We would." Kierden didn't deny it.

"Well, I don't want to be anyone's secret mate."

He lifted another bite of food toward me, and I snagged the utensil from his hand so I could feed myself.

I added, "In the extremely unlikely situation of us deciding we want to be together, I wouldn't be willing to do so in hiding. I was trapped for far too long to let the fear of someone's reaction hold me captive."

His expression darkened. "*Trapped*?"

I supposed I'd have to tell him about my past after all. I found myself actually *wanting* to tell him some of it, though.

"The tower you found me in was my prison. My mother ran the town, and she made sure I was kept starving and locked away so I could keep growing food for everyone."

His expression grew murderous. "I would've killed all of them if I'd realized. I thought the tower and guards were for your safety."

"They were for the *town's* safety. To keep everyone else from trying to steal their food source, and to make sure I wouldn't get more than a few feet away if I tried to escape on my own."

I scooped another bite of the cake. It was probably the best thing I'd ever tasted, and I'd had some incredible things in the time I'd been in Jirev.

"As soon as I'm free of the beast, I'll return to your town with a few of my warriors and end them all," he said. Though his voice was calm, I believed him completely.

"I don't want you to kill them all. The worst punishment would be to force them to relearn how to grow their own plants. But my plants shouldn't be too hard to tend to—and the town has so much money from selling my food that I don't think they'll even need to start any new farms. You should see the size of the gemstones the women have started wearing. A lot of them would've been big enough to feed the whole town with for months, before my magic came in."

"Then we'll burn your plants down, steal their money, and take their finery for ourselves," Kierden said bluntly.

My lips curved upward. "I appreciate that, but I don't want the kids in town to suffer. They don't know anything about the kind of hard work we put in before I was locked in the tower."

"Then they'll have to learn. Even if you leave them your plants and the gemstones you bought them, eventually, the money will run out. With the way humans age, it'll be the children in a few generations who suffer if you leave the plants, not the ones who wronged you. How long did they hold you?"

I grimaced. "Nine years."

His scowl deepened, his anger rising. "They *will* suffer for it. I'll ask a few warriors to remain in the Broken Woods to make sure the children don't go hungry, but the ones old enough to make a conscious decision to use you will pay."

"I just want to be done with my past, Kierden. I don't want to go back there for any reason, including revenge."

"Then you'll remain here, while I deal with it." He wasn't fazed even slightly by my reluctance.

"Alright." I leaned back against the wall.

He reached over, maneuvered my hand back to the cake, and scooped more food with my utensil.

We ate quietly for a bit, and my mind returned to what I'd said earlier about how I wasn't willing to be his secret mate. Kierden hadn't acknowledged that refusal—and I suspected it was because he had no solution for it.

Ultimately, nothing he'd ever said or done led me to believe he was willing to risk my life.

That put us in an impossible situation. The only way not to risk our lives was to keep any actual feelings for each other a secret.

According to Kierden, his people seemed to have accepted it when he told them that the bond was only to protect him from the Beast. That certainly didn't mean they would accept him taking me as a permanent mate.

"You didn't mention your father," Kierden remarked as I finished up with my food. I hadn't made it through everything he gave me, but I'd made a dent in it.

"I haven't," I agreed.

He waited.

I took another bite.

And another.

"You'll tell me eventually," he finally said.

Maybe he was right.

I guess that depended on what we decided to do when we were finally forced to make a decision about our mate bond.

We spent the next two days doing nothing of real worth. Kierden made me stay in his room to rest, since he was unconvinced that I'd already recovered. We chatted a little— him, mostly. I dodged pretty much all of the questions he asked me, since most of them were about my past, and I didn't want to keep talking about it. Particularly when he hadn't shared any pieces of his own history.

So, we settled on reading books and discussing them afterward, with our bonded esu snuggling up with us and offering the occasional thought.

It surprised me to find out how many emotions the king had when it came to fictional worlds. Especially because I had many emotions of my own. Many times, books had been what kept me sane in my tower, and they were the only real thing of value that my town had given me.

Then again, those books usually arrived after days where I'd gotten particularly agitated... and perhaps seemed slightly insane. So, my mother had probably been hoping the books would keep me docile.

On top of the reading, Kierden fed me a *lot*. We had five meals a day, and after I was certain I couldn't eat anything else, he fed me dessert.

It probably should've driven me mad to be stuck in his room, but I didn't feel trapped. I felt cared for, strangely enough. It was a foreign feeling, but one I loved.

And the fact that he slipped his hand between my thighs and gave me a climax every night before we fell asleep, without asking for anything in return, definitely didn't hurt.

CHAPTER 14

NISSA

When a knock came on the third day and Eisley said she needed us immediately, I was honestly a little sad.

We assumed the elves had arrived. As disappointing as it was, I'd known that life would eventually have to return to our version of normal, where Kierden ignored me, and I acted like I wasn't attracted to him.

I stepped into the bathroom to change, and took off the massive shirt I'd borrowed from the king. When I slipped into my orange dress, it caught on my hips. I had to tug hard to get it over them, which made me frown.

A glance at myself in the mirror made my eyes widen.

The dress *fit*.

Veil, it didn't even *fit*. It was *too tight*.

I beamed at my reflection as I turned sideways to see my profile, and the curves in it.

Damn, I looked good.

I definitely wasn't the same size or shape as any fae woman I had met, but I loved the flare of my hips, the softness of my belly, and the fullness of my breasts. They were healthy, human, and *alive*.

Kierden was waiting for me on the edge of the bed when I stepped out, and slowly, his eyes moved down my figure.

And then back up.

And then down again.

When they finally collided with mine, he couldn't have missed my grin.

His own lips curved upward slowly, until they formed a smirk. "Your dress is too tight; I suppose you'll have to wear the metal lingerie again."

I laughed. "Too bad you broke it."

We slipped out—him first and me second, with both esu behind me—but halted when we found a grave-looking Eisley waiting in the hallway.

"What happened?" Kierden's growl was immediate, every ounce of humor gone.

"We found another couple," Eisley said.

The sickness in her expression told me they'd probably found the couple mated and murdered.

Veil.

We'd thought she was there because of the *elves.*

"Who?"

Eisley gave two names I didn't recognize, but Kierden swore viciously.

Ice crept over his fists as he stormed down the hallway. Eisley kept his pace without a problem.

Death and Bright remained beside me as I stared behind them for a moment, then Bright bumped the side of my leg with her nose.

Right.

I needed to stick with them, because of the pain that would come from the bond if we were separated too much.

So I slipped onto Bright's back, leaning toward her and burying my fingers in her fur as she and Death caught up to the fae.

"You'll need to act indifferent," Bright murmured to me. *"Don't let anyone see that you and the king have gotten closer."*

I agreed.

Eisley and Kierden climbed onto the backs of their bonded esu, and then we were all moving quickly through the trees. I couldn't help but stare at the vibrant flowers that had spread through the jungle all around us. The further we ran, the more flowers I noticed.

None of them had been there before me. *I* had grown them and made the beauty of the jungle even more vibrant and alive.

I was proud of that, even if the tiniest bit of fear was curling in my belly at the fact that we were headed toward the bodies of two mated fae who had been killed.

We reached a small house built inside a tree. There were a few fae already standing on the platform just outside it. A few of them were crying, a few looked hollow... and a few looked absolutely furious.

Everyone parted for Kierden and Eisley, and their bonded esu stepped through the crowd and into the house.

Bright and I remained outside with the other fae. We hoped it would show respect for their dead and put distance between me and the king. A few of the fae glowered at me, and I tried not to shrink under the weight of their hatred. Most of them ignored me, so that made it slightly better.

"They're just mourning," Bright said quietly.

"She told me she wasn't going to seal the bond," one of the women near us said, wiping tears away with shaky hands. "She knew this could happen. Why did she seal it?"

"Why do any of them seal it?" another woman asked bitterly.

When no one answered, I realized it was a genuine question.

I remembered the itch in my mind to speak the words Kierden had said to me. The desire to seal the bond, even when I knew I didn't want that.

If I was in love with him, or actually wanted a sealed bond... veil, it would've been impossible to fight.

"They seal it because the magic pushes them to," I said quietly.

Everyone on the platform looked at me.

I explained, "There's an urge in your mind. It's unconscious, almost. You find yourself thinking the words you'd have to say to seal it, while the magic pushes you to speak them aloud. Even if you don't want it, you find yourself itching to do it. I'm so sorry for your loss, but it's not their fault; the magic most-likely made the decision for them."

Slowly, all of their gazes lowered to the glowing handprint around my wrist. Someone had taken my bracelet off me at some point while I was healing, and I hadn't thought about putting it back on.

My face warmed, slightly.

Kierden and Eisley emerged from the house, still on the backs of their bonded esu. Everyone was silent as they looked at the king.

There was something in his eyes—some combination of fury, horror, and guilt.

"Just like the last times," he said. His stance remained strong, and his gaze grew harder.

"The laws against sex helped prevent this," one of the male fae said.

"Refusing to start a bond in the first place is the only way to really stop it," another woman said solemnly.

"We should be free to create bonds if we want to." Eisley's face was pale, but her jaw was set firmly. "We should be allowed to take mates if it's something we desire."

"Not if it gets us killed," one of the men spat. "We need to catch the bastard who's doing this. We need to hunt again."

"We never *stopped* hunting, we just didn't find any damn leads," Kierden growled, his body tense.

"No one in the city could kill you," one of the women said. "If you sealed your bond with the human, we would have a chance of finally finding and ending the killer."

Everyone looked at me again.

Everyone except Kierden.

They wanted me to volunteer, to offer myself up as bait.

"No." Kierden's voice cut through the silence like a weapon. "Nissa is a human who's only lived a fraction of the time the rest of us have. After our bond dies with the eclipse, I'll mate with someone willing to risk their life for an answer."

His words stunned me.

And *veil*, they hurt me.

We'd been in bed together for days, talking for days, *touching* for days, and he just... volunteered to mate with someone else?

From what he'd told me, no one was killed until their bond was complete. And a complete bond was permanent.

I understood that what was happening was a tragedy, and that they needed a solution, but that didn't mean he needed to volunteer to mate with someone.

And he hadn't even *considered* choosing me permanently. After he'd spent days telling me he was attracted to me, he wanted me, he found me beautiful... the bastard may as well have slapped me in the face.

Nods went around the group of fae.

His people *approved* of his plan, and I couldn't question him without becoming either a target or a laughingstock.

I needed to get out of there. To get away from the king and clear my mind.

"The elves are approaching!" a voice called from somewhere deeper in the jungle.

"We'll comb the bodies and homes for any sign of magic or interference after I speak with the elves," Kierden said. He called three names and told them they would guard the home, and that they'd be working with him afterward. They agreed, and then Kierden, Eisley, and I headed off to meet the elves with our bonded esu.

Part of me wondered whether he'd even notice if Bright and I slipped away.

But then he glanced over his shoulder, looking me up and down. His voice touched my mind and he asked, *"Are you okay?"*

I stared at him.

What was I supposed to say?

Another mated couple had been murdered, solidifying the fact that Kierden and I could *not* seal our bond. Which I didn't want anyway, right?

And he had basically just told me we didn't have a future. We couldn't admit the truth of our developing feelings to his people, but if he really wanted me, he could've just gone along with volunteering me as the damn bait.

If we didn't have a future, what was I doing there at all? I couldn't watch him mate with another woman and just be friends with him after everything we'd done and been through.

Though I was nowhere near ready to seal our bond, some part of me had still been holding on to the possibility that I could be with Kierden in some capacity. Even if we were just lovers. I hated the idea of being mates in secret, but if we did break our bond, we could share a bed, share a home, share a life... it would have perks.

Perks that I could no longer allow myself to consider.

"I'm feeling sick," I lied. *"I'm going to go back to the castle and rest while you meet with the elves."*

His forehead wrinkled in concern. *"I'll ask Eisley to go with you."*

"No. I'd prefer to be alone."

He studied me for a moment, and then finally nodded and turned back.

"Let's go to the marketplace," I told Bright quietly. *"I need to get away from Kierden for a while."*

"We can ask Reo to make you dresses that fit," she suggested.

It sounded like the perfect way to distract myself for a bit, so I agreed, and she ran.

We reached the marketplace a few minutes later. The handprint on my wrist was throbbing thanks to my distance from Kierden, but I ignored it as well as I could. A lot less people were at the marketplace than the last time—and the ones who were there seemed much more subdued.

Kieren had told me he was certain the elves would agree to protect the fae kingdoms from their assassins when threatened with war. The elves weren't warriors. He also assumed they would send the other kings back to their own lands to make that protection easier, so the assassins couldn't work together. Because of that, I figured most people would be gathered together to hear how the meeting went.

Personally, I wasn't interested in fae politics, or elven politics, or... well, *anyone's* politics. I just wanted to live a peaceful life and spend the rest of my days with plenty of food to eat. How I was going to make that happen, I wasn't entirely sure.

Although if Kierden was going to mate with someone else, I supposed he was going to make my decision easy. I'd find a farm, convince someone to let me run it, and spend the rest of my life feasting on berries and vegetables.

I would miss the castle chef's incredible food and desserts, but I could sacrifice chocolate for safety and security.

There was no one in a few of the shops I passed, so I assumed those ones were closed. Reo's shop was open, so I slipped off Bright's back and walked toward a huge wooden bridge we'd need to cross to get there. Vines and flowers wrapped around nearly every inch of the bridge, but even that didn't really help my mood.

"What's wrong?" Bright asked me as we went.

"He said he was going to choose another mate," I admitted quietly.

"I heard. He may have just been trying to calm the other fae."

"I don't think so. He told me that the couples being murdered are one of his greatest shames. It doesn't seem like a stretch that he would risk his life trying to fix it, especially now that the war is over and the fae are trying to figure out how they want to live. A lot of them probably want to take mates."

"Perhaps. You'll need to talk to him, to find out," she mused.

"It seems like he'll say anything he can to get what he wants, though. I don't know if I can trust him."

"What does he want?"

"I don't know. Sex?"

"If all he wanted was sex, he would've asked or tried to make a move on you at night," she pointed out. Though she and Death always left when things got steamy, I'd kept her updated on the

developments between us because she was the only woman I could really talk to.

Or female, at least.

I would've liked to find Kaelle or Laeli and talk to them, but Kaelle was gone with Vayme, and Kierden hadn't let me out of our room since things started progressing. Eisley was obviously out too, since she was his sister. She wasn't hanging out in the room reading books with us or anything, so even if I wanted to talk to her, I couldn't.

I heaved a sigh. *"Stop being reasonable, Bright."*

She chuffed as we walked into the clothing shop. *"Esu are not like fae. We don't appreciate drama. If a male esu wants you, he tells you. Kierden has told you that he wants you, so trust him. He's never lied to you before."*

"But if there's really a chance he's going to mate with someone else after the eclipse, I can't risk letting myself develop any more feelings for him. I'd rather not have him than have him and lose him."

She rubbed her side against mine. *"I understand."*

We walked up to Reo, who was sitting in a chair with a book in his hands. The back of his chair was leaned up against a wall, and one of his ankles was draped over his knee. He lifted his eyes as we approached, and his lips curved upward just a tiny bit. "Hello."

"Hi. I need a few more dresses," I said apologetically. "Mine don't fit. I don't have any money, but—"

"You're keeping our king alive, from what I hear. I'll send him the bill." He winked at me, and I relaxed. "Come with me."

Bright and I followed him into the room where he'd taken my measurements the last time. At his command, I stripped. My face heated as I looked down at myself.

Yeah, *everything* was too tight. Scanties included.

"This will only take a moment," Reo said absentmindedly, as he started measuring my different parts. I fixed my gaze on one of the lights moving lazily through the room, and for the first time since I'd been in Jirev, I wondered what they were made of.

"Where do the lights come from?" I asked him, as he finished up his measurements.

He held up a finger, going back to the wall and scribbling some things down. When he returned, he said simply, "We call them glow bugs. In the language of the lost gods, they're named *huvin*." He held a hand out toward the creature.

After a moment, the bug descended slowly. Finally, it landed on his palm.

I stepped closer, eyes widening in fascination as I looked at it. We didn't have a human equivalent for it, but it was big and round, with a bit of fuzz on its body and two teeny antennae. Its entire body glowed, and seemed to brighten as he held it.

"What makes them glow?"

"They feed on our magic," he explained.

I blinked, resisting the urge to jerk away from the creature.

Reo's lips curved upward again, and he lifted my dress off the floor before he handed it back to me. "It doesn't hurt. The amount of magic they can take is so minute you won't even feel it. Quite handy to have around though, hmm?"

"Definitely." I tugged my dress back over my head. "Thank you for doing this. I should be able to get by with three more dresses, since I'm not sure if I'm finished growing or not."

He nodded, and we started walking toward the exit. "What colors?"

"Whatever you have that matches the flowers outside."

He assured me that wouldn't be a problem, and I headed out.

As I slipped onto Bright's back, I asked her, *"Do you know where we could go to talk to someone with a farm? I'd like to be able to use my magic to grow food for the kingdom, if they're interested in my help."*

"Of course." She headed down a bridge I hadn't crossed before, one just as covered in flowers and vines as the last one we'd walked. *"It'll be good for you to find your own place here, in case Kierden ends up being a worse man than I think he is."*

"You have a lot of faith in him," I grumbled at her.

She chuffed. *"I have a lot of faith in the power of mate bonds."*

I supposed that was good enough reasoning.

The pain in the handprint on my wrist grew fiercer as Bright carried me to the farm. It was on the ground, at the base of the town-sized tree the castle was built into. There was another farm in the treetops too, according to Reo, but it was on the far end of the city. That was too far from Kierden, so I knew it wasn't a possibility for me.

I ignored the stabbing pain as my gaze moved over the many rows of crops in awe. I'd helped my dad in the fields as a kid, so standing in front of them again felt a lot like coming home.

My town had been a mess of fruit and vegetable plants, all of which had been allowed to grow wildly and without reason so long as they produced something edible or sellable. In Jirev, even with my magic making everything grow better, they were still being kept neat and orderly.

I'd planned to walk out to the middle of the fields and sit down for a while, taking the time to try to figure out how to control my magic again. Staring out at the plants, I was no longer sure I could make my way out there without messing up any of the crops. And I really didn't want to piss off the farmer, so...

Guess we were staying near the castle.

Bright plopped down and closed her eyes, readying herself for a nap.

I noticed a wide door built into the tree's trunk and figured it must be the house of whoever the farmer was, so I walked up and knocked.

After a long moment, the door opened.

A beautiful male fae opened the door, his expression dark and grumpy. He had tousled, curly navy-blue hair, light brown skin, and wore nothing but a pair of shorts.

"Hi," I said, fighting the urge to take a quick step back and shrink in on myself a little.

"Ignore his attitude," a gorgeous female fae said, slipping out from behind him and giving me a massive smile. Her hair was tied in a thick, messy bun made up of small braids, her skin was dark brown, and her eyes glowed a soft purple color. All she had on was a pair of fancy scanties that looked as if they'd been pulled on in a hurry.

She looked happy, I thought.

Really, really happy.

His hand landed on her hip, and he stepped closer to her, eyeing me with less anger and more curiosity. "You're the human who's bonded to King Kier."

"Yes. I didn't mean to bother you—I was just wondering if I could sit in your fields while I practice with my magic. I figured I might as well grow something useful while I try." The pain in my wrist flared as I finished speaking, and I bit down on the inside of my cheek to stop from wincing.

Kierden must've started moving. He hadn't mentally demanded to know where I was though, so he hadn't figured me out yet.

Probably.

The woman's smile widened. "Of course; sit anywhere. Your magic has already made our job a lot easier. Don't be afraid to mess things up, either. We'll come out and fix anything we need to later."

"Thanks." I gave them both a quick smile, then turned and strode out into the fields as if my wrist didn't hurt like a fiend. The soil was soft and damp beneath my toes, and something about it made my lips curve upward.

Being there felt... right.

Something about the fields made my heart settle, and the ache in my chest calm.

I was exactly where I was supposed to be.

The pain in my wrist eased to just an ache as Bright followed me out. I figured Kierden was headed back toward the castle, and assumed he'd reach out into my mind all grumpy and growly when he realized I wasn't there.

But I needed the space from him, so I could think without the heaviness of his presence looming over me. While I liked that heavy presence, I had to be careful not to let it overshadow me and what I wanted.

"*I love it out here,*" I admitted to Bright, as I sat down on the soil before lowering my back to the ground. With the plants around me and the trees above me, it was calm and beautiful. I almost wondered if I'd somehow managed to cross the veil and find a more perfect world than Evare without realizing it.

"*It suits you.*" She licked my arm.

"*I wish there was a way to stay here. The fields still feel like home to me.*"

"*The last time I was here, the fae were arguing about who would be stuck tending the gardens when the rest of them went to fight. Perhaps they'd still like someone else to take over.*" With that, she put her head back down on her paws and fell asleep quickly. Esu needed more sleep than humans or fae, I'd realized—or maybe they just enjoyed it more than us.

I considered her idea as I stared up at the trees.

With the fields just below the castle, it wasn't an ideal living space. I'd be closer than I wanted to be to Kierden, considering we weren't going to be mated. But my mind gave me an image —a blissful one—of me spending my days in the fields and my nights in the castle with Kierden. We'd read and talk. We'd kiss, and bathe. We'd...

I closed my eyes and let out a long breath.

We weren't going to be together after the eclipse came around.

That was a hard thing to accept, but a necessary one.

And if I didn't create the life I wanted to live, I wasn't going to enjoy the one I ended up in.

So I formed a plan in my mind as I stared up at the trees above me and decided that I was going to make the farm my home, regardless of the cost.

I let a good chunk of time go by—without hearing from Kierden, though the pain had vanished—before I got up, dusted as much soil off my back and ass as possible, then walked back to the building.

I'd tried to make my magic respond to me again, but it was like there was no connection between me and it. I tried to stop it, and it ignored me. I tried to increase the flow of it, but that was useless, too.

I had a plan to persuade the farmers to let me take over their job. The chance of said plan succeeding was slim, but why not take the chance?

Rejection was the worst thing that could happen, and rejection was nothing compared to the misery I had already survived.

My fist rapped on the wood of the door again. This time, the tree's inhabitants opened it faster, and both of them looked slightly more put-together than the last time. The woman still wasn't wearing clothes, but I was used to seeing fae women in their scanties, so I really didn't care.

"Hi again," I said, giving them the biggest smile I could muster. "My bonded esu told me that you don't love working the fields, so I was wondering, would you be interested in handing the job over to me?"

They blinked at me.

"I'm sure you have a system, but I can learn it," I said quickly. "I'd—"

"It's all yours," the woman said, grinning broadly as she stepped back and gestured for me to come inside. "The fields, the house... veil, anything you want. Take it, please."

It was my turn to blink at her. "Just like that?"

She laughed.

The man grinned.

"The rest of the kingdom forced us down here because we refused to follow their laws against having sex during wartimes," she explained. "We're not mated, but we would be if we could do it without getting killed."

The look she gave my glowing handprint was a lingering one, and it made my heart ache a little for her.

"So this was a *punishment* for you?" I asked, a bit incredulous as I looked around the house. It was small but spacious, and looked cozy and comfortable.

There were two long windows built into the front walls and partially covered by thick, white curtains. The bed off to the side of the room was nearly as big as Kierden's. The kitchen was large and nice, the floors and walls were polished wood of course, and frames holding beautiful, dried flowers were displayed throughout the space.

"Yup." The man pointed to the kitchen, and I noticed one of the walls looked like it was covered in writing, like the one in Reo's dress shop. "There's the schedule for when people come to pick their produce. You don't have to harvest anything you don't want to eat yourself; your job is just to grow the plants. It used to be a lot more difficult than it is right now."

The woman winked at me.

My lips stretched widely. "I think I can manage that."

She laughed, crossed the room, and then pulled me in for a fierce hug. "Thank you so much. We'll just grab our things and get out of your hair."

The next few minutes were a whirlwind. They packed up much faster than I expected—even taking the sheets and blankets off the bed—and then left me alone.

Alone with the plants, the trees, and the esu who had become my most trusted friend.

"Well, that was easier than I expected," I mused to Bright.

She chuffed. *"I told you no one wanted the job."*

"I'm really glad you're right."

I opened the curtains and windows to air out the smells of strangers, and then went outside and picked a few of my flowers. They'd probably grow inside the house if I left them there, and I liked the idea of that.

I set them around the room, hoping they'd help freshen up the scent while I headed up to the castle to grab some bedding and my clothes.

There were a lot of fae moving around throughout the castle when Bright carried me inside again. A few of them waved at me, and though I waved back, none of them stopped me to talk.

I sat down and ate a meal in the dining room, surrounded by strangers, all of whom had a bonded esu with them. I took that to mean they were all from Kierden's kingdom.

A bunch of them were in the middle of a discussion, and I listened in long enough to learn that the king had been right. A few elves had agreed to go to each of the kingdoms to defend the land from the assassins, and so the fae from those kingdoms had all filed out with their kings, Laeli, and Kaelle.

The subject changed to the murders, and everyone's voices grew hopeful as they talked about Kierden agreeing to mate with someone after my bond with him broke. They all seemed certain that he would be able to end the murderer when that person came for him, easily.

I wasn't sure it would be that simple, but I tried not to let their emotions sway my own too much. It was a little difficult to hear them talk about Kierden mating with someone other than me, but I'd be fine.

I had to believe that.

When I'd finished my meal, I slipped out of the dining hall and headed to the nearest room. I knocked on the door and found the space empty of fae and personal belongings, confirming that it was open.

Quickly, I stripped the blankets off the bed, followed by the pillows. Tying everything in a bundle was a bit of a struggle, and it ended up nearly as big as me, but I managed.

After I grabbed some toiletries too, I made a quick stop in Kierden's room for the rest of my things, including the three big shirts of his I'd claimed. I packed all of it into a bag, then climbed up onto Bright's back, struggling to hold everything while maintaining my balance.

Her amusement swelled alongside mine as she carried me out of the castle. We got a few curious looks, but no one followed us down to the fields, thankfully.

My heart was beating fast and my lips were stretched in a massive grin when I slammed the door behind us.

I was already imagining Kierden's fury when he realized I'd moved out of his room without his permission... and veil, it made my grin even wider.

My excitement faded into peaceful happiness as I set up my new home. The blankets went on the bed, the toiletries in the bathroom, and the clothing in the closet.

When I was done, my happiness had faded too, and I found myself frowning at the home I'd claimed.

It was beautiful, and comfortable. Far more of a home than my tower had ever been. And the door worked properly—I'd made sure it couldn't be locked from the outside.

But something about it felt sort of... lonely.

I supposed that was to be expected, after sharing a bed with Kierden for nearly a month. I just wasn't used to being on my own anymore.

Deciding that I wasn't going to let that affect me, I threw myself into reading the couple's notes about the fields. When I finished reading, I walked the length of them on my own two feet, forcing myself to chat with Bright about anything and everything I could think of as we went. There were miles and miles of fields, and even though my wrist hurt, I kept moving.

If Kierden had changed his mind about wanting me, that was his problem. He had bigger things to deal with than a mate bond he hadn't wanted, and I did too.

Or at least, I tried to convince myself of that.

When the sun faded from the sky and the jungle grew quiet around me, I sat down on the edge of the bed and finally forced myself to admit the truth:

I loved the plants, but I was *lonely*.

I kept remembering the way I'd felt sitting in that bed with Kierden, talking about fictional worlds and characters as if they were real ones, and I missed that.

I missed it a lot.

Not just the conversation, though. The feeling that I wasn't alone. That someone liked me and cared about me, on top of it.

After spending nine years almost entirely alone, I'd finally spent a month living with someone else. Even when I hadn't liked Kierden, I had liked that he was next to me.

And... I wasn't willing to be alone any longer.

I wasn't willing to be his secret mate, and I wasn't willing to wait for him to reject me, either. When our bond disappeared, my magic would take control of me again without anyone's ice to slow it. If that happened, I'd only have a few solid hours of consciousness a day.

Which meant I was going to have to find someone else to bond with.

My stomach clenched at the thought, but there really wasn't an alternative. Even if there was, I didn't think I would settle for it.

I wanted a male to lay in bed with me and talk about books. To bathe with me when I felt sick and tell me I looked beautiful when I felt terrible. I wanted a husband; I wanted a *mate*. And when Kierden and his pretty fae woman stopped the murderers, I decided I was going to have exactly that.

Surely, I could talk *someone* into not despising farming. Some grumpy, battle-hardened warrior who needed a soft human to snuggle and take care of. Or some brilliant fae male who wanted a woman who'd discuss vague topics she didn't really understand with a great deal of passion and stubbornness...

I refused to admit to myself that Kierden functioned as both of those men in my mind.

So, I put on my pink dress and slipped back out of my house.

Bright carried me up to the nearest tavern. She seemed amused by my determination to meet a nice man. *"If you're really that desperate for a male, you can have one of my suitors,"* she drawled, as I climbed off her back just outside. It was near the marketplace, so my hand was aching something fierce, but I ignored the pain yet again.

Laughing, I said, *"Sure, I'll take Death off your hands right now."*

She gave me a feline grin. *"Not that one."*

"Think you might keep him?"

"Perhaps."

She was completely in love with him but still playing hard to get, which I got a kick out of.

We slipped inside the tavern, and I was surprised by the noise. It was large, and built into a tree like all the other homes in the city, which somehow made the whole kingdom feel like home to me. Some of my vines and flowers seemed to have invaded the place already, climbing down the walls and wrapping around the furniture.

One side of the space was taken up by a long countertop with a row of stools in front of it. Beside each stool was a cushion for an esu to sit on. Most of them were occupied, with only a few empty seats remaining.

The other side of the room was filled with tables of varying sizes, all of which were surrounded by multiple chairs.

Every table and most of the chairs were full of fae. Some were talking loudly and laughing. Others were quiet, seeming lost in their minds.

Off in the corner by the tables, a female fae was playing a smooth, soulful song on a stringed instrument I'd never seen before. The music filled the air and made the whole place feel more welcoming.

I didn't see anyone I knew in the tavern, so I just headed over to one of the empty chairs and sat down.

The man to my right looked over and grinned. "You're the king's human?"

Well, that was a *great* way to be identified. "For now."

He laughed.

A female fae brought me a drink, but stopped before she handed it over, and eyed me with some suspicion. "I'm not sure how our ale will affect a human."

"I'm not completely human," I said. "Other than the ears, of course."

The magic was a fairly distinctive difference.

The man next to me grinned, and the woman holding the ale looked curious.

Assuming that curiosity was for said ears, I dutifully pulled my hair away from one of them, turning to the side.

"Damn," the woman admired.

The man next to me ran a finger over the curve of my ear without asking permission first. I shuddered a little, but not because it felt good. Something about his touch just felt *wrong*. Especially after Keirden had dragged his tongue over that same curve.

"Don't touch her while she's the king's," the man on the other side of me growled, reaching past me to smack the other fae's hand away. "Do you *want* him to kill you?"

"He's just using me for my magic. I really don't think he'd care," I said, though the words felt bitter on my tongue.

I honestly wasn't sure how he'd feel.

"He'll be territorial with the bond between you, even though he doesn't want you," the man who hadn't touched me said.

I tried not to shrink at his words.

Even though he doesn't want you.

I reached over and took the drink from the woman's hand, and she leaned over the countertop for a moment. "If the king shows up furious and asks who served you, point to him." She pointed to a mean-looking guy handing out drinks on the other end of the counter.

I nodded.

But I was pretty sure that if the king showed up and got furious, his anger wouldn't be for the person who served me. It would just be for *me*.

"So what are you doing here?" the man who'd touched my ear asked. "Kier doesn't have you chained to his side while he looks into the murders?"

"Nope." I dodged his first question about what I was doing there, electing to lift the drink to my nose and sniff it.

It smelled so strong it made my eyes water, so I set it right back down. If I experimented with fae ale, I wasn't going to do it surrounded by strangers. For all I knew, they could lock me up and make me grow their crops too.

Then again, it wasn't as if I'd be difficult for them to trap if they wanted to. They were immortal fae warriors, after all.

The man who'd touched my ear took my drink, since his own was gone, and swallowed it in three loud gulps.

Maybe he wasn't the best choice to sit next to.

"You didn't say why you're here," he pointed out.

"I was lonely," I admitted.

He grinned at me, leaning closer. "I can keep you company."

The guy who'd smacked his hand leaned past me again and shoved at the other man's chest, hard. "Go home, or I'll kick your ass for the king."

The drunk man laughed, but he climbed out of his chair and swaggered off.

"Guess he's afraid of you," I told the man sitting next to me.

"Guess so." He grunted.

"I'm going to have to start a new bond after the eclipse," I told him, the words blurting out of my mouth. "If I don't, I'll lose control of my magic again, and I'll be unconscious most of the time."

"Damn."

"Yeah. I..." I bit my lip. "I'm Nissa." I offered him a hand.

He eyed it but didn't shake it. "Noin," he said. "And I'm sure the king will be here soon. I wouldn't mention looking for a new bond until after your current one is broken if you don't want to get locked in the castle."

He paused for a moment, then added, "And you should put ale on your ear; if Kier smells another man on your skin, he'll go hunting."

Veil.

"Thanks," I said weakly.

The woman who'd given me the first drink showed up with a new glass and set it down in front of me. "I found some weak ale in the back. It should be safer for you."

"Thank you." I gave her a small smile, and she left me with the ale.

I sipped a tiny bit, making a face at the strange, bitter taste.

Maybe going to a tavern wasn't such a good idea after all, because somehow, doing so had only managed to make me feel even lonelier. And the constant pain in my wrist only made that worse.

I wished Kierden was there... even though I knew I needed to move on.

CHAPTER 16

KIERDEN

I rubbed the exhaustion out of my eyes, staring at the sheet-covered bodies as if merely looking at them would produce the answers I needed.

After the elves had ridden in with their glittering magic and unreasonably delicate dresses, they'd formed an invisible shield over my city. The warriors and kings who'd been in my kingdom for the events had gone home soon after, thankfully.

When that was done, I'd gone back to the castle and spent the rest of my day trying to figure out the damned murders that had been plaguing us for so long.

I itched to go find my female, who must've been in and out of the castle all day if the ache in my palm was any sign. I knew she'd be safe with Bright, and I had a responsibility to my people to look for any evidence.

As always, there had been none.

The kings before me hadn't taken the killings seriously enough, and that gave the damn murderer time to perfect their method long before I was ever in a situation to find the killer.

The rest of the fae had already gone home or out to taverns, looking to drink away the stress of the day. We'd continue searching when morning came around, but the fact that we hadn't found anything was far from a good omen.

The door opened, and Eisley stepped in. Her expression was clouded as she sat down in the chair beside me.

A long, heavy moment passed between us before she finally said, "You didn't hear this from me, but I heard people talking about seeing Bright and Nissa in a tavern."

I blinked.

A *tavern*?

Why would Nissa go to a tavern?

I had no idea if our ale would affect her. Or if the other males would try to charm her in an attempt to share a bed with her. I'd lied to them about taking a mate, and they thought I wasn't interested in her. If any of them tried anything...

Veil, I'd kill them.

"Thanks," I told her, already striding across the room toward Death, who was sitting in the hallway.

He was up and waiting for me when I made it through the doors. I threw a leg over his back, and he took off through the castle. We were in the trees a moment later, running toward our females.

It didn't take long to get there. As soon as my feet hit the ground, I was striding into the tavern. My eyes landed on my female immediately, finding her small, soft form and her long, dark green hair without a problem.

She looked calm, with her hands wrapped around a glass of ale that was the wrong color.

Had someone drugged it?

I fought the urge to snarl at everyone and whisk her out of there, to make sure she was alright. She'd told me she wasn't feeling well—and when I stopped by the room to check on her after talking to the elves, she wasn't there. I had assumed she started feeling better and went out to do something, not that she'd gone to a *tavern*.

Apparently, I should've reached out to her mind or asked Death to find her instead.

There was an empty chair on one side of her, and Noin sat on the other. Rather than throwing her over my shoulder and stealing her away like I wanted to, I forced myself to calmly cross the tavern and take the seat next to her.

She glanced over at me, and then looked over again with surprise lighting those gorgeous green eyes. Her cheeks were flushed beautifully, but she said nothing.

If she wasn't bothering with a greeting, neither was I.

I plucked her glass from her hands, ignoring her weak protest as I lifted it to my nose and sniffed. It smelled like... watery ale. I only allowed myself to drink once or twice a year—usually at the eclipse—but I still knew the scent well.

"What is this?" I asked.

"Weak ale. It's gross, huh?" She tried to take it back anyway.

I hadn't smelled anything suspicious on the liquid, and I believed that.

I moved it away from her. "Why are you in a *tavern*, Nissa? You told me you were ill."

She opened her mouth to speak, then glanced around the room.

"Little human," I warned.

"I'm a farmer now," she finally said. "Farmers drink ale." She tried to steal the drink from me again, but the attempt was almost humorously ridiculous.

"What does that mean?" I was still itching to grab her and get out of there.

She huffed at me. "You don't care."

Before I could tell her she was wrong, the woman sitting beside me set her hand on mine. I jerked toward the woman with a growl as I ripped my hand away.

"Did you find any evidence, Kier?" Tal asked me, batting her eyelashes.

"Not yet." My annoyance flared.

"I would be willing to mate with you. If someone has to make the sacrifice, I'll do it."

"I have a mate," I growled back at her, the response so immediate and harsh that she leaned away from me, her eyes flooded with surprise.

"She's nothing more than a shield," Tal said. "You're a warrior, and you deserve to be mated to one too."

I didn't want a veil-damned warrior—I wanted my human.

I couldn't say that, though.

"I'll mate with whomever I choose should the necessity arrive. That is none of your concern, as you damn well know," I told her bluntly, turning away from her.

When I looked back at Nissa, I found her chair empty.

Bright was gone too.

"They left," Death told me.

"Clearly," I growled back. *"Where did they go?"*

"I don't know. Your female looked upset, and Bright told me she'd flay me if I followed her."

"You'd be thrilled if she flayed you." I abandoned the glass of human ale and strode toward the door as I reached out for my human's mind.

I'd find her—and I'd get the answers I wanted from her.

My lips curved upward wickedly as I considered the many ways I could do exactly that.

CHAPTER 17

NISSA

I slammed the door behind me and collapsed against the wood, breathing fast. The ale was not sitting well in my stomach—not well at all. I'd only had a few sips, and all it had managed to do was make me feel dizzy and flushed, which was miserable.

And then Kierden had shown up and made me feel all strange, and that *woman* had touched his hand...

I shuddered.

I'd never wanted to physically hurt anyone before. That really wasn't my personality. Sure, I had hoped my town would be burned down on many occasions, but I'd never actually wanted to do the burning myself.

And yet, I wanted to wrap my hands around that woman's neck and squeeze until the life had drained out of her.

Veil, what had possessed me?

Despite my horror at my own reactions, something inside me was still repeating:

He's mine.

He's mine.

He's mine.

"Veil," I groaned, squeezing my eyes shut and hoping Kierden couldn't hear those damn thoughts.

I never should've accepted that ale.

I never should've let myself start to care about the damn fae king.

What was I supposed to do now?

"Are you alright?" Bright asked me, sounding somewhere between amused and concerned.

At least one of us was enjoying the night.

"Fantastic," I lied.

She chuffed.

"Where are you, Nissa?" Kierden's voice echoed in my mind, low, growly, and making me shiver all over again.

I ignored him.

He wasn't getting a single damn answer from me.

Eventually, he'd follow my scent trail and find me.

Still, the longer it took him, the longer I'd have to try to gather my loose, ale-drowned wits.

I forced myself to remember why I'd moved out of his room.

He'd promised to mate with some random fae woman.

He hadn't considered even asking me if I'd be willing to just seal our bond instead.

He'd lied to me about wanting me—he only wanted sex.

Even if Bright didn't think that last part was true, I still felt like it was. Why else would he be so damn certain that he had to choose a fae female? Why else would he have told his people that he'd be in some other woman's bed as soon as the eclipse removed our connection?

My mind was moving too fast, spinning too quickly.

The room was moving a little, too.

Why did I think the ale was a good idea?

"Tell me where you are, or I'll have no choice but to start hunting you, little human," Kierden purred into my mind.

I shuddered yet again.

The mental bond was only getting more intimate, not less.

And what in the veil was I going to do about that?

"He's looking for you," Bright said, her voice almost... pleased.

"How do I stop him?" I asked her.

She chuffed. *"I don't think you do."*

I was in trouble.

Deep, deep trouble.

"Last chance," Kierden said into my mind.

He sounded just as pleased as Bright did.

"Just go home," I finally told him, a little desperation in my voice. *"I'm done."*

The door behind me flew open, shoving me forward with it. A thick arm caught me by the waist before I could land on my face, and then a hard chest was pressed to my back as my feet were lifted off the ground.

"You are *terrible* at hiding," the king growled into my ear. He stepped inside the house, and I heard him inhale deeply. "Why does it smell like you in here?"

I tried to keep my voice even as I said, "I moved out."

"You *what?*" His humor and playfulness were gone.

"I moved out of your room. The people living here offered me their house when I said I'd take over growing the food, and I accepted. I belong here, now. Among the plants."

"You're not a veil-damned *plant*, Nissa. You're not living among them," he growled into my ear, gripping my waist even tighter. "You're coming back to my room."

"I'm *not*," I shot back. "I'm *not* living with you for the next two months just so you don't have to deal with your own territorial feelings before you jump in bed with another woman as soon as the eclipse is over. I'm *not* going to let you touch me again before you abandon me. I'm *not* going to be the woman you only care about in secret, or the one you ignore as soon as you leave your bedroom, or the one you lie to just to enjoy a few months of sex with a bonded mate."

My eyes started stinging, and I reached up and wiped at them angrily. He was still holding me up off the floor, his lips near my ear, but he said nothing.

A moment of silence passed.

A long, long moment of silence.

I finally added in a shaky voice, "You don't get to use me, Kierden. No one gets to use me anymore. You're no better than my mother, using my magic to protect yourself without giving a damn about me. My feelings matter—I matter. Even if I'm not as important as you."

Another silent moment followed.

Despite the anger and bitterness I was feeling, getting the words out in the open made me feel... free.

Really free.

I felt like I could breathe again.

Kierden finally set me down on my feet.

I expected him to argue.

To tell me that I was wrong—that he thought I mattered, too. To say that he hadn't just used me or my magic, that he'd also protected me and taken care of me and more recently, fed me.

But he didn't.

Instead, he walked away.

I turned around in time to see Death disappear into the darkness of the trees.

My eyes stung more, they stung *worse*. A few tears dripped down my cheeks as I shut the door. Silently, I walked over to the edge of my bed and then sat down on the mattress.

I was fine.

I was going to be fine.

Kierden was only one man, and there were so many others out there. Others who would treat me better. Others I would like more.

But my mind kept going back to the way he had washed me in the bathing pool. To how gentle his hands had been, and how he hadn't been angry with me for risking my life when the Beast asked who was bonded to him.

My thoughts returned to the way he'd offered to wreck my mother's town, so the people could get what they deserved for the way they'd used and mistreated me.

A few more tears dripped out.

Despite the pain I was feeling, Kierden *had* been good to me. He hadn't—

The door opened again.

I blinked, wiping the water from beneath my eyes once more.

Kierden stood in the doorway with a bag thrown over his shoulder and steel in his eyes.

I blinked again.

He stepped inside.

Bright slipped out, knocking the door shut behind her and murmuring, *"Good luck."*

My throat swelled with emotion.

Why had he come back?

Neither of us said a word as he dropped his bag and then crossed the room in three massive steps.

He sank to his knees in front of me. The man was so insanely large that even kneeling while I sat on the bed, his eyes were only a few inches below mine.

He took my face in his hands, his grip firm and strong, but gentle too. "I'm sorry," he said, his voice low and honest. "I'm *sorry*, Nissa. When I first took you from your town, I *did* use you for your magic, and I am sorry for that. But I'm not your mother. I revel in the fire burning in your chest and the way you argue with me, as I always have. I care about your comfort, your health, and your happiness—and I have never tried to use you for sex, as you know well."

My eyes started watering again.

Dammit, he was right.

He hadn't tried to use me for sex.

It was an easy excuse to make, but not an honest one.

"It hurt you when I told my people I would mate with someone else," he said.

I squeezed my eyes shut for a moment, trying not to let my face contort with emotion. "It did."

His forehead met mine, the pressure comfortable. "I have never lied to you, and I never will. It didn't occur to me that my words might hurt you, but if I had told my people that I would mate with you to hunt down my killers, they would've realized what you mean to me already. I wasn't willing to take the chance that they could use it against both of us."

He admitted, "I don't know who the killer is; it could be anyone in my whole damn kingdom. If I give away my emotions, I put you at risk, and that's not something I'm willing to do at this point. Perhaps we'll decide to mate to hunt down the killer, and perhaps we won't. Either way, it will be *our* decision. Not theirs. I assumed you would see the deception for what it was, knowing that I care for you, and I'm sorry that I didn't make sure you understood. That was my fault, and it won't happen again."

My eyes stung. "That was a lot of apologies."

He gave me a rough, rueful chuckle. "I suppose I have a lot to apologize for."

"So you're not really going to mate with a fae woman after the eclipse is over?"

"No. I've been with my people for centuries, Nissa. If I were interested in pairing off with one of them, I would certainly have her in my bed by now."

My lips curved upward, just a tiny bit.

He had *me* in his bed. Which meant he was interested in pairing off with me, if his previous statements were to be trusted. I didn't know whether they were or not, but I still liked the sound of it.

"I have no experience with romantic relationships," Kierden squeezed my face between his palms lightly. "If I do something wrong, I need you to tell me so I can fix it. I won't get everything right the first time—veil, at this rate, I'll probably get everything wrong the first time. But I am trying, Nissa. I swear that to you."

"Is that what we have?" I asked him, still feeling vulnerable. "A romantic relationship?"

"Yes." He didn't have any doubt, and that made me feel a little more secure. "Though I seem to be failing at it, if you aren't sure. Perhaps I should spend more time in the nude so you can see exactly how you affect me."

My lips curved upward, slightly. "I'm sure that would help."

He tilted my head back slightly with his grip on my face, then captured my lips in his.

There was no hesitation. No pause. No fear. No question. Just his mouth on mine.

It was soft at first. He was giving me time to push him away, I supposed.

But I didn't want to push him away. I wanted him, the same way he wanted me.

It was my first kiss, but I wasn't nervous. Not with his grip on my face and his mouth on mine. I trusted him to take care of me.

He parted my lips, and we groaned together as his tongue stroked mine. The contact was strange, but perfect. Nothing like I'd expected, and yet so much more than I'd hoped for at the same time.

Kierden pulled away after a few minutes, and it made me fiercely proud when I saw his chest rising and falling almost as quickly as my own. He took a step back, burying his hand in his hair and gripping tightly, as if trying to resist grabbing me again.

His gaze was hot as it moved up and down my skin slowly. "How much ale did you drink?"

I lifted a shoulder. "Not much." Though I still felt flushed and a little dizzy, I found myself not minding it anymore.

"That was your first glass?"

I nodded.

"And it was watered down?"

"Yes. Why are you asking me this?" I eyed him, wishing he'd go back to kissing me already. While I looked at him, I debated the merits of throwing myself at him, so he had no choice but to start kissing me again.

"I'm trying to decide how much of an asshole I'd be if I stripped you bare and licked you until you unraveled on my tongue," he growled back.

Oh.

Ohhhh.

"Not an asshole," I said quickly. "Not at all."

Veil, I was *dying* to know how that would feel.

"A drunk female would feel the same way." He slid his hands into his pockets.

I was losing him.

If I didn't convince him immediately, my night was going to end in more talking.

And... I didn't want to talk anymore. I wanted to be distracted. Preferably by his fingers and mouth.

"You could touch me again," I said.

He narrowed his eyes at me. "A drunk female would say that, too. The last thing I want is for you to wake up feeling violated."

Damn him for caring.

Even though I really did appreciate that. I just... well, I wanted to be violated by him.

"I let you touch me before," I told him. "So technically, I already gave you permission to do that."

His gaze was skeptical.

I rose to my feet and stepped toward him until our chests collided. His hands landed on my hips, and his skepticism grew softer.

"That woman touched you," I said. "I saw it. She touched you and she offered to be your mate, so I left. What did you say to her after I was gone?"

His expression morphed into a scowl. "I told her that I already had a mate, and that I wasn't interested in her. I moved my hand away as soon as she touched me; it's not as if I encouraged her."

"I saw that part, too. You didn't hold her hand, which makes me feel better. But something inside me sort of... lost it when she touched you. I wanted to *kill* her, which obviously wouldn't work out, since she's a warrior and I'm a farmer."

His eyes gleamed wickedly. "If you wanted to end her, I would hold her down for you."

I laughed. "How romantic."

"She's been a thorn in my side for a long, long time. I suppose I should admit, she propositioned me once to spend the eclipse with her."

My eyebrows shot upward, and every ounce of humor and desire I'd felt vanished. "You had *sex* with *her*?"

"No. She propositioned me, and I turned her down. I haven't had sex in..." He thought about it for a moment and then finally admitted, "A long time."

"How long, exactly?" My curiosity was rising.

"Nearly four centuries, at my best guess."

I nearly choked on my own spit. "You're ancient."

"Time means little to me. So much of my life has been spent in war that I feel like I still haven't truly lived."

"Why did the war start in the first place?"

"No one remembers, yet we were all too old and too stubborn to stop, until recently. Vayme lost his twin brother a few years ago, and he came to me, pleading with me to consider putting an end to the fighting before we made ourselves extinct. It took a lot of time to convince our people, and ourselves, but it seems to have worked." He paused, and then added, "As long as you ignore that someone sent assassins after us as punishment for creating peace."

I gave him a sad smile. "I wouldn't live very long here if war broke out again."

He dragged me closer. "Actually, with your ability to grow food for us, you would be our highest priority to protect even if you weren't my mate. The other kingdoms wouldn't try to kill you—they would try to take you, for the advantage of your magic."

I grimaced. "Well, that might be even worse than dying."

Kierden chuckled, lowering his lips to mine and capturing my mouth again.

Chapter 18

Nissa

My thoughts vanished entirely as I wrapped my arms around the man's neck and deepened the kiss.

He began slowly walking us backward while our mouths moved together, stopping only when my ass met a wall. I hooked a leg around his hip, and he lifted me up without breaking the kiss. His erection met my core, and I wrapped my other leg around his ass as I ground against him. I was already wet with desire, and there was no way he hadn't realized it.

The kiss grew rougher, and Kierden lifted one of my hands to his hair. I dug my fingers into the thick, soft strands as he released my mouth to move down the column of my throat, sucking, licking, and biting me.

He eased my core away from his cock, unwrapping my legs enough to take a step to the side and open me up to him.

"Your skin is so damn delicious, little human." His lips worked their way back up my throat, then tugged my hair out of the way so he could trace the curve of my ear with his tongue.

I shuddered against him.

He withdrew for a moment—long enough to growl, "Why does your ear taste like ale?"

Veil.

"Must've spilled," I mumbled.

"Nissa," he growled.

"Just kiss me."

He chuckled, low and deep. His hand slid down the front of my dress, stopping to squeeze my breast lightly before following the curve of my hip and wrapping around my ass. I rocked my hips a bit. "Tell me, if you want me to keep touching you."

"Asshole," I breathed.

"Oh, I'll play with that too."

I arched as his hand slid between my legs from behind, his knuckles slowly teasing my slit without giving me the contact I wanted.

Considering we'd shared difficult truths already, I supposed I had to give him the answer he wanted. "Someone at the tavern touched my ear. I used the ale to clean it."

He snarled. "Who? I'll end them for touching you."

"It doesn't matter," I said quickly.

"It does. You are *mine* to touch."

"You don't even know if you want to be with me. I was looking for a mate, Kierden. If I don't take a mate when the eclipse comes, I'll be completely at the mercy of my magic, and I can't risk that again.

"You're wrong." His gaze was steady, his voice low and growly. "You belong to me, and I know what I want; I want someone I can ravage any time I feel the urge. Someone who will drench my fingers, tongue, and cock with their release day or night, whether in our bed, in an empty bedroom, or in the castle's pool."

My body only grew hotter with every word he said. "You want a mate."

His hand slipped out from behind me, and he moved me further to the side as he finally dragged a finger over my clit. Fabric still separated us, but damn, it felt incredible. "No. I want *you* to be my mate. Permanently."

I cried out as he slowly teased me, dragging slow circles around my clit while I gripped his hair tightly and panted. He made me want more, and more, until he finally pinched my clit, and I shattered.

Kierden gripped my core in his hand while my back arched, loud cries escaping me as I lost control. The pleasure seemed to go on forever.

When I finally slumped back against the wall, I was sucking in deep breaths of air, trying hard to recover.

He brushed a few strands of hair from my face with his free hand. The other was still gripping my core like it belonged to him. "Veil, you are *stunning* when you climax."

"Thanks, I guess," I murmured.

My eyes flew open when he carried me to the bed. The base of his palm moved as he walked, grinding against my clit. My body responded much faster than I expected it to, and desire swelled within me again as he lowered me to the edge of the mattress.

Kierden slid his shorts down his thighs. "Take your dress off."

I didn't respond to his command, my gaze fixed on his cock as it sprung free.

Veil, he was so damn thick.

"Dress off, Nissa." He slowly dragged his fist down the length of his erection.

My mouth dried at the sight, and I nearly shivered again.

He stepped closer, his cock bobbing for me as he finally grabbed the bottom hem of my dress and peeled it over my head for me.

The fabric hit the ground, and I glanced down at myself. My breasts were nearly bursting from the triangles of fabric that covered them. Even without looking, I knew my ass was the same.

Kierden growled, "Veil, look at those curves. Touch yourself for me, little human."

"I'd rather watch you," I breathed.

He grabbed my legs, tossing them up onto the bed before climbing up himself. He kneeled in front of me, his cock jutting out proudly as he opened my legs wide.

I nearly froze as he leaned forward and dragged his tongue over the fabric covering me. It was so thin that I could feel the heat of his lick—and I was so wet I knew he'd taste me.

His chest rumbled in appreciation as his eyes locked with mine, and he waited.

Need flooded me, hot and fast.

"Keep going," I breathed.

"No. If you want a climax or you want to see my release, you show me how you touch yourself."

I groaned, and his lips curved wickedly. We held each other's stare for a long, long moment as we both waited for the other to give in.

Finally, I slid a hand beneath the damp fabric covering me. My breath hitched as I slowly teased myself.

Kierden's gaze dropped to my hand, his eyes hot and needy. "How does that feel, Nissa?"

"So good," I whispered, my hips jerking slightly.

Something about having his eyes on me made it so much hotter.

"Show me how you touch yourself," I told him, my chest rising and falling rapidly. Unlike me, he didn't protest—he just kept watching me as he wrapped his hand around his cock.

My breathing grew frantic as I watched his powerful body react to every stroke of his hand. I was wetter than I'd ever been before, and dying to lose control, but the fabric of my scanties was in my way.

I pushed at them with shaky hands, and Kierden growled, grabbing the fabric and yanking it down my legs. He used my knees to open me up wider for him so he could see every wet inch of me.

My hand found my clit again a moment later, and then I was arching and crying out as I lost control.

Kierden stroked himself harder and faster until he found his release, roaring with me as he coated my core, ass, and the blanket beneath me with his pleasure.

His release felt blissfully warm on my sensitive skin.

I rubbed it around my clit, and my hips rocked.

Something about having his pleasure on me felt so damn right.

Desire curled in my lower belly.

I needed him.

"Touch me," I breathed to him.

"No. You drank the ale, you deal with the consequences. I don't know how it's affected your reasoning," he growled back.

I narrowed my eyes at him—then started touching myself again, too turned on to stop even if Kierden wasn't willing to participate.

His erection bobbed.

Human men needed to rest after climaxing, but I knew from the books I'd read that magical beings didn't have the same problem.

He took his cock in his fist and started stroking again.

The pleasure built up so insanely fast, it made my mind spin.

"Slide a finger inside yourself," the king commanded me.

I did as he said, and he snarled, "Another."

When I'd followed that one too, panting and rocking a little, he grabbed my wrist and tugged my fingers free so he could suck my pleasure off my skin while he touched himself.

He rumbled at the taste of me—of both of us—and a heartbeat later my ass was hanging off the edge of the bed. His mouth found my core, his face between my thighs as he devoured me. His tongue was so damn hot on my clit, his massive hands squeezing my thighs and ass as he worked me.

The feeling was absolutely surreal, and the sight was nearly as good. I lost control with another cry, and Kierden didn't pause for even a moment. He feasted on me, dragging my pleasure out and then reigniting my flame as his tongue carried me higher and higher.

I shattered again with more hoarse cries, and he finally let go of me—just long enough to stand over me and stroke his cock.

He climaxed again quickly, covering me in his release once more as he roared his pleasure.

My body was blissfully warm and relaxed as Kierden collapsed in bed with me. He held my back to his chest, wrapping his arms around me.

"That was..." I trailed off.

I wasn't sure I had words for it.

"The best moment of your life?" he murmured to me.

"Yes," I admitted.

"Mine as well." His arms tightened around me. "You'll never be free of me now. I intend to make you mine in every way there is."

"I still don't even feel like I know you," I whispered back. "I mean, I know your personality sometimes. But not well enough for me to promise you the rest of our lives."

"A mate bond is eternal. To seal ours would be to make a promise that would last far beyond our lives in Evare, Nissa. You would belong to me on this side of the veil and the next, regardless of what the future holds in this world or the one that follows."

"And you would belong to me too?" I asked, feeling slightly vulnerable.

"In every way there is." His grip on my abdomen loosened, and his fingers started moving slowly over my ribcage. The brush of them was light, gentle, and absolutely blissful.

"What would that really mean for us in real life, though?" I couldn't picture it. Or... any future for us, honestly.

"It would mean you could demand my cock, fingers, or tongue anywhere, at any time." He nipped lightly at my ear. A long moment passed, and then he added, "It would mean that I'd take care of you before myself. You would be fed the most delicious foods. Your closet would be full of colorful dresses, more than you could wear in a lifetime. I would brush your hair, feed you as often as you let me, and rub your shoulders when they're tight."

My throat felt thick.

All of that sounded incredible, honestly.

"What if I wanted to be a farmer?"

He made a noise of amusement. "Then all we would need to do is move the rest of my things down here. At this point, I'm not sure we'll ever be able to stop your magic from draining us."

My lips curved upward.

"If we were truly mated, I would do as much as I can to ensure that there's never a repeat of today," he added, a bit more quietly. "I should've told you what I was thinking about my people. I only stopped by to check on you once, and I didn't reach out when I didn't find you in our room. I regret that. I have a tendency to get slightly... obsessed, when I'm working on something or trying to solve a problem."

"You? Obsessed?" I teased him, my voice soft.

He chuckled, pulling an arm away enough to squeeze my hip lightly.

"If we were really mated, I would need to practice speaking my mind instead of getting angry or defensive," I admitted. "I should've stayed with you to talk to the elves, and offered my help with the murders, even though I'd probably be useless in that situation. And I definitely should've told you what I was thinking."

"I'd rather not have you near the bodies." He squeezed my hip again. "It's far too much risk, since we have no idea what killed them. And you are still human."

My lips curved downward. "Would it even be possible for us to be mated, considering my humanity?"

"Our magic has already connected. If we were to seal the bond, it would become one, and the magic fueling my immortality would fuel yours as well."

Well, I didn't hate the sound of that.

"Can you undo the back of my scanties?"

"Mmhm." He rumbled against me, and my lips curved upward.

Kierden undid it quickly, then slid it off my skin and pulled me closer. His arms wrapped around my middle again, his hands cupping my bare breasts, and I relaxed against his body. His cock was still hard, pressed lightly against my backside, and I loved the feel of it.

"Do you guys have the same birth control herbs that we have?"
I asked him softly.

"We do. Dirue, our healer, hands them out without blinking
an eye, as she always has, even when the law was in place."

"I think I'll visit her soon, then."

His chest rumbled in satisfaction, and his erection throbbed
against my ass. "I look forward to it, little human."

My heart about melted at the soft, sultry nickname. It had
seemed like an insult at first, but knowing that he wanted me
—not just for sex, but permanently, as his mate—erased any
bad feelings I'd had toward it.

"Will you tell me about your life?" I asked him. "I'd like to
know you as more than the battle-hardened king who loves
books."

He was silent for a moment, and then finally said, "When I was
a child, my parents were very vocal about wanting peace. They
led a small resistance, protesting our endless war. The incidents
they staged to demonstrate war's brutality cost many fae their
lives on every side. They were not good people, though
perhaps they had good intentions. The kings and queens at
that time hunted them for many decades without success."

"That was when people were still mated, and still having
children?" I asked.

"Yes. Mated couples began being hunted shortly before I was
born. The kings and queens who despised my parents were
eventually murdered by those hunters, which bought my
family a little more time. I was ten and Eisley was four when

members of the cult caught up to us. We were in the forest—
the four of us, and two cultists—but my father and mother
had sworn away their magic in their effort to create peace. My
mother didn't touch her power at all while she was pregnant
with Eisley, so my sister had no ice of her own. I had no idea
how to use my magic, but I could feel it in my veins, and I
knew that if I couldn't protect us, we were going to get
slaughtered."

My eyes were wide, my throat so swollen I doubted I could've
spoken even if I tried.

He admitted, "I threw everything I had at them, but I was an
untrained ten-year-old, and it wasn't enough. Their ice cut
through mine with ease, and it was all I could do to throw a
protective shelter over myself and Eisley before they could kill
us too. I left her inside when I knew the killers were gone, and
then buried our parents myself in earth and ice, the way our
people always do. With no other options left, I carried Eisley to
the nearest kingdom—this one. It was called Prive at the time.
A group of warriors led us to the castle, where we were housed
with the other orphans and taught to fight."

My eyes stung with tears. "*Veil*, Kierden."

"It was a long time ago. Don't weep for me, Nissa." He gently
wiped the tears from my cheeks. "You may be able to imagine
the rest. My magic was very strong, ironically. I became the
fiercest warrior in the kingdom, though I made certain that my
sister was a close second, since she had no magic to protect
herself with."

He continued, his voice still soft, "After one of our kings died, our people elected me to take his place. We vowed to put an end to all distractions, and our numbers stopped falling. We haven't lost a fae during battle in nearly a century."

"And I thought nine years in a tower was difficult," I said, wiping at my own tears.

He growled at me, captured my hand, and lifted it to his lips to kiss my palm. "Do not discount your own struggles because they sound less vicious than someone else's. If I were thrown in a tower for nearly a decade, I can tell you without question that I would come out a rabid, savage beast with little sense of myself. Losing all control like that would scar the fiercest warrior, and yet here you are, still sane, functioning, and *kind*."

"I don't sound so bad when you put it like that," I told him, still wiping away my tears.

"You are *not* bad, Nissa. Not at all." His grip on my hip and abdomen tightened. "I may have been terrible at proving it thus far, but I feel extremely lucky to have found you. After so many centuries without a shred of interest in the females I've known and fought with, I started to wonder if perhaps I'd never be capable of feeling for someone the way I do you."

"Maybe you should've started considering the males," I mumbled.

His chest rumbled with amusement. "I am not attracted to men, love. I've been alive long enough to be certain of that." He squeezed my hip again. "Tell me about your father, please?"

I grimaced. "It's not a happy story."

"Then it'll fit right in with mine."

I sighed. "My magic came in on my thirteenth birthday, and I woke up surrounded by vines, fruit, and flowers. It wasn't exciting; it was terrifying. I couldn't even get out of my room. My mother left as soon as she saw the plants, and my father spent an hour freeing me from them. By the time he finally got me out of the room, my mother had gotten the rest of the people in the town together. They held tools as weapons while she told me that my magic was a curse sent from the other side of the veil to punish me for the crimes of a past life, but that the town could use my curse to ease their struggles."

I continued, "My father tried to protest, but there were so many of them. When they started leading me around the town by my hand, he couldn't do anything but walk by my side until I collapsed after the magic had drained me dry. My feet were blistered when I woke up, and I could hardly move. We weren't in our home, but someone else's. When the people came to get me again, my father argued with them, but they shoved past him and took me anyway. We saw the base of the tower, then— and saw everyone working on it."

My eyes closed, and I let out a long breath.

Kierden's fingers massaged my hip gently, and the touch calmed me a little.

My voice was quiet when I admitted, "It only took them two weeks to build it. My mother told me and my father that it would be my new home the evening before it was ready. I told her I didn't want to live there, and she told me she didn't care, reminding me that I was cursed. That night, my dad woke me up before dawn and told me that we were leaving for my safety. He said that my mother had gone mad—that I was blessed, not cursed. He already had our things packed, so we left."

"She anticipated it, though. There were guards waiting for us at the edge of town. Everything happened so quickly. They swung at my father, and he fought back. There were three of them, and he was a farmer, not a fighter. I don't remember who stabbed him or what weapon they used. It felt like only a heartbeat later I was kneeling beside him, sobbing as he breathed his last breaths. He held me as tightly as he could, telling me he loved me while repeating over and over that I was a blessing, not a curse." Tears leaked from my eyes.

I had never told anyone any of that before, and getting it out made me feel... fresh. Stronger, too. Cleansed, maybe.

I felt like I could *breathe*, again.

So I continued. "They threw me into the tower, still covered in his blood. My mother and I had never been close before I got my magic, but she became the monster who stole everything from me. The town made her their leader, and she stayed away from me. I rarely saw her, even when they tied me up and led me around to make sure my magic would grow everything. I could be actively bleeding from the blisters on my feet, and no one would bat an eye. I meant *nothing* to them. They only cared about my power."

I squeezed my eyes shut. "I tried to escape every time I could, and I never forgot what my father said to me. I am *not* a curse. My magic is a part of me, but it's only one part. I knew you thought you were abducting me when you showed up in my tower, but you saved me. You saved my life."

"You would've figured out a way to save yourself eventually," he told me, his voice low and edged with fury.

That fury wasn't geared toward me, but to the people who had used me for so long.

"Maybe."

Even as I said the word, I knew it was a lie.

The only way out for me on my own would've been death.

"Tell me about your attempts at escape," he said.

He cared about what had happened to me.

He cared about *me*.

So I opened my mouth, and I told him.

With every story I told and every one he told me, I felt closer to him. By the time I fell asleep, I wondered if it was possible for a single conversation to change a person's life... because it felt like that one had changed mine entirely.

I woke with a gentle hand on my arm and a warm kiss to my cheek. Soft orange light streamed in from the windows I'd left open the night before, bathing my skin and the blankets around us.

"I have to go back to the castle to continue my search for the murderer," Kierden murmured.

Goosebumps broke out on my skin at the sultry tone to his voice. "Okay."

The words to seal the mating bond slipped into my mind again.

"Sillah ovim rett warum."

I ignored them.

He stroked my arm lightly. "Come to the castle for breakfast, and let me know when you're there. We'll meet for your other four meals as well."

"I think three meals is enough now. I haven't been as hungry."

"Four, then."

"Fine." I gave him a dramatic sigh.

The words repeated themselves in my mind again—

"Sillah ovim rett warum."

The urge to say them was getting stronger, but I could still fight it.

Kierden leaned over and captured my lips before reluctantly getting out of bed, oblivious to the way the bond pushed at my mind.

I watched him closely, my body warming as he moved. Noticing me watching him, he dragged a hand over his erection for me.

I bit my lip to fight a grin, and bit it harder when he gave me a gorgeous smirk.

Kierden pulled a clean pair of shorts from his bag and tugged them on before heading out. He stopped in the doorway to look back at me for a long moment before saying, "Stay safe, and let me know what you're up to so I don't worry."

I lifted an eyebrow. "I'm not going to update you every time I use the toilet, Kierden."

"Pity." He slipped out, and I snorted.

Bright stepped back inside as he left, and he gave her a friendly pat on the head in passing.

She jumped onto the bed and snuggled up next to me. I scratched her behind the ears absentmindedly, not in any hurry to get up.

"It seems like you worked things out," she said to me, eyes gleaming with interest.

"Seems like it."

I wouldn't really know how much the night had meant to Kierden until we had interacted in front of his people again—and even then, I didn't know how sure I could be, because he had to put on an act of some kind for them.

"Are we supposed to pretend we don't like each other in front of everyone else again?" I asked him mentally. The connection seemed to come much easier than it had the last time I used it, which was nice.

"No. I've been aiming for neutrality," he said.

"Damn. If that's your definition of neutrality, you must've been a miserable bastard to be around for the past century or three."

He laughed into my mind—loudly. *"I never claimed to be cheerful or polite, Nissa. My people are not the kind who obey calm, measured words. If you want them to get their asses in line, you bark, yell, or snarl at them. They're used to it; it doesn't offend them."*

"So you're going to bark at me?" I checked.

"No. I'm done pretending not to have feelings for you. There are a few couples in the kingdom who have been lovers very openly for hundreds of years. The murderer hasn't touched them because

they haven't created a bond. He or she only cares about a permanent connection—it seems to be the only thing that inspires them to kill."

"Are there people in the other kingdoms with mate bonds?" I asked curiously.

"I don't know. If there are, they won't dare come here. To do so would be a death sentence."

"Have the mated couples tried leaving the city?"

"Yes. We find their bodies buried with our other fallen, identified by their ice gravestones."

"Well, that's terrifying."

"When you and I decide to seal our bond, there will be nothing that can peel me from your side until the killer is dead," Kierden vowed.

Surprisingly enough, I didn't hate the sound of that.

Even though I wasn't quite sure whether to be excited or alarmed by his use of the word *"when"* where I would've put an *"if"*.

"Alright. Good luck," I told him.

I sort of *felt* it when his mind disconnected from mine, and the feeling was an unpleasant one that made me shiver a bit. There was no pain in my wrist, at least. Just a slight ache.

I stayed in bed for a little while, lounging around while I convinced Bright to give me the details about her night with Death. As it turned out, he had propositioned her, she had refused again, and then they'd spent hours running through the trees together, fighting and playing. He had tried to convince her to be his mate once more at the end of the night, and she'd turned him down yet again.

"What are you waiting for?" I asked her curiously.

She flashed me a wickedly sharp grin. *"Eventually, he'll grow certain enough to tell me that I belong to him and will no longer accept my refusal. That will be my guarantee that he won't change his mind."*

A laugh escaped me.

She *did* have a point.

We spent an hour or two walking around in the fields, when we finally got out of bed. They were among the most peaceful hours I'd ever lived.

Though my stomach rumbled a few times, I was enjoying it so much that I only headed back when Kierden's mind touched mine. *"You'd better not be trying to skip a meal, little human."*

My lips curved upward, my fingers sliding over the bumpy rind of a huge citrus as I passed it. It shuddered at my touch, swelling much larger. *"I'm not skipping a meal. Just enjoying my new life as a fae farmer."*

He chuckled. *"I'm glad."*

"I'm heading up now. Did you find anything?"

"Nothing." His voice grew frustrated. *"My sister is bothering me about socializing with the elves. Would you be willing to eat in the dining room?"*

"Sure. I guess she's the diplomatic one between the two of you."

"Undoubtedly. There has never been much need for diplomacy before, which makes it that much worse now."

"I can imagine. Will the elves be offended by my curved ears?"

"Only if they want my swords in their chests," he grumbled. *"They're aware of my bond to you, and most elves pride themselves in being graceful and polite."*

"So the opposite of fae?" I teased.

"Exactly. One of the elven leaders is here too—Alida. She's half shifter, so less uptight. She's the one who told me and the other kings that we needed to mate with humans. Unlike the rest of the elves, she's trustworthy, and visits the fae kingdoms often."

"Have you asked the elves for help with your murders?"

"Yes. The killer doesn't seem to use magic, so the elves haven't found anything. He or she also doesn't use weapons, so we believe it's some sort of poison, though we have yet to find any proof of it."

"I could take a look," I suggested. *"If it's plant-related, maybe I could find something?"*

"If we don't find anything in the next few days, I suppose it's worth a try." His response was grudging, but I already knew he didn't like the idea of having me around the bodies. It wasn't

that he didn't want my help, he just thought it was risky for me because of my humanity.

Bright reached the castle, and I looked around the entrance in surprise. My vines were spreading much farther down the hallways than they had been the day before—and the flowers on them were bigger, brighter, and more vibrant.

Kierden and Death waited for us near the entrance, and the king greeted me with a fierce hug that made me smile.

"When did the flowers get like this?" I asked, gesturing to the vines as he lifted me off Bright's back like I didn't have legs of my own.

"Last night." The look he gave me was wicked, and my face heated at the memory of what we'd done together. "The fruit looked much bigger, too."

I supposed it had.

I flashed him a grin. "You must have a really great farmer."

"The best."

When he took my hand in his and started down the hallway, I noticed a few of his warriors, both men and women, were gaping at us.

The heat in my cheeks flared a bit, but I did my best to ignore it. If Kierden was willing to hold my hand in public, he must've accepted the consequences of it.

"They're staring at us," I told him as we walked.

"They should. You're too damn gorgeous in that dress not to." He glanced over at me, making a show of looking me up and down.

"Reo is making me a few that fit better," I admitted.

"I know. He sent a fae over earlier to ask me if I had any color preferences." Kierden adjusted his grip on my hand, pushing his fingers between mine. The hold was comfortable—really comfortable.

"What did you say?"

"Black."

"Asshole." When I flashed him a glare, I found him smirking and realized it was a joke. My lips curved upward.

"I told him to give you whatever colors you asked for, with a little less fabric," he said.

I rolled my eyes at him. *"You didn't."*

He chuckled. *"Alright, I told him that your clothing is your choice. I'm sure he'll make you something you love; he's famous among the fae for that, and travels back and forth between the kingdoms. I think it's just his way of avoiding fighting a battle, but I can't say I blame him."*

"Neither do I."

We walked into the dining hall, and more eyes turned to us.

Kierden squeezed my hand lightly, not stumbling for even one beat as we walked toward the large table Eisley was seated at.

I knew male elves didn't exist, only females, and my gaze slid over all five of the women as I tried to determine which of them was Alida. They had a variety of skin and hair colors, all of them soft-looking and curvy in the same places a healthy human was. Like mine, their builds were a direct opposite to the slim, muscular ones of the female fae.

"Look at that pretty, glittering bond between you two," one of the elves purred, leaning over the table toward us. Her long, straight hair was a deep shade of black, her skin was light brown, and her eyes glowed a stunning hazel. Her gaze landed on me, and lingered. "Veil, the magic just *pours* off of you, doesn't it?"

"Unfortunately. I haven't figured out a way to control it," I admitted, taking the only remaining empty seat at the table. Kierden left for a moment to grab another chair.

"No, and I don't think you will," she mused.

"Well that's encouraging," Eisley drawled. "Thanks for bringing the sunshine, Alida."

"Some magic isn't meant to be controlled," the elf said simply. "It's not a bad thing. It just *is*. The wilds around you thrum with the energy of your power now. It's quite beautiful."

"We could certainly use some of these flowers in our corner," another elf murmured.

"Nah, we're going to keep them." Eisley slung an arm over my shoulder, tugging me close. "I don't know if my brother's going to let her go."

Kierden put his chair beside mine, sat down, and set his hand on my thigh possessively. "I'm not."

Eisley grimaced. "Just don't do anything insane, like sealing that damn bond."

Alida's eyes glittered. "Oh, but bonds are *meant* to be sealed. The magic will grow stronger, and the urge to say the words will become irresistible."

"You knew this was going to happen, didn't you?" Eisley asked Alida.

The elf grinned wickedly. "You'll never know."

"Alida sees the future," Eisley explained, looking at me. "She's a pain in everyone's ass."

Alida cackled.

"She only sees the tiniest flashes of the future," one of the other elves corrected. "But she can see mate bonds—both fated and nonfated ones. And relationships between people too, both positive and negative."

"Fated?" I asked, curious.

When I glanced over at Kierden, he shook his head. "Fated mates are just a legend." His mind touched mine. *"Don't tell them anything about how our bond started."*

"To some people. Not to me." Alida's eyes flashed green. "A mate bond between a fated couple will ignite before they've said the words to create a connection. Did yours?"

I thought about it, but wasn't sure what the sign was of a bond igniting.

Kierden drawled, "No, Alida."

Her eyes gleamed. "Is that so?"

"Yes." His gaze met hers, steely.

"What's special about fated mate bonds?" I asked her. Since Kierden was worried about them knowing the truth about the beginning of our relationship, I had to guess that meant we were fated, and he didn't want anyone to know.

"It's said that the souls of fated mates choose each other in the life before this one," one of the elves explained.

I found that concept absolutely beautiful.

"What does it look like when fated mates meet, then?" I asked them. "How does the bond ignite?"

"It always starts with a handprint." One of the women gestured to my glowing wrist. "If a couple is fated, the print appears the first time they touch. It's the place their souls meet again for the first time in this world, and that makes it sacred. If you're not fated, the print forms after you say the words, marking the place your souls meet for the first time as mates."

My mind whirled.

I could distinctly remember Kierden grabbing me in my tower, before he said the words that officially started the bond between us. And when he grabbed me, the handprint appeared.

"It has to stay a secret," he said to me.

I held the elves' gaze. "The handprint definitely appeared *after* he started our bond."

One of them looked slightly suspicious. Alida didn't look even a little bit convinced.

"Fated mate bonds are known to be more powerful than normal ones," Alida said, studying us. "If the couple seals their bond, their power not only combines, but grows stronger as well. It makes them great rulers—and incredible villains."

"Then the cult probably went after them first, right?" I asked.

Expressions around the table grew grim.

"Indeed," Alida said quietly.

"Do fated bonds still disappear when the eclipse comes?"

"They do. A bond can only be sealed by choice, even if that choice is made under the influence of the bond's magic." Alida gave me a small smile. "An unwanted bond will never become permanent."

I nodded.

My first instinct was to be angry with Kierden for keeping that secret from me, but ultimately, he had been determined that he wasn't going to seal the bond with me. And if we didn't seal the bond, knowing we were fated would only hurt me more.

That made the secret feel like more of a kindness than anything else.

One of the elves remarked, "The strongest males and females of all magical beings usually have fated mates out there somewhere. Alida sees the connection stretching away from them."

"It's true," Alida agreed. "I saw the king's bond; he has a fated mate."

Interesting.

If she could see bonds, and she was known for visiting the fae fairly often, maybe she could be the killer...

Then again, he said he trusted her, and he didn't trust easily.

"Well, I suppose Kierden had better get out and start looking for him or her, then," I said, flashing him a teasing smile that I hoped everyone thought was real.

He chuckled. "Not going to happen, little human." Squeezing my thigh, he said into my mind, *"How angry are you?"*

"Not angry. I understand why you didn't tell me." I paused before adding, *"And I don't think it really changes anything, unless you're only with me for the hope of an eventual boost to your magic."*

"Without a war to fight, I have no need for more ice, Nissa."

"Then I don't have any reason to be angry."

Eisley changed the subject, thankfully. "Have you seen any sign of the Beast outside your forcefield?" she asked.

"Not yet, though I'm sure he's here," Alida said easily.

I grimaced. "How long can you hold him off?"

"Two months, we hope."

"How did they get so powerful?" I asked.

"We made an error when we created them," Alida began.

Someone interrupted us as they brought our food out, and we all paused for a moment to thank them before we started eating.

Alida resumed, "It's a long story, but we made them dependent on their contracts to stay alive. They gain energy through killing, and it keeps them functioning. We didn't factor in the possibility that the energy wasn't their own by nature, so it won't ever fade from them."

My eyes widened. "So they're constantly getting stronger?"

"Yes. What an error to make, right? Eventually, those bastards are going to be strong enough to destroy our world—and we have no way of knowing exactly when that will be."

Damn.

"I need to get back to our work as soon as we're done eating," Kierden told the elves, changing the subject again. They offered to help look at the bodies again, and he agreed readily.

We ended up talking about the differences between clothing styles in all the different lands while we ate. And honestly, it was a lot more fun than I expected.

CHAPTER 20

NISSA

The next two weeks passed by quickly. Kierden spent most of his time with the elves, looking into anything and everything that could possibly be a lead. They found nothing, though none of them gave up.

Eisley left soon after the elves started helping Kierden and the other fae search. Neither she nor her brother would tell me where she was going, but she took a group of fae with her. Though I didn't voice my suspicion, I was guessing that Kierden had sent her to my town for the revenge he had mentioned.

Part of me hoped my suspicion was right, because that part of me wanted them to suffer for what they'd done to me.

Another part of me hoped I was wrong, and we could all just let go of what happened. I wanted to be done with it more than I wanted revenge.

Kierden most definitely didn't feel that way, though.

I spent my days in the fields, growing plants and helping harvest them. We had an excess of crops, and they were all getting too big, so we sent two groups of fae out to the other kingdoms with massive carts full of produce. I worried the esu would be grumpy about pulling the heavy carts, but they were excited to have something to do, and really excited to see the kingdoms without being at war.

When we finished harvesting, it would be time to replant my fields. It would take me *weeks* to get everything planted, and I was absolutely thrilled that I'd get to spend all that time with my hands in the dirt. I never felt more at ease than I did surrounded by my plants.

Kierden and I spent every night together, splitting our time between his room in the castle and my home just off the farm. I'd started considering them both *our* homes, but it felt like a stretch since we hadn't officially bound ourselves together in any way.

The itch to seal our bond grew stronger, and I had to fight harder not to say the words with every damn day that passed.

The desire to have sex grew stronger too—we made love every night with our fingers and mouths but hadn't taken it any further. I was putting off a visit to the healer, Dirue, because it just seemed awkward.

I kept hoping a fertility-suppressing plant would just appear outside my house overnight, but that had yet to happen. Kierden had offered to go, but he was busy with the elves, so I turned him down.

After one night when we had a particularly hard time restraining from graduating to full-on sex, I finally decided it was time to swallow my discomfort and visit Dirue.

Bright and I made our way to the healer's house. She was amused by my reluctance... so at least one of us was entertained by my misfortune.

I knocked tentatively on the door. It was on the far end of the kingdom, so my wrist was hurting something fierce. Kierden had assured me mentally that she wouldn't want to chat for long, so I was ignoring the pain. He and Bright both insisted that she wouldn't mind the intrusion, but I was still a bit nervous.

I scratched Bright lightly behind the ears as I waited.

The thick wooden door opened a moment later, and my gaze collided with that of a beautiful fae woman with light skin and vibrant pink hair. She was nearly as tall as Kierden, though obviously not as large.

"Nissa," the healer said, her voice warm as her mouth curved upward. "I wondered when I'd get to see you healthy."

I blinked.

"I was the one who sent for Kierden, so you could drink his blood and recover from your meeting with the Beast," the woman explained.

"Thank you, then."

"Of course. Come in." She opened the door, and I walked inside a bit cautiously.

My eyes slid over the interior of the large tree she had made her home. It looked a lot like all the others, with the smooth wood floors and walls. There were no dividers between the bed and living area.

My gaze was drawn to three large shelves of plants at the far end of the space, near a slim window that let in just a tiny bit of light. The bright green plants sat in matching white pots. Their leaves were small and delicate, growing off long, thin branches that stretched over the sides and grew down toward the ground.

"I'm Dirue," she said. "What can I help you with?"

My cheeks warmed. "I'm hoping you might be willing to share some of the fertility-suppressing herb, actually."

Her smile widened. "Of course." She picked up a fabric bag from a pile to the left of the plants, and slowly looked over all of them. "You don't intend to seal your mate bond, do you?"

"Oh, definitely not," I said quickly.

She nodded.

A moment of silence followed. It was an awkward one, honestly.

"Have King Kier and the elves found anything about the murders yet?" Dirue asked, making conversation as she slowly and carefully began pulling a leaf from one of the plants.

"Not yet, but I'm sure they will." Another awkward silence followed, and I felt inclined to fill it. "It's surprising that someone here is willing to kill people just because they fall in love. Among humans, love is treasured."

Or at least in an ideal world it was.

"Love isn't what's getting them killed," Dirue said absentmindedly. "The cult never feared or hated love—they just believed a mated pair could destroy our world."

Kierden had told me that, but he hadn't given many other details. "How was the cult destroyed?"

"Oh, the elves' numbers were being decimated by the cult. The elves used to form mate bonds with the gargoyles; it was a vital part of their culture, so they were a large target. They grew desperate after their queen was killed, and created their assassins to hunt the cult members down. The cultists were picked off one by one until the elves lost control of the assassins, and that gave the rest of them time to go into hiding."

"Damn, that's terrible," I murmured. My eyes swept over the plants again, lingering on one in the middle. Though it looked identical to the others, something about it just sort of *felt* the tiniest bit different to me. When I focused on the flow of my magic and followed it to the plant, I realized its energy was different than the others.

I assumed it was the original plant, perhaps one that had been taken from the human lands since the fertility-suppressing herbs grew wildly there. "Would you mind if I took a clipping so I could grow my own?"

"Unfortunately, these plants are too delicate to clip, even for someone as gifted as yourself." She winked at me and finally tied the top of the pouch. "You're welcome to come back any time you need more. Tuck a leaf beneath your tongue for about ten minutes once a week, and you won't find yourself with child. Swallow it if you want, or discard it. It'll work the same either way. And you can take them twice a week for extra protection, if desired."

"Thank you." I gave her a quick smile as I tucked the pouch of leaves into the top of my dress. Reo had come through with some gorgeous ones that actually fit me, in colors that made me ridiculously happy. "I've got to get back, but it was nice to meet you."

"And you as well." She led me to the door, waving at me as I slipped onto Bright's back. I waved too, and then held on as Bright began to move.

"That was odd. I'm sure her plants aren't that delicate. The herbs taste good—we plucked wild ones all the time as children without damaging anything, and we were never careful."

"She's probably just protective of them because they enable her to hold her role as healer," Bright mused. *"If you started growing them for everyone, no one would need to visit her, and she might feel purposeless. Magical beings are known to start losing their minds when they get too old. Given how long the wars have been going, there may be some insanity beginning to brew for a lot of the warriors. They call that insanity immis."*

She pronounced the word ihm-iss.

Well, that sounded terrifying.

"Immis doesn't happen for esu?"

"Oh, no. We're smart enough to take mates before immis begins to set in," she said with a chuff. *"And we have our bonds with the fae to ground us, too."*

"Taking a mate prevents insanity?"

"It does. Your mate becomes your purpose. Even on your worst day, you feel a drive to make sure they've had enough to eat and drink. You feel a desire to spend time with them and experience things together. Having a mate enriches your life enough to protect against immis entirely."

"Maybe a lot of the fae will start taking mates now that they don't have any more wars to fight, then," I murmured.

"Maybe the wars were started in an effort to avoid immis without taking a mate in the first place," Bright countered.

I wondered if she had a point.

"Would it be terrible if I grew my own plants from the leaves Dirue gave me? I don't want to take her place or make her lose her mind, but I don't want to be reliant on her plants either."

Bright chuffed. *"No. I wouldn't want to return to her in a few weeks when those run out either. She only put four in there."*

My lips curved upward.

We neared the castle, and I reached out to Kierden. *"Are you ready for me to look at the bodies?"*

He and the elves had exhausted their ideas, so he was finally ready to take the "risk" of having me see if I could sense anything. It was unlikely, but my magic was unique so there was always some small chance it would work.

He sighed. *"Unfortunately. They're frozen, and I've covered them with sheets; if there are any plants, you should be able to sense them without seeing them, right?"*

"I think so."

"We'll find out, then."

I didn't want to see the bodies unless I had to, so I was grateful that he covered them.

When we reached the castle, I slipped off Bright's back, and she led me through a maze of hallways.

Bright didn't want to go in with the bodies, so when we reached the room and found Death already sitting outside the doors, the two of them decided to slip into the jungle together for a few hours. She still hadn't admitted that she was in love with him, but everyone knew, including Death. He wasn't sure why she still wouldn't mate with him, but he was getting closer to refusing her "no" every day, just like she wanted him to.

The room was much emptier than I'd expected. There were no elves in sight; it was just Kierden and a few other fae I didn't know. On one side of the space, there were a few long desks. On the other side, there were two tables set up parallel to each other, holding two bodies hidden beneath sheets.

I could see the bright golden glow of their bond showing through the fabric covering them.

"Their bond is still glowing?" I asked Kierden mentally, not wanting to disturb the grim silence in the room.

"A sealed mate bond doesn't break with death, little human. The magic of it holds through every world and every life that follows."

My throat swelled with emotion.

He'd told me that before, but it never occurred to me that a bond could be so eternal that the glow of it didn't vanish.

What had happened to them was horrible, but at least they were still together, permanently.

Kierden stepped up to me, his hand landing on my lower back as he waited for me to decide whether I was going to approach them or not.

I let out a slow breath, and finally walked over to the tables. Despite the nausea in my stomach, I was there for a purpose.

"Do you feel anything?" Kierden asked me quietly, as we stood between the fae. I assumed he'd spoken aloud for everyone else's sake.

"Give me a minute," I murmured.

Closing my eyes, I focused on my magic. I was usually surrounded by so many plants that I had never bothered with trying to find them individually.

As I followed the energy of my magic, I could feel the life in the walls and floors of the room, along with every other inch of the tree that made up the castle. Whoever created it had done so with extreme care, making sure not to hurt the tree in the slightest, and had put magic into place to prevent its growth from contorting the castle's shape. My magic had rejuvenated the tree, strengthening it without affecting the shape or size of it.

It took a few minutes for me to guide my mind through the massive flow of my power. Navigating through it as I tried to pinpoint smaller bits of growth felt like running uphill.

I felt the vines and flowers, growing over the walls inside the castle.

I felt the large variety of herbs growing in the kitchen, bursting with life even as someone plucked a few of the leaves.

Finally, I felt the room I was in. It was nearly empty as far as plants went. Besides the living, breathing being that was the tree we occupied, and the herb pouch tucked in my dress, I felt only two tiny twinges.

Both seemed to have been set on the table furthest from me. The twinges felt familiar; I recognized the plants, though I couldn't say what they were from where I was in the moment.

"There's nothing in the bodies that I can feel," I said quietly. "Just two things over there." Letting out another long breath, I pulled my mind away from my magic and opened my eyes. "What are they?"

"The fertility-suppressant plants. Most males take them too, when they're with a partner."

I nodded. "Can I see?"

He captured my hand and pulled me over to a small tray with two leaves on them.

I slipped my pouch out of my dress and pulled one of my own leaves from it, leaning closer and comparing them. Visually, they looked identical.

"And you studied them to make sure no one has poisoned them?" I asked.

"Dirue does every time," he confirmed. "We check for magical tampering, too, but haven't found anything."

My throat swelled. "What if she's the killer?"

"Dirue? No. She's been alive longer than any of the rest of us, and has been taking care of our people with medicinal herbs and plants throughout the years. The woman has an entire garden dedicated to it."

I held my leaf between two of my fingers, and picked up one of the other ones with my free hand.

"Veil, Nissa," Kierden growled, trying to rip the leaf from my hand. I took a few quick steps back and closed my eyes, focusing on the tiny blip of energy coursing through both leaves.

"These are *not* the same, Kierden. They grow the same and look the same, but their energy is different. I noticed a strange plant between the others in Dirue's house—and this feels like it came from *that* plant."

He ripped both leaves from my hand and dropped them on the table as he covered my fingers with ice, like he was trying to cleanse them. The ice cracked and fell away quickly, vanishing before it could clatter to the ground.

"She's not the killer—And don't risk your damn *life*." He snarled that last part at me, grabbing my pouch of the herbs off the counter and shoving it in his pocket.

I could feel the eyes of every other fae in the room on us, but I didn't let myself acknowledge that. "I didn't say she's the killer," I told him, my voice calm and even. "I said that those leaves came from two different plants. Which they did. Maybe mated couples need stronger fertility suppressants; I don't know. But the plants she gave me are not the ones she gave the couple who died."

He stared at me, eyes narrowed and chest heaving.

I met his stare without flinching.

"I'll get mine so we can determine which ones are different," one of the female fae in the room with us said quietly. I turned my head, looking away from Kierden and meeting her eyes. They glowed a brilliant teal, a gorgeous contrast to her vibrant purple hair and dark brown skin.

"I need to go back for more," one of the men said. He had tan skin, purple eyes, and gleaming white hair. "I'll mention that I wish I could make Eiva my mate, and ask her what she knows of the bond outside of the murders, so we can find out if fertility increases."

"My house is close enough to hers that I can sit on my porch and read while keeping an eye on her without raising suspicion," another female offered. Her amber gaze met Kierden's glowing blues as she stood and slipped her hands into the pockets of her simple, black dress. "None of us want to believe Dirue could be behind this, but this is the only real clue we've *ever* had. And when you think about it, haven't all of the bodies had the same leaves? If they're really different than the ones the rest of us take..." she shook her head, her eyes pooling with tears. "We've lost too many people. No one will make sense as the murderer after this long."

She turned and left the room, her words hanging heavy in the air around all of us.

"It *could* be a coincidence," the male fae with the white hair said. "But we'd be fools not to look deeper into it. Nissa doesn't know any of us; she's perhaps the only person in our kingdom who could see the deaths from a neutral perspective. I'll report back after I've talked to Dirue—we all need to spread the word that we've given up on our search without finding any clues."

Nods went around the room, but I looked at Kierden.

He jerked his head too, and finally admitted, "It's a good idea. Thank you. Come and find me if you have news."

Murmurs of agreement followed, and the rest of the fae filed out of the room until it was just me and the king.

I braced myself for his anger as I turned toward him.

Instead, I saw him rake his fingers through his hair as he swore under his breath.

"I'm sorry," I said quietly.

"It's not your fault. None of this shit is your fault." He grabbed me by the hips and dragged me to his chest. I realized he was hugging me a moment later than I should've, and wrapped my arms around him too.

I wasn't sure we'd ever just *hugged*. Maybe when I was recovering from the Beast's bite? I wasn't sure. But honestly, it felt incredible. I could definitely get used to hugs.

"It's going to be a long few hours." His voice was weary.

"No one would expect you to go to a tavern to drink away your worries?"

"No. I only drink on eclipses, and only to dull the desire," he rested his chin on the top of my head, holding me securely. "I usually just sit in here and pace, trying to work out a damn solution in my mind until I'm exhausted enough to collapse. Then I return the bodies to their loved ones, and I mourn with them."

"You're a good king," I murmured.

"They'd flay me if I wasn't." His voice was tired. So damn tired.

He let go of me long enough to lead me out of the room with a hand on my back, and then dragged me into his arms again as he leaned up against the wall in the hallway. The space was empty, but I didn't think he would've done anything different if it wasn't.

"You'd probably enjoy the challenge if they tried to flay you," I teased him lightly.

His lips curved upward slightly. "I suppose."

"What do you do when you want to relax?"

"I read, remember?" He dragged a hand slowly over my back.

"What else?"

"I train a lot, though that feels nearly pointless without a battle in our future."

I got the feeling those were *really* the only things he did for relaxation.

"Alright. Well... you have a pool here, don't you? You mentioned that before, but I've never seen it." He'd mentioned a library too, but I didn't think books would be a good enough distraction at the moment.

"Yes." His chest rumbled. "It's a large hot spring the original king paid the elves to create a millennium ago, and the only source of warm water in the city. Most fae don't enjoy the heat, so it's rarely used."

"Well, *I* would enjoy the heat. And maybe it would take your mind off everything while we wait?"

As the words slipped out, I found my cheeks warming a bit.

I'd asked him to do something with me, for what was probably the first time in the entire month and a half we'd known each other.

"I suppose it's worth a try." He let out a long sigh. "Alright. Let's go to the pool."

"You sound positively thrilled," I teased him.

He chuckled and took my hand, sliding his fingers between mine without hesitation as he led me out of the room.

CHAPTER 21

NISSA

Steam rose off the swirling water in the hot pool, and I stared at it in utter fascination. Something in the water foamed enough to cloud the surface completely, and it smelled strangely good. We hadn't had anything like that in my town—just a small river off to one side.

The pool was in a massive room that also contained the training area, so when we'd walked in, I got an eyeful of gorgeous fae warriors fighting with weapons of ice.

"Why don't you guys use your magic for anything other than weapons?" I asked Kierden, as I tugged my dress over my head. He took the fabric from me and folded it smoothly before setting it down on the side of the pool.

I couldn't help but watch him as he took off his shorts and put them by my dress. He still had on the tight undershorts he always wore, but the view certainly didn't disappoint.

"Because we have no need of it." He captured my hand as I started to step down toward the water. *"Be careful. I don't want you bleeding again."*

"Why don't you need your magic?"

"Ice magic is death personified," Kierden said, stepping into the water after me and wincing at the heat. As I sank further into the warm bliss of it, he remained standing on one of the steps, adjusting to the temperature the way I would've needed to adjust to cold water before I was bonded with him. *"It's not a magic that can help someone. Ice is hard and cruel. It asks no questions and gives no answers. Even if we were to create our city with it, like our ancestors did in Ravv's, it wouldn't feel alive the way our jungle does."*

"Ice can be beautiful, I'd imagine," I countered.

"Of course. There's something beautifully final about death, isn't there? Even knowing that life continues beyond the veil, the permanence of it is still poetic."

I eyed him with distaste as I settled down on the deepest seat beneath the water. *"Maybe you're the killer."*

He chuckled, finally sitting down beside me. *"I am far from innocent, little human. They didn't choose me to be king for my gentleness."* My hair moved around me in the water, and Kierden snagged a few strands, rubbing them softly between his fingers. *"You, on the other hand..."*

"The picture of innocence?" I drawled back.

He dragged me onto his lap, wrapping a possessive arm around my waist and placing the other on my thigh. *"Oh, yes."*

"You'll ruin me, though." I leaned my head back against his shoulder. *"As long as I don't drink ale."*

His chest rumbled against me as he chuckled again, his hand sliding further up my thigh. *"In every way there is, Nissa."*

Veil, I loved the sound of that.

His erection throbbed against my ass, and his hand slid higher, until his knuckles brushed my clit through the fabric covering me.

I inhaled sharply, my gaze snapping to the warriors on the far side of the room. They were pretty far away, and completely focused on their fighting, but there were at least fifteen of them over there. Maybe even more.

"They could see us," I hissed at him, as his fingers brushed my clit again and desire swelled in my lower belly.

Veil, I wanted him to keep going.

"Only from the waist up. Stay still and quiet, and they won't notice," Kierden said, his tone almost wicked.

I started to protest—but then his fingers brushed my core again, and I had to clamp my mouth down to stop myself from crying out.

"Kierden," I growled into his mind.

"You wanted to distract me, Nissa. This is the only distraction I want."

Damn him.

And damn me for wanting him.

I clenched my jaw tighter as he hooked a finger in the top of my scanties and pulled. The thin triangle of it rolled up and rubbed against my clit as he pulled it higher and higher.

My breathing hitched at the pressure, and my fingers dug into his arms as he lazily dragged a finger down my clit, pressing on the tight fabric.

One of the pairs of warriors strode toward us.

My body tensed, but Kierden's fingers continued slowly stroking my core over the thin roll of fabric, and the tension in my shoulders relaxed even as my lower body clenched tighter.

The warriors nodded at Kierden without stopping to chat, and I felt him nod back.

"You are dead to me," I hissed into his mind.

"You'll change your tune when you're unraveling on my fingers." He kissed my shoulder lightly as he finally eased the fabric away from my core.

"You're supposed to be territorial," I shot back, trying to ignore the short-circuiting in my brain as he slid the cloth down to my knees.

"Oh, I am," he rumbled back. *"Every male who looks this way sees me holding you. He doesn't know that I'm touching you like this, but he knows that you're mine—and that if he tried to take you from me, my blade would tear him to shreds."*

"I thought possessiveness would mean you want my skin covered more—not that you'd risk touching me in a damn public pool."

His chest rumbled as he chuckled, and *finally*, he dragged his finger over my clit. *"They can look at you and envy me as much as they'd like, so long as they remember that I'm the only one who gets to taste you, fill you, and make you scream."*

My body trembled as I bit back a cry of pleasure. *"You're obsessed."*

"Entirely." His growl and fingers dragged me over the edge, and I shattered with a silent cry. He held me in place with a firm hand, preventing me from bucking or rocking against him the way I so desperately wanted to. Though the fingers on his other hand remained over my clit, he'd stopped stroking me. *"Are you going to take my cock tonight, Nissa?"*

I didn't even have to think about it. *"Veil, yes."*

He made a noise of approval. *"How wet will you be for me?"*

"As wet as you make me."

He chuckled again, his erection throbbing against my ass. *"Good answer."*

My breathing had finally started to level out when he dragged his fingers down my clit again—just as another pair of warriors strode through the room, headed toward the others. They nodded at Kierden like the others had, and he nodded back again.

"What are you doing?" I asked him.

"I'm nowhere near done with you. If you want my cock, you have to take my fingers first, and prove that you can still feel pleasure with them stretching you."

The way my tense stomach fluttered at his words was ridiculous, but I couldn't suppress it.

"What if I can't?"

"Then I get to feel you shatter on them over and over until you can," he growled.

One of his thick fingers brushed up against my slit, making my breath catch.

"Ready?" he asked me.

"Yes."

His finger pushed inside me, so, so slowly.

I clutched his arm, digging my nails into his skin as he slid deeper and deeper, until he was filling me. He stopped when his finger was fully sheathed inside me, his thumb stroking my clit lightly. *"How do you feel?"*

"Incredible," I breathed.

"Good. Show me how well you can climax on my hand, little human."

I bit my cheek to stop myself from groaning. He continued working my clit—and started slowly stroking the inside of my channel, too.

Another pair of warriors walked by, and I barely even noticed them.

Kierden continued touching me, stretching me, and bringing me pleasure until I shattered. A soft cry escaped me, but by some miracle none of the warriors turned toward us.

"We can't keep doing this here," I told Kierden.

"Would you prefer the dining hall?" he purred to me.

"You're a damned exhibitionist," I spat.

"And I will be, until everyone in my kingdom knows that you belong to me." His voice was casual, but there was more steel in it than I would've expected.

"Stop, Kierden," I hissed at him, as he rubbed my clit harder.

To his credit, he stopped immediately.

My chest rose and fell too rapidly—I was feeling too out of control.

"You don't get to make me climax just to make a statement. If you touch me, it's because you want to make me feel good." I caught his wrist and tugged it away, so his fingers slid out of me. Though I winced at the loss of him, it was the right call.

"Of course I want to make you feel good," he growled back at me. *"A man can have more than one motive."*

"Not if one of them is proving a point." I tried to slide off his lap, but he held me firmly in place.

"I am not human, nor will I ever be. I will always feel a drive to dominate and conquer. As the king, that drive becomes a visceral need. You are either willing to accept that part of me, or you aren't. The time to decide that is now."

When I tried to climb off him again, he released me, though he did so with great reluctance. As I reached for my scanties, he did too—pulling them up my thighs and then smoothing them, making sure they covered me.

The gesture was confusingly sweet after our little argument.

My stomach growled as I stood, and Kierden rose to his feet with me. He took my hand again to steady me as I climbed out.

"I'll train for an hour or two while I wait for my fae to return with news about Dirue. Eat something and think about it." His voice was gentle again.

Something told me he already felt confident that I was going to accept his *drive to dominate and conquer.*

"Tell me as soon as you hear something. I want to be there for all of it," I warned him.

He agreed, and I believed him.

I tugged my dress over my wet skin and walked to the dining hall on shaky legs, wondering what I had been thinking when I decided to develop feelings for a fae king.

Eisley was sitting at a small table in the corner of the dining hall when I got there, both of us completely alone for once.

She grinned at me when I sat down across from her. "Hey."

"Hi." I gave her a small smile of my own. "Back from your secret mission?"

She winked at me. "I'll never tell."

My smile grew slightly more genuine.

"You look stressed," she remarked.

"Confused, mostly."

She waited.

I sighed.

"Come on, Nissa. I need the distraction." Her words were slightly playful, but the sadness in her eyes told me they were genuine. I had a feeling she was still struggling with the loss of the couple that had died; they had been her friends.

And the fact that her words mirrored Kierden's didn't pass my notice. I felt a little bad for leaving him when he was struggling, but he had upset me. I couldn't just ignore that, or the man would start to think he could make all the calls about everything.

I looked around.

There were only a few other people in the room, and they were far enough away that they wouldn't hear me as long as I didn't raise my voice.

"Kierden told me he feels a drive to dominate and conquer," I said quietly.

She made a face. "Do *not* give me details."

"Sorry," I replied quickly.

She gave me a long look, and then leaned in. "Fine, tell me. Still, no details."

I leaned closer too. "He wanted a distraction. I distracted him. But he pushed me a little too far and I got mad, so he said the thing about needing to dominate and conquer, and told me I had to decide whether I could handle it or not."

She nodded. "Kier has always been very, very intense. I know the reason he hasn't been interested in anyone in so long is because he feels things too strongly. He won't accept casual or half-committed relationships. If he wants something, he's all in, permanently. I'm sure he's shitty at expressing it, but that's the truth. If he wants you, he wants *everything* with you."

"What if I don't like *everything*?" I asked. "What if he tries to do something—" I saw her face and added hastily, "Like cooking me breakfast—and I don't like it? Do you think he'd be angry? Would he push me for more? Would he insist that I keep letting him cook me breakfast because of his desire to dominate and conquer or whatever? I don't want to be trapped, or forced into anything. I really couldn't handle that."

Her eyes softened. "With a sealed mate bond, it would be impossible for him to hurt you. I don't know much about the connections, but I do know that. Even the cruelest, most violent kings couldn't hurt a hair on the heads of their queens. They were teams—as wicked and dark as that sometimes was for everyone."

Maybe that shouldn't have made me feel better, but it did.

"I don't want to make him unhappy, though," I said quietly. "I don't want to agree to this and then change my mind, and have him regret it."

She flashed me a smile—a genuine one. "Kier has never regretted a decision in his life. He's far too *dominant* and *conquering* for that. If he picks you, he's yours, no matter what."

My heart warmed rapidly.

Her gaze lifted to the dining hall's entrance, and her smile grew. "Whatever he did, he must've realized he screwed up."

My head turned just as a thick, warm hand landed on my shoulder.

"I'm sorry," he said into my mind. *"Veil, I am terrible at this."*

"It's alright. I think we just need to talk about it."

"I agree." He sat down next to me.

"You're talking mentally, huh?" Eisley asked knowingly.

"Of course not." Kierden snagged my fork from my fingers, loading it up and lifting it to my mouth. I stole it back from him and ate the food.

"We would never," I agreed as I chewed. "You need to eat something too," I told him.

"Don't worry about me, Nissa." He dropped a hand to my thigh and squeezed.

"I'm supposed to worry about you. We're mates."

He made a noise of disagreement. *"You're my female."*

"And you're my male, right?"

"You guys are *totally* talking mentally. If you weren't so damn adorable, I'd be annoyed," Eisley said, interrupting our conversation.

Err, the conversation we *weren't* having.

"We aren't," I protested as Kierden said into my mind,

"You know I'm yours, little human."

"Mmhm." Eisley didn't sound convinced in the slightest.

Kierden got up for a moment, and she shook her head at me while he was gone. He returned quickly, with a plate of food in his hands.

"So I take it you didn't learn anything about the deaths today?" Eisley looked at her brother.

He inclined his head to the side a little, and I realized he was gesturing toward the room we'd been in earlier. "No, we didn't."

"That's disappointing," she said calmly, though her eyes had widened slightly.

"We'll talk after we tell her what happened," Kierden murmured.

I agreed, and we both focused on our meal.

CHAPTER 22

NISSA

Eisley made conversation while Kierden and I both ate. When we were done, all three of us went back to the room the bodies were in. One of the fae woman from earlier was already waiting for us inside, and when we entered, she pulled a small pouch nearly identical to mine out of her pocket. She tossed it to me, and I caught it.

"Don't touch the other leaves again," Kierden warned me as he pulled my pouch out of his pocket and handed it to me.

"It'll be easier to match them if I hold them."

"I will drag your ass back to my room if you even think about it," he growled.

Though I gave him a dramatic sigh, I had to admit that he had a point.

I wouldn't touch anything.

"What's going on?" Eisley asked.

"When Nissa was in Dirue's home, she realized one of the fertility-suppressing plants wasn't the same as the others around it. They look the same, but their energy is different," the female fae who'd returned with her leaves explained. Kierden was too busy watching me to make sure I didn't touch any of the leaves to explain it himself.

"Veil," Eisley breathed. "You think *Dirue* is the murderer?"

"We think someone has been murdering couples for a long, long time, and this is the first clue we've ever had," the other woman said.

They continued talking while I set my leaves and the other woman's on tables a few feet away from each other, and then stepped back and closed my eyes.

Letting out a slow breath, I forced myself to follow the flow of my magic again.

It took some time, but eventually, I managed to find the plants in the room again.

I paid close attention to the individual leaves for a few minutes before finally withdrawing from the magic. I'd made sure I was absolutely certain—I wasn't going to be responsible for condemning someone for something they hadn't done.

All three pairs of eyes in the room were focused on me when I opened mine.

"Mine match hers." I gestured to the woman who'd brought hers for comparison. "The couples' leaves feel different than ours."

Eisley's expression grew grave.

"It could still be that the mated couples need stronger plants," the other woman reminded us, though she didn't sound convinced.

"She's the killer," Kierden said, his voice low but sure. "It doesn't make sense, but nothing else does either."

Eisley's grimace deepened. "She supported the unmated couples more than anyone else, and opposed the anti-sex laws more loudly, too. I don't know how she could go from that to murdering all newly-mated couples."

"She told me that the cult didn't have anything against love, they just thought mated couples could destroy Evare," I said quietly.

"Veil." Eisley pushed her hair out of her eyes.

There was a long moment of silence.

Finally, Kierden said, "We don't act until we've heard back from Govind. It'll be a few hours; he's going over there to ask her about the fertility of fully-mated pairs."

The women nodded.

"We'll keep an eye out for him and come find you when he shows," Eisley said, looking at Kierden.

He nodded, grabbing my pouch of leaves and the other woman's too. He tossed hers back, then tucked mine into my dress like I had earlier. My face warmed at the brush of his knuckles on my breast, but he withdrew quickly before taking my hand and slipping his fingers through mine.

"At least this nightmare is almost over," Eisley said quietly, as we slipped out of the room.

"For that, we can thank the veil," the other woman agreed.

Kierden's shoulders were heavy as we walked back to his room. I didn't ask if he was okay; clearly, he wasn't. Some things were far too terrible to ever be okay with.

"Are we moving down to your farm after this ends?" he asked me as he pulled the door to his room open. I got the feeling he was just trying to lighten the mood a little, but he didn't need to do that for me. I was used to dealing with the darkness, and it hadn't overwhelmed me yet, by some miracle.

Or some amount of strength, as silly as that seemed.

"I don't know. Are we?" I glanced at him.

"Perhaps we'll just keep both homes, so you have somewhere other than the tavern to run to when I inevitably screw up."

My lips curved upward a bit. "You didn't screw up in the pool. You just took me by surprise, and I didn't react well. Being defensive seems like my automatic response. I don't think either of us handled it perfectly."

He nodded, and I noticed him eyeing the bathing pool. Though we'd only just been in the water and some of my hair was still damp, I tugged him toward the bath. He'd used it to relax after long days on a few different occasions, so I thought it might calm him. I wasn't hoping for a repeat of earlier—I just wanted to help him feel a little better.

"Haven't you had enough water for the day, little human?" His voice was tired, but slightly playful.

I flashed him a smile as we reached the edge of the bath. "Not yet. Take your clothes off and get in."

He gave me a small grin. "You just want me naked."

"I won't deny that."

After a soft chuckle, he stripped completely, then slipped into the water.

Rather than following his lead, I sat down right behind him with my legs on either side of his arms as he leaned back against the wall of the pool.

He flashed me a curious look as I set my hands on his shoulders. "What are you doing?"

"Attempting to give you a massage. I'm sure I'll be terrible at it. The last massage I even saw was one my father gave my mother when I was eight or nine, and she looked absolutely miserable. He did too."

His expression morphed to surprise. "I'm sure I wouldn't know the difference. I've never had a massage before."

My eyebrows lifted. "Really? But you've had sex before. We always spend a little time in bed together, touching each other a bit, so I assumed it might've happened before for you." I lightly pressed my thumbs into the thick muscles at the base of his neck.

He groaned at the pressure, and I moved my thumbs around a bit. "Veil."

"It's okay?"

"It's incredible."

I grabbed the soap and rubbed it over my hands, so they'd be slicker. He groaned again, even louder, when I set them back on his shoulders and resumed the motions.

"I told you, the sex was only physical. There was no emotion involved. I didn't smell the female's hair, tell her she was beautiful, hold her, or particularly care if she climaxed, just as she didn't care if I did. For the fae, sex is always very selfish. I've never taken pleasure from making a woman unravel the way I do with you—and I've certainly never wanted one's hands on my skin like this before."

I liked that a lot, though I wasn't sure I should admit it. "When have you ever sniffed my hair?"

He groaned again when I slid my hands a bit further apart to massage the tighter parts of his muscles. "Every chance I get."

I didn't bother asking if it felt good, since he was so clearly showing me that it did. "Do I smell good?"

"Better than anything." His words sounded almost reverent.

"And you really think we're fated?" My words were soft, but I wanted to hear him say them aloud.

"I know that we're fated. I can feel it in my chest, my magic, and my very soul."

His words made something within me settle a little.

We both grew quiet, other than Kierden's soft groans and murmurs of how good my hands felt on his skin. I wasn't really thinking about anything, just focused on trying to make him feel good.

After a little time had gone by, he said in a voice so low I could barely make out the words, "I dread what this night will hold, Nissa."

"Do you want to talk about it?"

There was a long pause.

I assumed he was going to say no.

Instead, he admitted quietly, "It's my duty to kill her for what she's done. Though she deserves to die for her actions..."

"She's your friend," I said quietly.

"She's my friend," he repeated, his words slower and heavier than mine.

"Did you have sex with her?" I asked him. If he had, I wouldn't be jealous; it would've been a long time ago, and I only wanted to know so I could be aware of whether it was a factor or not.

"No. We have never been attracted to one another."

"But she's still your friend."

"Indeed." He leaned his head forward for me, and I slid my hands back to the base of his neck, earning a low, rumbly groan.

"I'm sorry," I said softly. "If there was a way for me to make it easier for you, I would do it."

"Thank you." He lifted a hand to rest on my knee. The gesture wasn't sexual; it was one of gratitude, and companionship.

"Is it lonely to be the king? I know you have Eisley, but she's your little sister, and I've never seen you vulnerable with her."

"Eisley is the only person I trust entirely when it comes to the kingdom, but you're right. I don't share my emotions or my burdens with anyone, and it has been lonely. Until now, I suppose."

"Does sharing them feel like ripping your nails off?" I teased him gently.

He chuckled. "Surprisingly, no. It feels like a weight is being lifted off my shoulders. Then again, that could just be those pretty little fingers."

I laughed. "Still flirting with me, huh?"

"As I will be until the bitter end, little human." He squeezed my knee. "We should talk about what happened at the pool earlier."

"Alright. Want me to stop touching you?"

"Never." His answer was quick, and firm. "But if your hands are getting sore, I'd rather you stop."

"I'm alright." They were a little tired, but in a good way. I loved the way he was reacting to my touch, and the way his muscles felt beneath my palms, so I had no desire to let go. "I can accept your need to *dominate* and *conquer*, but if something makes me uncomfortable, I have to be able to draw a line. And I'm not comfortable with you using me to make a statement to your people. If your drive for those things is too strong to accept that, this will never work between us. I'm not an object to be used."

"I know you aren't, and I'm sorry. I like to be in control, but I can only enjoy it if it brings you pleasure too. It wasn't my intention to make you feel like I cared more about the statement I was making than about pleasing you; my focus was on you, not my warriors."

I nodded. "I get it. And the dominating and conquering thing doesn't surprise me, or scare me away. If it gets you off to touch me in random places, I'm not against it, as long as no one actually sees anything and it's about us having fun."

"I can agree with that." There was a gorgeous, growl to his voice that I loved. "Despite my poor reaction, that was among one of the most pleasurable moments of my life."

My body warmed a little. He hadn't even climaxed. "Mine too," I admitted. "I have to admit, I'm curious how we could possibly have sex in the dining room."

He chuckled. "I suppose you'll have to wait and see."

My lips curved upward.

I continued massaging him for a while before I finally stopped and rested my hands on his shoulders. He leaned backward until he found my chest with his shoulder blades, and then tilted his head back so he could look into my eyes.

The gorgeous, dark blue orbs held me enraptured for a long moment before I blinked.

His lips curved upward, just the tiniest bit. "I'd like to spend the next few hours in our bed, holding you in my arms."

"That sounds nice." I brushed some hair off his forehead, and he closed his eyes briefly.

"Despite everything else, I'm not sure I've ever had a moment this peaceful before. I feel... happy." Kierden's voice was soft, his eyes still closed. "Thank you for giving me this."

My throat swelled. "You're welcome."

He opened his eyes, then caught my hand and dragged it to his lips. I gave him a small smile when he brushed a kiss to the backs of my fingers.

After a moment, Kierden released me and turned so he was kneeling on the pool's seat. His hands landed on either side of me, and his lips met mine in a soft kiss. Our tongues tangled, the movements slow and intimate enough to make my toes curl.

He pulled away a few minutes later and scooped me into his arms before he climbed out of the water. I leaned my head against his chest as he crossed the room, and a moment later, I was tucked beneath the blankets. He left me while he dried off, and my gaze lingered on his form as he pulled on a pair of tight shorts and then returned to me.

I moved over to give him room when he slipped under the blankets—and then he pulled me right back to him before putting me completely on top of him, so my chest was pressed against his. His heat warmed me through the thin fabric of my dress, and I lowered my head to rest against his neck.

"If we really decide to complete the bond, our entire lives will change," I whispered to him.

"A warrior without something to fight for is a hopeless wanderer. You give me something to fight for again, so I welcome the change," he murmured back.

"But what if your war starts again?"

"Then I'll finally have a reason not just to fight it, but to end it." His hand stroked my back lightly. "I don't see that happening, though. It's been so long since we've had peace that I think everyone is looking forward to the quiet. We plan on having the friendly fights here every year, to give our people something to train for in case they aren't interested in finding something else to do with themselves."

"Do you think any of them will want to have kids?" I asked, curiously.

"I'm certain that many will. There are couples in the kingdom who have been together for centuries without mating or starting a family, and I would guess that at least a few of those females will be pregnant before the year's end."

"And what about you?"

"What about me?"

"Do you want to have kids?"

He was silent for a moment.

A long, long moment.

"I suppose I've never considered it," he finally admitted. "I've longed for a partner at times. Someone to hold, confide in, and laugh with. A child never even crossed my mind."

"Well, you were so focused on war that you outlawed sex. Kids seem like an impossibility when no one's having sex."

He made a noise of agreement. "Do you want children?"

A soft laugh escaped me. "I have no idea. I feel like I haven't even lived yet. I need to figure out who I am before I so much as *consider* having a kid."

"You know who you are." His voice grew soft, and slightly playful. "You're a farmer."

I smiled; I did love my farm.

"You're as stubborn as any fae warrior," he added, his hand moving gently over my back, as if he were tracing a shape. "Braver, too. Certainly tougher. A sentence in that tower would've driven any of us mad, and yet here you are."

My smile grew a bit wistful. "I didn't know how much longer I was going to make it. I'm glad you showed up."

"As am I, little human."

"If we seal the bond, I won't really be human anymore."

"Regardless, you will be mine." His lips brushed the top of my head.

"Why are you so certain of that?" I asked him. "What do you even see in me?"

He was silent for a moment.

Part of me cringed, waiting for him to admit that he saw nothing, or just some potential.

Instead, he said, "I see many things when I look at you, Nissa. The one that truly stands out is *hope*. You make my world look brighter, and I need that."

I grew quiet as those words set in.

"What do you see in me?" he asked.

"Physical strength, mental strength, emotional strength... you have everything. When I think about the person I want to spend my life with, I think about someone I can lay in bed and talk about books with, and someone strong enough to protect me, if anyone else ever comes after me for my magic. Someone who will hold me when I need it and push me when I need that too. At this point, it doesn't even work when I try to picture anyone else but you in that place."

"Good. I'd hate to have to behead one of my warriors just because you pictured him as your mate."

I laughed again. "You wouldn't really."

"Perhaps not. I'd want to, though."

"That's fair." I closed my eyes, taking in a deep breath of his scent. My body was completely and entirely relaxed, and I was getting a little sleepy.

"You should rest. I kept you up late last night, and you're still fragile."

"I'm not fragile; I'm thicker than most of your fae," I mumbled back.

"In the best places." He slid his hand down and gave my ass a possessive squeeze. "But it will take more time than this to recover from those years of starvation."

"Unless you convince me to drink more of your blood." My words grew softer as he started stroking my back again.

"I thought I'd have to work up to that."

My lips curved upward. "It was fun. You should try drinking mine too, sometime."

"Definitely thought I'd have to work up to *that*," he said, chest rumbling a bit.

"We'll figure it out later."

He made a noise of agreement and continued to rub my back as I drifted off.

CHAPTER 23

NISSA

Kierden woke me up an hour or two later. His expression was so solemn that I didn't need to ask whether the male fae had come back from Dirue's house with news.

Both of us were silent as he pulled his shorts on and I adjusted my dress. He took my hand, slipping his fingers between mine while he opened the door.

Eisley and a few of the fae I'd met earlier stood outside with their bonded esu, including the man who had gone to talk to Dirue.

Their expressions were all grave.

"What happened?" Kierden's voice was low, but not angry.

The man who'd visited her explained, "She told me fertility doesn't change after sealing a mate bond, but that taking extra leaves doesn't hurt, so she usually sends them home with more.

I went back and searched the couple's home afterward but couldn't find their pouches anywhere."

Kierden grimaced, "She didn't mention giving them different leaves?"

"No."

He nodded slowly. "Is she still home?"

"Yes."

"I'll confront her and give her a chance to explain. Ready?" He looked at the others, and they all nodded.

Then he looked at me.

I was a little surprised he didn't ask me to stay back but nodded too.

"I asked Death to bring Bright back with him while you were sleeping," Kierden told me as we walked.

"Thank you."

"Of course." He squeezed my hand, and I squeezed back.

Our bonded esu reached the castle's entrance as we did, and we slid onto their backs while the other fae with us did the same.

I filled Bright in on what we'd learned while we moved through the city as a pack. She mentioned catching the Beast's scent while she was outside the elves' shield—which terrified me a little, though there was nothing we could do to keep him away from us.

The Beast would keep hunting Kierden until the eclipse, and there was no way around that. According to Kierden and the elves, shifters didn't believe in hurting animals, so the esu were safe outside the magical shield.

When we reached the healer's house, Kierden and Death stopped on Dirue's balcony, and Eisley and Sharp did the same. It made me feel better to know they would watch each other's backs.

Bright stopped on the porch of a tree near Dirue's, close enough that we could see her porch and far enough that she couldn't reach us.

I saw movement in the corner of my eye, and then noticed more fae already gathered in the trees around us. They waited silently, their expressions dark. Someone must've spread the word about Dirue's potential guilt, but since she was still in her home, it obviously hadn't reached her.

Kierden rapped a fist on her door, then gave her a moment to answer.

She opened the door with a smile—but when her gaze met Kierden's and then lifted to the trees, it vanished.

"Please step outside," Kierden told her.

Despite the "please," I knew it wasn't optional. And the look on Dirue's face told me she knew it wasn't either.

She stepped outside.

Kierden's mind touched mine. *"Which plant is it?"*

"The middle one," I said.

He strode into the house, sending me a mental image of them as he grabbed the pot. I confirmed it was right, and then focused my magic just to make sure.

"Be careful," I told him quietly.

Ice covered his hand and arm to keep the plant from touching his skin.

"What's this about?" Dirue asked, her expression a calm neutral the whole time Kierden was gone.

Eisley stared her down. "The murders."

Dirue didn't look surprised, though she didn't say anything incriminating.

Kierden emerged with the pot.

"Please be careful with my plants. Not all of us grow things as easily as the human you brought here," the healer said curtly. The argument was a pointless one, considering my magic had already sprouted massive flowers all around us. There was no way it hadn't affected her plants too.

"Her name is Nissa." Kierden stepped up to Dirue and held out the pot. "Eat one of these leaves."

She studied him.

"The only reason you wouldn't be willing to eat one of your own plant's leaves is if you knew it could kill you, the same way it killed Freive and Woan."

She stayed silent for a long, long moment.

"Do you deny it?" Kierden asked.

She held his gaze. "I do not."

The trees around me seemed to inhale as one as the fae's shock rolled through the air.

"You've killed every mated couple for centuries, when they trusted you. Why?" The king didn't lose his temper, and I respected him for it. My heart was beating rapidly, and I wasn't even really involved in the situation.

"A sealed mate bond gives a couple too much power. Look at you and Nissa. Between her life magic and your death, you could ravage our world. It's a risk no one should be willing to take—one you should be killed for, should you choose to seal your bond." She gestured toward me.

Kierden's eyes flashed with anger. "For murdering our friends and family in cold blood, Dirue, I challenge you. Does anyone protest the challenge?" He raised his voice as he asked the question, but the jungle was thick with silence.

Another look around showed that even more fae had gathered. Nearly the whole damn kingdom had to have been there; I could even see the elves in one of the trees nearest to the ground.

"Can I say a few words, first?" Dirue asked, her voice calm and measured.

Kierden set his jaw, but jerked his head in a nod.

She looked up at the trees. "I have loved all of you and been honest with all of you. I wept for the lives I ended, and mourned their deaths, even though they were necessary ones. I saw the wicked, corrupt power of a mated fae king and queen as a child. They wounded without reason and killed without question. I pray to the veil that one among you will consider taking up my mantle, and—"

A sharp blade of ice sliced through her throat, and her words cut off abruptly. She grabbed at her neck as blood poured from her, and I watched in sick fascination as she fell to her knees.

"Close your eyes," Bright and Kierden both told me.

I closed them.

"May the souls of our lost make your next life a painful one," Kierden growled. "And may the guilt on your conscience turn your future to ash."

There was an awful squelching noise, and then I heard Dirue's body hit the ground.

Silence reigned in the jungle for a long moment.

I opened my eyes.

Kierden dropped the potted plant on the porch, beside Dirue's body. He turned to face the warriors in the trees and said, "We will burn her in her home with her poison, and pray that she's tortured in the next life by the people she murdered so coldly. Should anyone else attempt to hurt a mated couple for no other reason than the bond, we will take great pleasure in tearing them limb from limb, over many weeks. We do not fear strength, we *celebrate* it. And no one's past dictates our future—*we* do."

Murmurs and growls of agreement seemed to echo through the jungle around us.

A male fae brought a burning torch forward as Kierden and
Eisley went back into the house for the non-poisonous plants.
They emerged quickly, but my gaze remained fixed on Dirue's
body while a few other fae joined the man with the torch.
Their hands were out as they used their magic to spread their
ice over the wood, so they could burn the killer without
hurting the tree.

A few more fae brought large bottles of something that looked
suspiciously like ale, and slowly drizzled it over Dirue's body
and her poisonous plant, before stepping into her home to
spread more of it inside.

I watched quietly as they finished and slipped off the porch
and into the tree branches—and I stayed silent as the man
finally tossed his flaming torch onto the healer's body.

There was a moment's pause before everything went up in
flames, and no one said a word as we watched it burn.

A flash of gold off to my right made me turn my head. The
couple from the farm was standing together, her back to his
chest, and his arms wrapped securely around her middle. A
golden handprint rested on her hip, glowing much brighter
than the silver one on my wrist—and I could see the glow from
the man's hand, too.

My lips curved upward just a tiny bit at the sight. Though my
heart was still beating quickly, and there was still a lump in my
throat from the violence I'd seen, knowing that mated couples
weren't in danger anymore brought me peace.

Eisley and Sharp wove through the branches until they landed next to the couple. She exchanged a few words with them, then all three of them nodded.

I imagined she was inviting them to stay at the castle so she and Kierden could keep an eye out, just to make sure Dirue had been working alone.

"Are you alright?" Kierden asked me quietly.

My eyes met his over the blazing fire below us. He stood on a bridge across from my branch with Death and a bunch of other fae and esu. His arms were full of plants, and if the situation had been different, the sight might have turned me on. *"I am. Are you?"*

"Not really. I've never had to kill one of my people before."

"Do you think anyone's going to try anything because of what she said?"

"I don't." He didn't hesitate. *"If she had been working with anyone, we would've caught them by now. It's much harder for two people to keep a secret than one."*

"I hope you're right."

We all stayed where we were and remained silent until the fire died completely. Though no one spoke for a long moment, everyone was looking at Kierden, waiting for him to give them instructions.

"Nissa will plant the herb throughout the city," Kierden said, looking at me.

I nodded.

"If you want to grow your own, do it. You are in control now. We all are. Our fates are ours to decide, and if we choose mates, we will defend them."

Murmurs of agreement rolled through the trees around us.

Kierden's mind touched mine. *Follow me.*

I didn't look back at what we'd left behind as we disappeared into the jungle.

When Death headed toward my farm, Bright followed. He stopped at one of the far edges of my recently-harvested land, and Kierden held out one of the potted plants he'd been holding.

"Ready?" he asked me.

"Mmhm." I took a small clipping of the plant—he gave me a small pair of sharp scissors made of ice when I asked him to— and then crouched down.

It only took a moment to make a small divot in the dirt, tuck the plant in, and rebury the roots. I felt my magic wash over it instantly, and saw the plant perk up.

We repeated the motion a few more times around the farmland, far enough from the crops that their roots wouldn't overlap as they continued to grow.

"There are a few high-traffic places we should put them, if you're okay with it," Kierden told me after we'd nearly planted all we could from the first pot. His voice was still low, and though he hadn't said anything about it, I knew he was itching to go back to the castle and to bed. Not to sleep, but to give himself time to process everything that had happened and everything he had done.

I agreed, and our bonded esu took us to the marketplace. I tucked a few of the plants' stems into deep crevices that existed in a few of the tree trunks, where they could grow freely. They wouldn't grow there naturally, but my magic wasn't exactly natural.

When we were done there, Bright and I followed Kierden and Death to a residential portion of the city I'd never seen before. Some of the fae in their homes watched us as we planted, and I waved at them when I saw them. Most waved back, too.

Eisley joined us as we were nearing the end of our stash. She and Kierden exchanged a few quiet words while I continued going through the last of our plants, and then handed him the ones she had picked up too.

She gave me a quick hug before she left again, and Kierden led me to another part of the city that was also full of homes. He watched me for a moment before he began helping me tuck the plants away to get them ready to continue growing.

As we did, I noticed my vines and flowers had somehow managed to grow all the way out where we were. It was much further from the castle than the edges of my town had been from my tower.

That meant my magic was either growing stronger, or it was simply spreading further when the plants near me were strong enough. I hoped for the latter.

We went to a few more locations, planting the herbs everywhere we went until we only had a few small sprouts left. Kierden stopped at the forest's floor to fill two of the pots with dirt, and then we finally went back to the castle.

I didn't bother asking him if he wanted to go to my house by the farm. He needed the comfort of his long-time home, and I needed to be somewhere in the middle of all the new plants. The castle was about as central as it got, and staying central would help make sure my magic reached everything so the herbs would start growing the way they were supposed to.

The door to his room closed behind us, and Kierden let out a long breath. He kneeled near the door, and quickly dumped half of the dirt from the two full pots into the other two, so all four were half-full. After he tucked the sprouts into the soil and buried the roots, he rose to his feet. I leaned over and carefully took one of the few remaining leaves from one of the sprouts, slipping it into my mouth and tucking it under my tongue.

It didn't hurt to be prepared, after all.

The taste was sweet and tangy, reminding me of my happy childhood, before everything had changed. I wasn't sure whether to smile at the memories or embrace the sadness of knowing just how far in the past they were. But, after so many weeks in Jirev, the sadness felt much more distant than it used to.

My gaze moved back to Kierden. He looked absolutely defeated.

I could help him with that, though.

"I think I need a bath. Come with me?" I asked, wrapping my hand around his gigantic bicep. There was a fair amount of dried blood on his skin, and I wasn't climbing in bed with him until we'd washed it off.

Kierden nodded absently, so I led him to the bathing pool.

Bright murmured to me that Death had asked her on a run in the forest, and when I assured her that we'd be fine, the two of them slipped out of the room.

I tugged my dress over my head, dropping it at my feet. Kierden's eyes lowered to my skin and trailed over me slowly as I took off my scanties too—and they heated when I stepped up to him and pushed his shorts down his thighs.

When his erection sprang free, I wanted to touch him, but didn't want to push him after what he'd had to do to Dirue.

"Keep looking at me like you want to eat me, little human, and your tongue and teeth won't be the only things in your mouth," he murmured as he took a seat on the edge of the bathing pool.

My gaze jerked to his, and I found his lips curved slightly, his eyes a little playful. He'd taught me how to please him with my mouth when I demanded it a handful of days earlier, but it wasn't his favorite way to get off. Not because I wasn't good, but because I took control from him, and he was a little obsessive about retaining it. I didn't mind, because he was damn good at being in control... though it did make me feel powerful to be in charge of his pleasure like that.

Though his words had been a joke, I'd been with him long enough to know that a joke about something related to sex meant he wanted it. He was too prideful to ask me to go down on him—and too polite to demand it. I had a feeling the politeness would vanish with the newness of our bond, though.

I kneeled beside him and leaned over, wrapping my lips around his erection. His eyes closed, his head tilted back, and a low groan escaped him. "You suck my cock so damn well."

I made a noise of agreement, bobbing and gripping the base of his cock as I took him deeper. His hands dug into my hair, and he gripped my head firmly. Even when he started moving me the way he wanted me, I still knew I was in control. If I'd resisted at all, he would've stopped and let me take the lead again.

"I fit so perfectly in that little mouth," he growled, as he neared the edge of his climax. I squeezed him, then took him deeper until he hit the back of my throat.

He snarled, his hips jerking and his hands fisting tightly in my hair as he flooded my mouth with his release. I swallowed his pleasure, licking the head of his cock as I slowly pulled away.

Kierden pulled me into his arms, sitting me on his thigh and holding me against him. I listened to the rapid beat of his heart as his chest rose and fell quickly.

"Thank you," he said, his voice low. One of his hands started to slip between my thighs, but I pressed down on it, holding it where it was.

"I did that because I wanted to, Kierden. Not because I wanted you to reciprocate."

He pulled his hand free, and used it to wipe a bit of his pleasure off my lip before slipping it inside my mouth. I sucked, and his lips curved upward slightly. "Veil, you're cute."

I laughed softly. "I hope that's a compliment."

"It is."

He slipped into the water, still holding me tightly to his chest. A few more minutes passed peacefully before he murmured in my ear, "Thank you."

"You already thanked me." I leaned back against him, enjoying the feel of his skin on mine.

"Not for bringing me pleasure; for bringing us the closure we've been seeking since before I was king." His lips brushed the side of my head. "And for letting me hold you like this while pretending you need a bath."

A soft laugh escaped me. "I did no such thing."

"Mmhm." He pressed another kiss to my temple. "Tell me a story from your childhood. Something happy."

It took me a minute to come up with something, but I eventually remembered a day I'd spent helping my dad in his fields, and launched into the story.

CHAPTER 24

NISSA

A few hours and a few dozen stories later, we emerged from the bathing pool and got dressed again. I think we could've lasted a bit longer, but my stomach started growling, and my hunger made Kierden grumpy.

So, we headed to the dining hall.

Despite the horror of what had happened a few hours earlier, I felt closer than ever to the king. We'd talked like old friends, and something about hearing stories of the stupid things he'd done when he was younger made him feel more real to me.

"The cooks will have brought out the ale, so prepare yourself," he warned me as we walked. "My fae will be drunk. Very drunk."

"Noted."

Despite my confirmation, I wasn't really prepared for what we walked in on.

The dining hall was absolutely full—I didn't see a single empty seat, anywhere. The walls were lined with even more people, too. They were everywhere.

A group of men and women in one corner were singing loud and drunkenly, at least a dozen of them strumming stringed instruments. They were completely out of rhythm, and the clashing sounds made me cringe a little.

In another corner there were a handful of fae crying together with a pile of tissues on the table in front of them.

The third corner held fae who were playing games with cards and dice, some of them roaring with laughter while others looked angry or grumpy.

The last corner held a buffet of food, and there was another table beside it with dozens of glasses of ale lined up on it.

I whistled.

He pulled me behind him as he began weaving around the tables. Some of the people moved for him, but some were just too drunk. *"The goal is to get food and get out before too many people notice us."*

"What happens if they notice us?"

"They'll convince me to drink with them," he grumbled.

My lips curved upward. *"I kind of want to see you drunk."*

"You will eventually."

When we reached the buffet table, we both loaded our plates quickly. Kierden wasn't satisfied with the amount of food I put on mine, so he piled more on it before he snagged it from me and then started back toward the door.

"King Kier!" one of the male fae exclaimed, his voice extremely slurred.

"I'm busy," Kierden said, as we neared our escape.

"It's okay if you want to spend the evening drinking with them. They knew Dirue the same way you did, and you could all talk about her. It might give you closure," I told him. *"It won't offend me. I understand, and can spend the night with Bright and Death, or—"*

"I don't need closure." He led me out of the dining hall. The noise faded as we walked further from it. *"I got that when I saw her go up in ashes, and I've had all day to accept the truth. Now, I want to be distracted. Preferably by your body."*

I didn't really believe him about having accepted everything, but if he wanted a distraction, I could give him that.

"Alright. If you change your mind, that's okay."

"I'm not going to change my mind, Nissa. I want you bare and writhing with pleasure through the whole damn night." He pushed the door to his room open with his shoulder, and held it for me while I stepped through too.

"Sounds like fun."

"Mmhm." He turned just slightly, only enough for my hip to brush against his erection as I walked past him.

Veil, he was hard.

"Do you think Bright and Death are going to mate soon?" I asked him as we walked to the bed together.

Perhaps it was strange to eat in bed, but it was a habit I hoped we'd never break. Something about having plenty of food to eat, while lounging beneath the blankets, felt like the pinnacle of luxury to me.

Kierden chuckled. "He's going to lose his damn mind if they don't."

I grinned. "She'll give in soon."

We sat down and ate, and though we were quiet, his hand brushed my knee and thigh every now and then, making me feel... well, like I mattered to him.

It was one of the best feelings I'd ever had.

When we finished, he took my plate and set it on the floor before tugging my dress over my head. He dragged my barely-clothed body into his arms before the fabric even hit the floor.

"You're going to take my cock tonight, little human," he murmured to me, moving his hands slowly over my bare thighs and ass as I settled against his erection. I could feel the thickness of his cock against my clit, despite the fabric of his shorts and my undergarments that separated us.

"Sounds like fun." My clit grinded against him as I moved my hips.

"Oh, yes. You'll be drenched and desperate for it long before I fill you." He nipped at my shoulder. "Remember the way my finger feels inside you?"

My body flushed at the memories. "Of course."

"You'll take two when I lick you to climax."

He was right; I was already soaked for him, and achy too.

"Will I?" I managed to ask.

His hands finally found my core, and he dragged a finger lightly up and down the center of me. "Yes. You'll take three after the second climax."

Oh damn.

He hooked a finger in my scanties and tugged them downward. My body rocked at the brush of his skin against my clit, and his chest rumbled in satisfaction.

With one smooth motion, he rolled me to my back. Our eyes were locked as he pulled the fabric down my legs and then tossed it to the floor.

He freed my breasts next, tossing that fabric too before he took thick handfuls of my tits and squeezed. Releasing them, he slid further down my body until he settled between my thighs, opening my legs wider. His burning eyes took in every inch of me like it was the first time he was seeing me, the same way they always did.

He dragged a finger slowly over my clit, and my hips rocked in response. "When you're drenched in your own pleasure, you'll part these gorgeous thighs even wider for me and watch my cock sink inside this pretty little body of yours. Ready, Nissa?"

"Yes," I breathed.

His lips curved upward wickedly. "Good."

He lowered his tongue to my clit and licked me, slowly.

The world stopped.

Everything stopped.

Everything, except my body and Kierden's.

His chest rumbled in approval. "You're absolutely delicious."

He licked me again, and I cried out at the sensation.

"I can see and taste how much you want me, little human. Look how slick you are for me." He dragged a finger down my center, and I cried out again. My hips rocked desperately as he slowly slid a finger inside me while his tongue made love to my clit.

My cries grew more desperate as I shattered, the pleasure hitting hard and fast.

I was panting when I came down from the high, flushed and relaxed but somehow still wound up. Probably because his tongue was still moving lazily over my clit, like he just couldn't stop tasting me.

"That was perfect, Nissa. You're going to take another finger now. Get ready."

Something about the simple way he gave the order was insanely erotic to me, and I found myself nodding.

He slipped his finger out of me—and then slowly slid two inside me.

My body went still at the pressure of it.

His tongue dragged over my clit, and I let out a long, shaky breath. He stretched me further and further, until his fingers were buried deep inside me.

Kierden slowly stroked my inner walls, and I let out a slow moan as my body tensed. The pleasure was fierce, building up rapidly until I lost control with another cry.

He sucked lightly on my clit, making me dizzy as I struggled to catch my breath. "Just one more, little human. Then you'll be ready for me."

I already felt ready for him, but if he was going to keep licking me and touching me, I'd do whatever he wanted.

When he slowly worked his third finger into me, I gasped, reeling at the pleasure of it.

If his fingers felt that good, how would his cock feel?

I moaned at the thought, the sensations, and everything else.

He licked and sucked on my clit, giving it so damn much attention as he filled me with his fingers. The need built again, more slowly but more fiercely, until I unraveled with another desperate cry of pleasure.

I was so unbelievably sated.

So unbelievably drained, too.

But when he slid his fingers out of me, I still whimpered just the tiniest bit at the loss of him.

Kierden gave my clit one last flick with his tongue before he stripped his shorts off, then leaned back over my body and captured my mouth. He kissed me slowly, his hands moving over my skin as he opened my thighs wider. His erection rubbed against my core, and the thick heat of him made me want more, despite everything we'd just done.

He growled against my lips, "Ready, little human?"

"Completely," I breathed.

The head of him pressed against my slit, and everything didn't just stop—it ceased to exist.

The world.

The room.

Even the bed.

Nothing mattered except me and Kierden.

He slowly slid inside me, and all thoughts faded from my mind.

It was just me and him.

Me and my king.

Me and my friend.

Me and my *mate*.

And veil, we fit together perfectly.

My breathing was fast, my body flushed and needy as I wrapped my legs around his hips, pulling him even deeper inside me.

"You're so damn wet and tight. So damn *perfect*." His words were low and gravelly, his lips moving against mine as he spoke them. I struggled for air while he throbbed inside me, staying still while I adjusted to the thickness of him. "How do you feel?"

"So good."

His rumble of approval made me feel even better.

He slowly slid out and back in—and the intensity of it made me gasp.

So he did it again.

And again.

And again.

Until I was bucking my hips, crying out at the ferocity of the climax that took control of me.

It was everything.

He was everything.

Kierden roared with me, slamming into me as he took his pleasure too. The sensation of him flooding me with his release was so damn surreal—and I wanted more before he was even done.

He tried to pull out of me, but I grabbed him by his thick, muscular ass and held him in place. My nails dug into his backside, and his eyes burned into mine as his cock throbbed inside me.

"You need a break," he told me, wiping a bead of sweat from my forehead and then licking it off his thumb.

"No," I whispered, holding him there. His release was leaking out of me, wet and warm on my core and the insides of my thighs. "I want more."

His eyes burned hotter. "Nissa..."

"Give me what I want, Kierden." I squeezed his ass, and he growled at me. In one sharp motion, he'd rolled us over so he was below me.

"*Take* what you want, little human."

Ohhh.

I liked that a lot.

"I don't know what I'm doing," I warned him, as I propped myself up on his chest and rolled my hips a little.

"You're doing it *perfectly*," he growled, grabbing my ass and squeezing, *hard*.

I rolled my hips, and he squeezed my ass again. "Use me for your pleasure, little human. I belong to you."

One of his hands moved to my breast, gripping and massaging as I sat up higher so I could watch our bodies connect as I rode him slowly. The pleasure was building again—he'd made me so damn insatiable.

I rocked my hips, panting as the pleasure grew. Kierden's fingers brushed my back entrance, making me gasp as we neared the edge together.

The touch shattered me. I made sounds I hadn't even realized I was capable of as the climax went on, and on, and on. He lost it with me, flooding me with his release again.

When the bliss had faded, I collapsed on Kierden's chest, catching my breath as he held me tight.

"That was incredible." He squeezed me tightly. "Damn, little human."

I grinned against his chest. "It was. I think you're holding back on me, though."

His whole body rumbled with a deep belly-laugh. "Of course I'm holding back on you. I wasn't even sure you'd like my cock."

My grin widened. "Asshole."

"You're tiny, Nissa. A man my size has to worry, so consider it a compliment."

"How could I consider it a compliment?" I peeled my face off his chest, propping myself up on my forearms as I attempted to give him a dirty look. It failed, because he was still buried inside me, and I was still grinning.

Kierden lifted his hands to cradle my face. "I was worried because I care about you. If I didn't care, I wouldn't worry."

"Okay, you win. It's a compliment."

His lips curved upward, and he pulled me down for a slow, soft kiss before releasing me and tugging my face back down to his chest. "Fate clearly chose right for us. When I'm sure I can stop holding back without hurting you, I'll do exactly that, with great pleasure. Until then, I'm going to hold back."

I sighed dramatically. "Overprotective fae bastard."

He chuckled. "I'll wear the title with pride."

"Kierden Jirev, King of the Fae, Overprotective Bastard of a Mate," I drawled.

"Suits me perfectly."

"It does." I patted him on the chest.

He laughed again for me, and my grin returned. "You are *stunning*, Nissa. I may be holding back, but that was still the most incredible sex I've ever had."

"Liar."

He rolled me over, pinning me to the bed as his body pressed into mine.

Damn, I'd forgotten how *big* he was.

"I've never had sex with a woman who means something to me, and that makes this the most intimate, pleasurable connection I've ever had. Doubt that, and there will be consequences."

"What consequences?" I shot back. "You'll stop holding back?"

He rocked his hips, and a soft groan escaped me as his cock hit the back of my channel. "Consequences like me freezing your wrists above your head, so you can't touch me while I drag you to the edge repeatedly without letting you climax," he growled, thrusting into me again. "Consequences like me sitting you on my face and holding you there while I feast on you until you *beg* for release."

Veil, that sounded hot.

"In all seriousness, I think the bindings might be too much for me," I admitted. "After being tied up so many times…"

"Then there will be no binding until you want to try it." He stroked my hip lightly with one of his hands. "Your pleasure is what matters most to me, little human. Remember that."

"It would bring me pleasure if you stopped holding back."

He studied me. "You're serious about this."

"Of course I'm serious about this. You have tons of experience, and I'm new. I don't want you holding back and then thinking later tonight, '*damn, Nissa is really terrible at sex… I should go back to one of my old fae lovers.*'"

He barked out a laugh. "I never had a *lover.*"

"I feel like you just missed the point of the whole conversation," I grumbled.

"I didn't. You want me to treat you like you have experience, to take what I want from you the way I would if you were a fae woman."

"Yes." I nodded emphatically.

He rocked his hips, bottoming out inside me. I swore as I jerked mine in response, and my channel clenched as he pulled out entirely. His arms were under me a moment later, and then he was striding across the room.

CHAPTER 25

NISSA

My feet hit the ground as we reached the wall, and he spun me around until my breasts kissed the wood. My cheek pressed against it, and Kierden lifted one of my hands up above my head, followed by the other.

"Leave them there," he commanded.

"Okay, I—" The words died in my throat when he grabbed me by the thighs, opening me up before he slammed into me.

I choked on air and pleasure, my breasts smashed against the wood as he slammed into me again and again. His fingers dug into my thighs, and the need inside me built much slower, but it *did* build.

"After a female has given him permission, a male fae takes what he wants, when he wants it," Kierden said into my ear. "If a female needs more, she demands it."

"How?" I gasped.

"Commands. *Slower. Harder. Touch my clit. Don't climax until I have. Fill me with ice. Stop for a moment.*"

"Slower," I breathed.

"Louder, Nissa. You're the queen; act like it."

The title he'd given me didn't process at all.

"Slower, Kierden," I snarled at him.

"Perfect," he growled back, slowing his strokes immediately.

I groaned as he bottomed out inside me.

Even after following my command, he was driving into me harder and faster than he had on the bed. It wasn't better, but it was still incredible—just different.

His breathing was more ragged, his hands rougher on my skin as he grabbed my breasts, hips, and ass whenever he wanted.

"Touch my clit," I ordered him breathlessly.

He ignored me, so I repeated it louder, commanding him again.

He didn't hesitate to give me what I'd wanted, his fingers working me as he slammed home.

The pleasure hit me, and I shattered on his cock even harder than before. A scream tore through my lungs at the fierce intensity of it, and Kierden snarled as he lost control with me.

"Veil," I moaned, collapsing against his chest. "You should never hold back again. I did like it slower too, though. It was more emotional, in a way. So maybe holding back isn't the worst."

"Noted," he rumbled against my back, his hands moving slowly over my breasts. "And I agree."

I huffed a sigh. "I am so damn exhausted."

"I should let you sleep," Kierden agreed. He started lifting me off his cock, but I protested immediately.

"I'm not ready."

"Good; I want you to fall asleep with me buried inside you." He carried me into the bathroom and grabbed a towel, then dampened it as he slid me off his cock. When he set me on my ultra-wobbly legs, kneeling in front of me, I stared down at him. He gently cleaned me off, then leaned in and kissed my clit like he just couldn't help it.

And then he buried a few fingers inside me, like he couldn't help that either.

A laugh escaped me. "Kierden."

"Stop looking and smelling so damn good, and maybe I won't need to touch you so much," he grumbled at me, withdrawing his fingers and licking them clean.

If I wasn't so exhausted, the sight would've turned me on.

Kierden stood back up when I was clean, lifting me off the ground. After a stop in the closet for one of his old shirts—which he tugged over my head himself—he carried me back to the bed.

When he sat down, he tugged the fabric up out of the way so we could both watch as he pulled me down onto his cock again. I sank down much easier than before, and veil, it felt so damn good.

"If you sleep like this, I'm going to wake up partway through the night to get you off. Probably more than once," Kierden warned me as he lowered us both to the bed.

"Feel free," I breathed.

He brushed a kiss to my forehead. "Sleep well, Nissa. Despite the misery of this evening, I'll cherish the memories of tonight as the best of my life."

Emotions swelled in my chest. "Me too."

He kissed my shoulder, and I drifted off with the soft words of our bond echoing in my mind, itching to be spoken.

"Sillah ovim rett warum."

"Sillah ovim rett warum."

"Sillah ovim rett warum."

I pressed my lips to his chest to keep myself silent, and the urge passed as I fell asleep.

Kierden woke me with his face between my thighs an hour later, and rolled me onto my abdomen before he drove his cock into me from behind, bringing my pleasure to new heights before we fell back asleep.

I woke him an hour after that with my mouth on his erection, tasting us both on his skin before he seated me on his cock backward and slammed into me again, again, and again.

The night passed by in a haze... and quickly rolled into the next day.

The next handful of weeks went by in a whirlwind of farming, delicious food, and sex. We explored the library a bit, but Kierden joined me in the fields most of the days, learning how to harvest and plant with me.

Our breakfasts were spent in the castle's dining hall, conversing with the other fae. Our lunch breaks were full of fresh fruit and conversation, alone in my house just off the farm. Our dinners were always back in the castle, laughing with the elves as they and the fae told story after story of the long lives they'd lived.

They were the most blissful weeks of my life.

We didn't discuss making our bond permanent, but Kierden had told me he planned on reigniting it after the eclipse so my magic didn't overwhelm me.

Bright and Death spent most of their time in the jungle together. Though we missed them, we were thrilled for them. He was pursuing her with every damn ounce of effort he had, and we kept waiting for them to come back mated. They frequently smelled the Beast while out in the Wilds, but as everyone kept reminding me, he wouldn't go near the esu.

. . .

A few nights before the eclipse, Bright's panicked cry cut into my mind in the middle of the night, waking me up suddenly. *"Nissa!"*

Jerking upright, I sucked in a deep, staggered breath. *"What happened? What's wrong?"*

"The Beast took Death. We just mated a few hours ago—he's my mate." The fear in her voice was thick. *"He's hurt. I don't know how bad. I can smell Kierden in the Wilds; I think he's on his way. We need to get the elves—they're the only chance we have."*

My head jerked to the side, and I realized the bed was empty.

Terror crashed into me.

The Beast couldn't kill Death, though he could wound him badly.

But he could kill Kierden.

He *needed* to kill Kierden.

It was his last chance to do so, because when the suns eclipsed in the morning, his vow would break if my mate was still alive.

"I'll get Alida," I said, scrambling toward the door in nothing but the massive white shirt I wore as a nightgown. There was a thin layer of ice over the door—Kierden's quick attempt to stop me from going after him, the absolute bastard—but when I rammed it with my shoulder, I broke through easily.

He knew better than to truly trap me anywhere. I would kick his ass to the veil and back, and still be absolutely furious.

My hair and massive shirt swayed and bounced with me as I sprinted down the hallway. I knew the general direction of the elves' rooms, but I'd never been there before, so I yelled as I neared them, "Alida!"

I continued shouting and running until the sleepy, pissed-off elf-shifter burst out of a room as I neared the door.

My chest rose and fell rapidly, my heart beating like a drum in my chest. "The Beast is here. He hurt Death—Kierden's running toward him right now. You have to stop him."

She blinked. "You want me to stop Kierden?"

"No, the Beast. Please, you have to help." Images flickered in my mind, memories of my dad taking his last breaths while I held on to him as if I could anchor him to this side of the veil myself.

That couldn't happen to Kierden.

I couldn't let it happen to Kierden.

Alida's expression darkened. "If there was anything we could do to stop our assassins, we would've done it centuries ago. You'll have to stop the king yourself, or say goodbye."

She took my hand and squeezed lightly. "I'll strengthen the defenses on the city just to be safe."

With that, she disappeared back into her room and left me standing in the hallway alone.

"They can't help us," I whispered to Bright.

She snarled into my mind. *"Then we'll have to save them ourselves."*

"How?"

"The beast wants power, right? You're more powerful than any of the fae in the city. If you offer to mate with him after the eclipse so he can have your power too, it might buy time. We only need a few hours."

"Or it might get me killed," I whispered.

"He can't kill you. Not completely."

He could get really damn close, though, and let my humanity do the rest.

When it came down to it, it was a choice between certain death for Kierden, or a chance that we could both live.

There was no question what I had to do.

Alida burst back through the door, her eyes wide and bright. "Our assassins hunt through magical connections; that's why your bond hides Kierden from the Beast. If you seal it, his magic will meld with yours and change permanently. The beast's contract will dissolve, and he won't be able to kill the king no matter how badly he wants to."

I went still.

If I sealed my bond with Kierden, it would save his life.

But it would change mine permanently, and that was a massive commitment.

If it came down to it, and there was no other choice...

Well, I'd do whatever I had to, to save his life.

"I'm coming," I told Bright.

She picked me up at the castle's entrance a few minutes later and streaked into the Wilds faster than she'd ever run.

"I'll grab Kierden and get him out of there as fast as I can," Bright told me, her voice hard. *"He's on foot, and not far ahead of us. Do whatever you have to. The Beast thought you smelled good, so use that."*

"I probably smell like Kierden now," I whispered back.

She inhaled, and then swore.

"I'll figure something out."

"We're all going to survive this," Bright growled. *"We haven't made it this long to lose our lives to the damn Beast."*

I agreed, though my confidence was fading alongside the distance between us and the Beast.

It was a terrible plan, but if we didn't go, no one would. And we couldn't just sit back and let our mates die; veil, that wasn't even an option.

"Here I am," Kierden's snarl echoed through the jungle ahead of us.

Fear clutched my stomach as the Beast's laughter cut through the Wilds.

Finally, we saw Kierden, the Beast, and an unconscious Death in a small clearing on the floor of the jungle. There was only a short distance between the men—and Death separated them.

Bright launched toward the clearing as the Beast lunged for Kierden, moving so fast I couldn't even see him move. The fae king's ice swords appeared in his hands as he whirled out of the way, slashing his weapons out.

The Beast roared as ice cut through his arm—and his claws caught Kierden's side.

The men spun together, the scent of their blood flooding the air as they fought. I couldn't see who was winning, but Kierden wasn't anywhere near as fast as the Beast, and I knew that meant he would eventually be overtaken.

"Death is breathing. He's unconscious, but I don't smell any blood," Bright said. *"You have to intervene now, if you want me to get Kierden out of here."*

She was right.

Though it went against every one of my instincts, I slipped off Bright's back and called out, "Beast, I have something you'll want more than a fae king's energy."

The asssassin appeared in front of me.

"Get Kierden out of here," I whispered to Bright. *"I don't care what you have to do to him—just get him out."*

She practically flew at the fae king, ramming him. He landed on her back, and she bit down on his leg to hold him there as she sprinted back into the jungle with him.

Kierden was snarling into my mind, but I didn't let myself listen to what he was saying. If I listened, I might get worried, and I couldn't allow myself to be afraid.

I forced myself to focus on the real threat—the man in front of me.

His lips lifted in a feral grin that told me I was going to regret sacrificing myself the way I just had. "You must be very powerful to think you're worth more to me than the man I've vowed to kill. Or just very stupid."

Or a little of both, maybe.

"What do you know about mating?" I asked him, fighting hard to keep my voice even.

"Your mating won't keep me from killing your king, sweetheart."

"Not my mating; *yours*."

His gaze became slightly... curious. "I'm listening."

"Did you know that mating connects two people's magic? If I seal my bond with Kierden, I'll have access to his power, and he'll have access to mine."

The Beast's eyes narrowed.

I added quickly, "The elves' magic changed you. What if you mated with a shifter? Would it balance out that magic so you don't have to take contracts anymore? Would it make your power even stronger?"

His eyes narrowed even further.

The words poured out of me, "I've been where you are. You're trapped by the spells the elves put on you; I was trapped in a literal tower for most of my life. But what if there's a way out? What if taking a mate would free you? Isn't that worth more than this?" I gestured to the jungle around us.

The Beast lifted an eyebrow "You're defending him."

Kierden had grown silent in my head, which worried me, but I couldn't let it distract me. "Of course I am. He's my *mate*."

"Yet he stole you from your home and started a bond between you against your will, to protect himself."

"Most people will do whatever they possibly can to stay alive. I think you're proof of that."

The Beast laughed darkly. "Indeed. I'll even use a fragile little human as bait."

He lunged too fast for me to dodge. One of his arms pinned my hands at my side, and the other gripped my throat as he held my back to his chest. I couldn't breathe with the way he held me, and the pain warred with the panic of being trapped.

"I have your female, Kier," the Beast bellowed into the forest. "For every minute you make me wait, I'll remove a limb. Will you let her bleed for you?"

"I can't stop him," Bright snarled into my mind. *"He's coming for you."*

My eyes collided with Death's.

The esu was conscious, and staring at me.

"When Death moves, duck," Bright commanded me, speaking for her mate.

In the blink of an eye, he launched toward me and the Beast.

My heart lodged in my throat as I threw myself forward. The Beast didn't so much as blink at the weight of my effort—but then Death's body slammed into him, throwing us both backward.

His claws dug into my hip and throat, and a scream burst from me in response to the pain. Death tore into his shoulder, and with a snarl, the Beast threw me aside.

I slammed into a tree, *hard*.

The impact knocked the breath out of me.

I felt something crack—before I felt nothing at all.

When I landed on the jungle's floor on my back, my breathing felt shallow, and feeling slowly started creeping into my limbs again. It wasn't just feeling, it was *pain*. Insane, intense pain.

The scent of my blood flooded the air, and slowly, the pain grew more intense.

Shock clouded my mind as I watched Death fight the Beast. Both creatures bled and snarled, until a moment later, when Kierden and Bright joined the fight.

It was a flurry of blood and pain.

One simple, clear thought crossed my mind as I watched them tear into each other, claws colliding with fangs and swords of ice:

I was dying.

I had no future anymore.

If I sealed our bond I could give Kierden a chance of surviving *hundreds* of years.

And if I did manage to make it through by some miracle...

Well, I would want to spend my life with him. He'd proven that he was willing to try anything if it kept him at my side, including *farming*. And most importantly, he wasn't someone who would change his mind. After he said we belonged to each other, he never wavered. He would fight for us no matter how bad things became.

It would've been terrifying to promise him my life, no matter how long I knew him or how sure I was that everything would work out between us. A bond like that was so much bigger than I could ever understand from our side of the veil.

But there was so damn much hope in it, too.

Even if I was dying, even if I wouldn't see him until he joined me on the other side of the veil in a few centuries, I *wanted* that bond with him.

And I wanted to save his life.

So I parted my lips, and finally whispered the words that the bond had tried so damn hard to get me to say.

"Sillah ovim rett warum."

The handprint on my wrist burned.

The magic in my chest swelled.

I gasped at the pain, at the intensity—and then watched helplessly as everything faded around me, until the world itself was gone.

And perhaps I was gone too.

CHAPTER 26

KIERDEN

I was covered in blood as I spun and slashed, fighting as one with my bonded esu and his mate.

Death and I had never fought a battle we couldn't win, but perhaps we'd finally found one.

At least when I passed, I would do so fighting for my female.

The Beast was gaining ground on us, wounding us more than we were wounding him, without waning in the slightest despite his own blood loss.

He was a monster, created by magic and fueled by it too. I was simply a warrior, honed through battle but kept alive by the blood and ice in my veins, the warring of life and death.

A whisper sounded behind me—one I shouldn't have heard with my focus trained on the fight. Nissa's voice, softer and weaker than it should've been.

"Sillah ovim rett warum."

Time slowed—and then went still.

Fierce pain burned through my palm—and then Nissa's magic burst to life in my chest, over my skin, and through my blood. It cleansed the dark magic of the brand on my hand as it knitted with mine, her life and my death.

Battle cries echoed through the jungle as my warriors launched into battle. I didn't know who had woken them, or how they'd found us. I didn't have time to be glad they were there, either.

Because as they charged the Beast, I staggered backward. I could feel the fading consciousness of my mate through my mind... and all the way to my damned soul.

She was dying.

My mate was dying.

Nissa was dying.

There was no time to think.

No time to consider my options, or pray to any of the lost gods who might still be listening.

I shoved through the mass of my warriors until I reached her. As I dropped to my knees, I didn't let myself look at her broken body, her bleeding wounds, or the sickly paleness of her tan skin.

There wasn't time for that either.

I sliced through the place my neck met my shoulder with one hand as I hauled her upright with the other, and dragged her face to my bleeding wound.

"Bite me, Nissa," I snarled into her mind and ear with every bit of force and power I had.

She didn't respond.

I refused to accept that.

Diving into our bond, I found the place our minds met. There was a thin wisp of a wall separating us, but I cut through it ruthlessly.

She could hate me for it later.

Later, when she wasn't going to die.

I wouldn't let her leave me.

"Drink my blood," I commanded her, all but taking control of her body with the force of my will.

Her body jolted slightly, and I held her face to my neck.

Finally, she swallowed.

It was the tiniest sip, but it was all the assurance I needed.

It was going to work.

She *was* going to survive.

"Again," I snarled directly into her mind. She couldn't block me out, not while I was inside her so damn intimately.

She took another small swallow.

"More, Nissa."

She drank again, again, and again, until she was sucking my blood down desperately, taking all I had to offer.

My energy faded as she drank, but veil, I couldn't have cared less about myself. As long as she was breathing, as long as she was *living*, I'd walk through that damn veil with pride.

"My fiery little human," I murmured into her mind, stroking her hair lightly as I turned so my back met the tree behind us for support. *"Our months together have been the best of my life. I love you more than I could ever find the words to say."*

Her beautiful eyes were cloudy as they collided with mine, and their appearance stunned me. One was the same gorgeous green it had always been, while the other was my dark blue. My chest burned with pride and relief as I slipped into unconsciousness.

She was alive.

And she was mine in this life, the one that had come before, and every damn one that would follow.

CHAPTER 27

NISSA

"Veil. What happened?" Eisley's voice snapped me out of the daze I was in, staring at Kierden's face. His chest was still rising and falling, though slowly, and he looked paler than he should've. He was unconscious—but just unconscious, I hoped.

"I almost died," I rasped. I could feel Kierden's blood moving through me, *healing* me, but it would take time. "He saved me. Again."

"You saved him first. And then again, too," she pointed out, kneeling next to me and putting two fingers on his throat. She was checking for his pulse, I thought.

Near-death experiences were probably expected for her, at that point. After so many centuries of battle, it must've been inevitable. I supposed that was enough to keep anyone calm when another one arose.

"Slow, but healthy," she told me. "He'll be just fine." She carefully wiped at a bit of blood on my neck, her lips turning down in a grimace.

"Where's the Beast?" My head turned back to where he'd been.

"Even he wasn't fast enough to handle an army of fae warriors. When it became clear that he couldn't win, he took off. With the eclipse coming in a few hours, I doubt he'll attempt to return." Eisley's gaze dipped to Kierden's hand, and her gaze lingered. "The brand's already gone."

I nodded, still a little shaky. "Alida said if we sealed it, the brand would vanish. The connections are through magic, and our magic changed permanently when the bond solidified."

Her eyebrows shot upward. "Damn."

I looked back at Kierden, watching his chest rise and fall again just for the sake of my sanity.

Bright and Death shoved their way past the fae and stepped up on either side of me and Kierden, sniffing both of us as they pressed up against us. I leaned against Death a little, scratching Bright lightly behind the ears as my eyelids started to grow heavy.

"I think I need to rest," I whispered to Eisley.

"Let's get you back to the castle," she agreed, eyeing Bright and Death. Both of them had wounds and were bleeding in multiple places, but they seemed fine otherwise.

Death ducked a head under Kierden's arm, and Bright growled at him.

He stopped and gave her a long look.

She growled at him again, and he lowered his head toward her before he stepped up close to me and inclined his head. My arm went up over his neck, and Eisley lifted me onto his back as he bent down a bit.

My face buried into his fur, and I felt the warm stickiness of his blood against one of my arms as I carefully wrapped them around him.

"I'm sorry," I whispered to him, realizing why Bright had gotten mad at him when he tried to take Kierden. He was more injured than she was.

He licked my arm lightly, and my guilt softened.

"He still wants to help. Stubborn bastard," Bright grumbled as she bent down. Eisley helped shove Kierden's massive body onto Bright's back, and then Bright slipped into the jungle, her movements smooth and careful. A few bands of ice wrapped around her and the other four of us followed.

It took a lot longer to get back to the castle than it normally would've, but I didn't complain.

I was alive and well, and Kierden was too. We needed rest— probably a lot of rest—but we were okay. And that was what mattered.

When Death reached Kierden's room in the castle, I was shivering a little, and could barely keep my eyes open. He carefully placed me on the bed, and Bright did the same with

Kierden. My side met his, and I curled toward him as my heavy eyes started to close.

"I'm going to bring you food soon and check on you frequently," Eisley warned me. She brushed a few strands of hair off my face, then placed the back of her hand against my forehead to check my temperature. "I don't know much about how humans heal, but you seem alright," she said. I thought it was more to herself than to me.

"I'm a fae now," I murmured to her, finally giving up on the fight with my eyelids. "Kierden's magic will have changed me in all the ways that matter."

She flipped my hair away from my ear and lightly tapped on the gentle curve of it. "Not here."

My lips curved upward slightly.

Kierden loved my ears.

She smoothed my hair back into place carefully, despite the blood and dirt in it. "Get some rest. I'll be back soon."

I was already lost to sleep.

Eisley woke me up to eat sometime later, and attempted to wake Kierden too. He didn't so much as flinch. When I reached out to his mind to make sure he was alright, I didn't feel anything concerning, so she gave up on it and left us to get more sleep.

. . .

Kierden's blood must've worked well, because the next time she woke me up, I already felt much, much better. When we looked at my wounds, we were shocked to find them almost entirely healed. Though I still felt sore, I was no longer in terrible pain.

Bright and Death woke up just long enough to scarf down the food Eisley brought them, then fell back to sleep almost instantly when they'd finished.

Once again, we couldn't get Kierden to wake up. Eisley was starting to worry, though she was trying to act like everything was fine for my sake.

"I'm almost healed," I told her quietly, so I wouldn't wake the esu. "If he's not up in a few hours, I'll make him drink my blood the way he made me drink his."

"He'd kill me if I let you do that so soon after you've recovered," she protested. "I'm sure he'll wake up soon."

I didn't argue with her, because she was taking care of me, and I didn't want her to worry that I'd take it into my own hands. But I wasn't concerned with Kierden's potential anger; I could handle it. And if my wounds were healed, I wouldn't die if he drained me the way I'd drained him.

I nodded my agreement, eating the food she'd brought me quickly before handing her my plate. She fussed with my hair, the way she'd taken to doing, and then slipped out of the room.

Though I fell asleep quickly, I did so with one thought in my mind:

Making sure Kierden was alright.

The next time Eisley fed me and the esu, she was even more worried. I didn't mention her concern, because I was going to wake him up as soon as she left.

After the esu went to sleep and she slipped out again, I waited a few minutes to make sure no one else was going to barge in, and then I carefully rolled on top of Kierden. His wounds had only healed a tiny bit, but none were actively bleeding, so I hoped that was a good sign.

He didn't react to me laying on top of him, so I carefully leaned down, pressing the top of my shoulder against his lips as I reached toward his mind.

Instead of his mind, I found... him.

His whole *being*.

I shivered at the intensity of finding him there so completely. His thoughts and emotions were silent because of the deep unconsciousness, but it wasn't just his mind I'd found; it was his *soul*.

We'd have time to explore that part of the bond later, though. After we were both healed, and conscious.

"Kierden," I said quietly, into his mind.

His body stirred below mine, and a huge hand landed on my lower back.

"Bite me, Kierden."

He groaned beneath me.

When I repeated the words louder, making them a full-on command, he finally reacted.

His teeth sank into my neck, and I gasped at the intensity of the feeling. It didn't hurt at all—honestly, it was one of the most pleasant things I'd ever felt. It wasn't like the Beast's bite, where an unfortunate bliss washed over me. Instead, I just felt some mixture of joy, pleasure, and desire.

His hands found my hips as my life flooded into him. He'd given it to me first, though, so the trade only seemed fair.

Some amount of time passed; I wasn't keeping track.

But then he jerked his head away, gasping for breath and rolling me off of him.

The world spun around me as he snarled at me—I was getting a lecture, I thought—but I couldn't keep myself awake. My eyes closed, and I went back to sleep immediately.

"Nissa," Kierden growled into my mind. His hands were on my hips, and I felt my bare chest pressed against his. A thick blanket had been pulled over the top of me, but it didn't feel nearly as nice as the warm body I was laying on. *"You need to wake up and eat."*

"Hmm?" I struggled to rouse myself from sleep.

"Open those pretty eyes, little human." He still sounded angry at me, but I wrestled them open anyway—and then froze when I saw his eyes staring down at me.

One was his gorgeous dark blue... and one was my typical green.

"Veil," I breathed.

Kierden swept hair off my face, then leaned forward and kissed my lips softly. He pulled away before the kiss could grow intense, unfortunately, and growled, "I am *furious* with you."

I closed my eyes again. "Tell me later. I'm tired."

"You can sleep after you've eaten."

I sighed heavily.

"Thank you, Eisley. I'll make sure she eats," Kierden told his sister, in a voice much kinder than the one he'd been giving me. Guess I earned his anger by letting him drink from me so soon after my brush against the veil.

I opened my eyes long enough to wave at her, and she winked at me before she closed the door behind herself. She looked much calmer than she had the last time I saw her, so I was glad at least one person appreciated what I'd done.

Kierden plucked that thought right out of my mind.

"I *appreciate* you worrying about me enough to feed me your blood." He set my plate on my lap then picked up a sandwich and lifted it to my lips.

I reluctantly bit into it.

He added, "But you should've stopped me before you passed out. You should've snapped me out of it and made sure I didn't hurt you."

"It definitely didn't hurt," I said after I swallowed the food in my mouth.

He let out a long breath, leaning back against the bed's headboard. "You scared me, Nissa. Veil, I've never been so terrified in my damn life."

"You didn't seem scared. Just thirsty." Though I knew he was talking about my near-death experience, I would rather discuss the blood drinking.

He gave me an exasperated look, and I matched it with one of my own as I plucked the sandwich from his hand and took another bite.

He stared at me while I ate it.

I stared back at him.

Finally he shook his head and raked a hand through his hair.

I noticed the dried blood all over him, and the fresh skin where his injuries had been. "We need to bathe."

"I'm worrying about you," he growled at me. "Let me worry."

I put my plate on his lap and tossed the blanket off my body, turning a bit so he could see me. "Look, Kierden. I'm fine. My wounds are healed. My body doesn't hurt anymore."

"You're still pale and covered in dried blood." He tossed a hand toward me. "You were *dying*, Nissa. I felt you *dying*." The grit in his voice was a clear sign of what he was really worried about.

There was nothing I could say to take that memory from him, or to prevent him from worrying. But, I could prove that I was alright.

I slipped out of bed, patting Death's head lightly and scratching Bright behind the ears as I passed them.

Kierden set our food down on the bed and followed me across the room. "What are you doing?"

"Taking a bath. There's nothing like a pool of cold water to revive you after a near-death experience."

He scowled. "It won't feel cold to you. My magic is yours now. I—"

"Ohhhh." I sank into the water, closing my eyes.

Somehow, it felt *warm*.

I leaned back against the inner edge of the bathing pool. "This is even better than the hot pool."

"I know," he grumbled, reluctantly stepping into the bath with me. He had me seated on his lap a moment later, and I leaned against his chest as his arms wrapped around my abdomen.

"I'm sorry I almost died," I told him quietly. "That wasn't my intention. The Beast needed to kill you, and I hoped I could persuade him to leave me alive while Bright saved your life. It clearly didn't work as I hoped."

"Bright told me you were planning to offer yourself up as his mate," Kierden growled at me, his grip tightening.

"It was an option. But Alida told me just before I left that sealing our bond was an option too, so I wasn't rushing into offering myself to him. I didn't know if I was really ready for the bond, and I didn't want to force you into it when I wasn't sure you wanted it, but I was dying. I figured I might as well seal it to save you."

"Veil." He gritted his teeth.

I sighed, leaning my head back against his shoulder. "I'm sorry."

"No. I just—" he cut himself off, growling, "How could you think I wouldn't want the bond? How could you think I'd be *upset* about having your magic in my veins and your thoughts in my mind? I feel blessed, Nissa—so damn *blessed* to be your mate. I hate that I got you hurt, and I despise that I couldn't protect you from the Beast, but I am *thrilled* that you sealed the bond."

Emotion swelled in my chest, lodging itself in my throat.

There was a moment's pause before he admitted, "I probably deserve to die for it, but I'd do it all again if I knew it would bring me back to this moment. Holding you in my arms, smelling my scent on your skin, feeling your heart beating against mine... You're my mate, Nissa. My *mate*." He pressed his lips to my shoulder once, then again, like he just couldn't help himself. "It's surreal."

"It is," I admitted, and he brushed a kiss to my shoulder again. My emotions were thick and fierce, a verified whirlwind. But the strongest of them was relief.

Relief that he wanted me and wasn't angry I'd sealed the bond. That he hadn't changed his mind without the threat of the Beast hanging over our heads.

"Do you feel ready for the connection now?" he asked me.

"I think so? I'm not sure. If we had the option, I would've waited longer. Not because I doubted you, but because I worry I'll decide I want to leave your kingdom and become a nomad, or do something entirely different with my life, while you're tied to the castle."

"I'm tied to nothing but you now, little human. If you want to see all of Evare, we'll see it all. If you want to farm plants and continue growing an absurd amount of flowers all over my kingdom, that's what we'll do. You are my first priority— nothing and no one else. Eisley would be a better queen than I am king, anyway." He kissed my shoulder again.

My lips curved upward. I had no current intention to ask him to sacrifice his throne, but his words made me feel a bit better about my place versus his kingdom's.

"You'll feel more confident after you've recovered," he told me, running a hand lightly down my thigh. "I'm going to wash you, get you fed, and put you back to bed."

My smile grew. "That sounds nice."

"Mmhm." He kissed my throat, and then my cheek, before he started scrubbing me.

As he washed me, I decided that even if shared baths for the rest of my life were the only benefit of a sealed mate bond, I had made a very, very good choice in sealing ours.

CHAPTER 28

NISSA

I slept for most of the the next two days. When I finally woke up long enough for more than a meal and a short conversation with Kierden, I found myself in bed with the gorgeous king, draped over his lap while he read a book.

"When did I become your table?" I murmured to him, looking over my shoulder at the edge of the book he had resting on my back.

He chuckled and his body rumbled against me, making me smile a little. "When you became my mate."

My body felt strangely warm.

A yawn stretched my lips. Kierden lifted his book when I slipped off his side, spreading my arms and legs out to stretch a little. I frowned at the increasing warmness in my body. And... wetness between my thighs? "Why am I horny?"

"Welcome to the eclipse, little human." He slid his hand into my hair and massaged my scalp lightly. I closed my eyes and groaned at the blissfulness of it.

"Has there been any sign of the Beast coming back?" I asked him.

"Luckily for him, no." Kierden's voice was playful, though we both knew it would be no laughing matter if the Beast really did come back. "A few of our warriors followed his trail back toward the Broken Woods."

"Oh, damn. I mentioned mating with a shifter when I was trying to buy time—you don't think he's actually going to do it, do you?"

"I think the shifters can defend themselves just as thoroughly as the fae can. Don't worry about them."

I sighed. "Alright."

"Reo dropped some new clothing off for you yesterday. I put it in our closet, if you'd like to see it," Kierden said, still massaging my scalp.

I sat up quickly. I'd finally stopped gaining weight a few weeks earlier, and my curves had been a little too much for the last batch of dresses. I was *dying* to know what he'd created now that he knew I wouldn't need something new in a few days—pun not intended.

"Let's go."

Kierden grinned, tossing his book to the bed as he slipped out from beneath the blankets with me. I grabbed his hand and towed him to the closet, halting in the doorway. My lips parted when I took in a full row of vibrantly-colored fabrics, in all of the same shades as my flowers. "I love them," I whispered.

Kierden laughed. "You haven't even tried them on." He opened a simple set of drawers and pulled out a pair of scanties, dangling them toward me.

I snagged them from his fingers, then grabbed the first dress I saw—one in the same shade of orange as my old favorite. Stripping out of the simple shirt I had on took all of one moment, and then I tugged the scanties on, followed by the dress.

Kierden followed me to the bathroom as I went to see myself in the mirror. He leaned up against the doorway while I stared at myself for a long, long moment.

I looked... good.

Healthy.

Strong, too.

The dress was cut perfectly to the shape of my body, with sections missing from the sides to show off my figure. The thin, soft sleeves hung off my shoulders and over my arms, and the part over my breasts was heart-shaped, emphasizing the weight of them.

"Veil," I whispered. Slowly, I lifted my eyes to meet Kierden's in the mirror. He wasn't looking at my face when I did, though. "What do you think?"

"It would look a damn lot better on the ground, with you bent over our bed," he said.

My lips stretched in a wide grin, my fresh scanties already damp thanks to the heat of the eclipse. "I'll take that as a compliment."

"You should."

My gaze dipped to his shorts. More accurately, to the fabric tented at the front of them.

My body warmed. "It's been a few days since we've had sex."

"Believe me, I know." The low tone of his voice made me hotter.

I grinned and tugged my dress back over my head. As I did so, my gaze caught on the handprint around my wrist.

My eyes widened as I finally gave it the attention it deserved.

The damn thing glowed, and it glowed brightly.

"Let me see your hand," I told him, tugging it out of his pocket without waiting for him to give it to me, and then staring down at the glow in wonder. "Damn."

"Miraculous, isn't it?"

"It's beautiful," I admitted—and then nearly choked on my own damn spit when he sent me a mental image of his glowing hand between my thighs as he pinned me to our bed and toyed with my clit.

Heat flushed my cheeks when the mental image progressed into a full-on fantasy of us having sex, his hand glowing against my body while we moved.

The eclipse must've been going for a while, if he was already fantasizing about me.

Then again, we'd been having a *lot* of sex before we both nearly died, so he could've just been horny.

He hooked his fingers in the waistband of my scanties and used them to tug me closer. My chest met his, and his lips curved upward. "The suns haven't even overlapped yet, little human —and the eclipse affects fae far more than humans. The wetness between your thighs is just the beginning."

Well damn, I liked the sound of that.

"So should we hold off as long as possible?" I checked.

He dipped his fingers deeper into my scanties, and my body arched as he dragged them lightly over my clit.

Veil, that was more intense than it should've been.

His gaze met mine, and there was a challenge in it. "I'd prefer to get an early start."

"It *is* our first eclipse together. We should make it count."

"Precisely," he rubbed my clit again, his touch still light. I leaned against him, my eyes closing as I grabbed his arms and held on. My body was far more reactive than usual—and it was always reactive for him.

"Veil," I whispered, my breaths coming out rapidly as I already neared the edge of my first climax.

Kierden slid a finger inside me, and I cried out, so damn close to losing it. His finger went still though, and his hand held my hips securely to stop me from using his hand.

I hissed, "Dammit, Kierden."

He chuckled, low and deep. "If you want pleasure today, you take it on my cock."

"Fine." I pushed his shorts down, freeing his cock. "Fill me, then."

His eyes gleamed, and he didn't wait for another invitation. He lifted me up and spun me around until my back met the bathroom wall, hard, as he ripped my scanties off and yanked me down on his cock. The motion was harsh, but with the eclipse already affecting me, it felt incredible.

"You feel so damn good," he growled at me, thrusting into me and taking me over the edge.

I cried out as the pleasure hit me—and then screamed when his teeth sank into my shoulder, dragging the climax out longer and making it insanely intense. His body quaked as he filled me with his release.

I sucked in deep breaths of air when I came down from the high. He released my shoulder, licking the wound clean before capturing my mouth in his. His cock throbbed inside me as he kissed me, our bodies still intertwined as our tongues danced.

His hands lowered to my ass, and one of his fingers brushed my back entrance. I sucked in a harsh breath as another one of his mental images hit me—this one, of me on my hands and knees in front of him. My legs were spread wide, his cock was buried deep inside me, stretching my wet, pink skin... and he held a cylinder of ice inside my ass.

"Veil," I moaned, as his fingers slicked over my asshole. We hadn't tried that yet, but he'd mentioned it in passing. I'd never thought I'd like it...

"You would love it," he growled, answering the thought I hadn't voiced. "There's nothing more intense."

"Prove it," I breathed.

He hauled me back to our bed and set me down on the edge, sliding his cock free before he kneeled in front of me. His pleasure dripped down my thighs, but I knew from experience that he didn't give a damn about the mess unless he thought it might bother me.

He parted my thighs, lowering his face to my core and tilting me back. My forearms collided with the mattress, but I caught myself as he said, "You'll take my finger first."

I opened my mouth to reply, but then his tongue was on my clit, and he was sliding a piece of ice shaped like his cock inside my channel. It wasn't cold; just smooth, and hard.

He worked my clit slowly with his mouth—I could tell he didn't want me to climax again yet, but enjoyed it anyway. His fingers dragged the slickness of our combined pleasure to my back entrance, and then massaged the sensitive skin there lightly.

My pleasure heightened with the touch, and heightened further when the slick tip of his finger stretched me.

I sucked in a sharp breath, and he stopped.

"Don't stop," I demanded.

He licked my clit again, but pulled away before I could climax.

I swore and bucked my hips as his finger sank deeper inside my ass, stretching me wider and wider. The need for release was borderline painful, but in a way I was absolutely feral for. I cried out as ice covered his finger, stretching me further.

"You are so damn beautiful like this," he said, leaning back to look at me. An image from his point of view hit me—my legs spread wide, my body bare, and my channel and back entrance both full of ice. My hips were rocking with need, and his hands were on my thighs, holding me in place.

"Don't torture me," I panted to him.

He chuckled, grabbing the ice in my channel and slowly sliding it free. "I feel your emotions bleeding into mine, little human. You love this."

He was right.

My hips bucked desperately against his grip, my body clenching around nothing as I snarled at him, "Give me your cock, now."

Kierden's eyes burned. "That's right, little human. I'm yours to command—don't forget it."

He flipped me onto my stomach with one motion and tucked my knees up beneath me, before he lifted my ass and slid home slowly enough to make me detonate.

I screamed, my body jerking as he thrust into me harder and faster. The ice in my ass swelled larger, and the pleasure was so intense I could've sworn I touched the veil.

When my climax ended, I collapsed to the mattress with a groan. The eclipse must've been beginning, because my body was somehow even hotter and needier than before.

Kierden slapped my ass lightly, and I shuddered. "How long is the desire going to last?"

"All day and all night. You'll be deliciously sore tomorrow." He thrust in and pulled out.

I shuddered again. "I already want more. This is absolutely insane."

"Soon, your thoughts will fade, and you'll do nothing but *feel*. Prepare to embrace the insanity, Nissa Jirev. You're my mate now; you'll never spend an eclipse out of my arms again."

Heat flooded my body, and I clenched around Kierden's cock, making him growl. "I like the sound of that."

"Good. Now, open your eyes and tilt your head so you can watch me slide in and out of your channel. I want you to see yourself climax."

More heat flared as I did as he said, and sure enough, I watched my body writhe with pleasure only moments later.

There was no thinking that day—only feeling.

And veil, I definitely understood why the fae celebrated eclipses.

CHAPTER 29

NISSA

It was the middle of the next day before we finally made it into the dining hall, exhausted and sore, but ridiculously content. We talked with the elves—they were heading out later that day—and then chatted with Eisley and a few of the other warriors.

When we were done eating, we headed down to my farm with Bright and Death. They kept brushing up against each other's sides and making these adorable purring noises. Kierden flashed me a grin from where he was planting seeds, and I mirrored his with my own.

Our bonded esu went off together, leaving me and Kierden to the plants near the front end of my farm.

"Have fun," I told Bright.

She chuffed. *"Oh, I will."*

My grin widened.

We finished planting where we were, and then headed out on a short walk. He captured my hand, lacing his fingers between mine and lifting my hand to his lips as we went. *"Thank you for saving me,"* he murmured into my mind.

"You're the one who saved me, remember?" I tilted my head toward him, and a soft breeze caught my hair, dragging the long strands into the air. It made me think of Kaelle. The fae brought me news of her and Laeli when they returned with their empty carts after taking the extra produce to the other kingdoms, but they hadn't told me anything that made me think anyone really knew what was happening to the human women and their kings.

I liked to believe that they were determined enough to forge themselves lives that they loved in those kingdoms, but I'd reach out soon myself to make sure.

Kierden said, *"We saved each other on multiple occasions. It's a good way to begin a life together, though I pray to whatever gods still remain that you never have to risk your life for me again."*

My lips curved upward. *"I'll add my prayers to yours, then."*

He chuckled, and we continued walking. My eyes scanned the jungle above us, following the vines and flowers down every tree trunk. My magic had flooded everything with life, making the colors richer and the plants more energetic. The fruit grew thick and rich, the vegetables monstrous and full of flavor.

Like the jungle, I was still the same as I'd been in my mother's town. I had the same breath in my lungs and heart in my chest, but since I'd come to Jirev, I'd been brought to life.

Thinking of my town... I looked at Kierden. "Did you send your fae to raid my mother?"

His lips curved upward wickedly. "Of course I did."

I heaved a sigh, but it turned into a laugh as I shook my head. "No one died?"

"Not even your mother. My fae distributed the money and produce among the towns nearby that looked worse for the wear. I wanted to do it myself, but Eisley warned me that you may not forgive me for tearing out your mother's throat, so I decided to stay."

"Probably a good choice," I said with a soft smile. "Thank you. And for what it's worth, I love you."

"It's worth a great deal, little human." He leaned over and brushed a kiss to my cheek. "And I love you."

I smiled up at the flowers above me as we continued walking. My magic still emanated from me without my control, but something about it felt settled alongside our mate bond.

I couldn't wait to keep practicing with it, to see if I could learn even a shred of control.

It was a simple thing, really, to look forward to a future. But it was a simple thing I'd never had before—and one I would cherish for the rest of my life.

Bonus Scene

Nissa—a few weeks after the eclipse

"*This is a terrible idea,*" I whispered into Kierden's mind, as he sat me down on his lap in the corner of the dining hall. It was early in the morning, so we were all alone, other than the chefs in the kitchen. I'd finally met them a few days earlier, and they were ridiculously nice.

There was no way of telling how long it would be until someone else walked into the dining hall though—which was what made this idea terrible.

"*This is a fantastic idea.*" He set our plate down in front of us before dropping a hand to my thigh.

Dipping his fingers beneath the hem of my dress, he dragged them lightly over my clit, making me flush. I wasn't wearing any scanties, which had been his idea—and honestly, I supported it.

I grabbed a pastry off our plate and took a big bite of it to keep myself quiet.

Though I was in my longest dress, my longest dress was still extremely short, and that made our current escapade very, very risky.

"My good little human, already drenched for me," Kierden growled, slipping his fingers into my channel, then dragging them over my clit again.

I fought a groan. *"You're already hard for me, too."*

"I'm always hard for you." He rocked my ass against his erection, just a little.

He also wasn't wearing any undergarments. I was still unsure as to whether we'd actually be able to have full-on sex in the dining room, but we'd figured we might as well be prepared.

"Eat, Nissa." He snatched the pastry from me with his free hand and lifted it to my mouth.

I took a bite, choking on the food as I nearly inhaled it when he pinched my clit.

"You're so damn bossy."

He pinched me again. *"You love it."*

I really did love it.

He continued teasing my clit and feeding me. I gripped the edge of the table for dear life, letting him have his way with me as I edged closer to my climax.

Just before I lost control, he lifted my ass for a moment—and then slid me onto his cock.

I choked on a cry at the intense pressure of the tight fit. My legs weren't parted much, thanks to our position and my lack of undergarments. *"Veil."*

"So tight and slick," he growled into my mind as he moved my hips until he was fully sheathed inside me. *"You're too good to me, little human."*

My body trembled.

I wasn't sure I could put words together even if I tried.

His fingers found my clit again. *"Bite the bread and I'll let you climax."*

I bit it, and he worked my clit. His fingers stilled just before I lost control, and I started to growl at him—but then the doors opened.

A pair of male fae came in, their fingers intertwined and their hands glowing gold.

My body went stiff as a board while I tried to reign my need in, and Kierden tugged my skirt down, so it covered us both.

There would be no doubt about what was going on if they came any closer.

They nodded at Kierden, and he nodded back as they grabbed food from the kitchen and then settled in the other corner of the room.

They faced away from us as they ate, and my king's fingers slid to my clit again.

"This is so risky," I hissed at him.

"If you didn't love it, you wouldn't be soaking my cock right now." He sucked lightly on my throat. *"Give me a climax, and I'll let you go."*

I groaned silently. *"Kierden."*

"Nissa." He nipped at my shoulder. *"The longer you wait, the more people will show up."*

"We're going to be sitting here all day then," I said bluntly.

He chuckled. *"Alright. If they don't leave soon, I'll get us to an empty room."*

"Deal."

He stroked my clit slowly, and the pleasure began to build again. Whenever my gaze flicked to the men in the other corner, Kierden would send me a mental image of his cock sliding inside me—or of his tongue between my thighs—or of me, sitting on his face.

The heat built, and built, until I was nearly panting. I started moving my hips a little, clenching around his cock, and he picked up the pace on my clit.

Just before I lost it, the men at the table got up—already done.

I snarled into Kierden's mind as we both froze, and he lifted another piece of bread to my mouth.

I took a violent bite, and we both waved at the men as they left.

As soon as the doors shut behind them, Kierden flung a hand out toward them to freeze them shut. He did the same to the doors to the kitchen as he hauled me up onto the table, pushing the food out of the way. My tits met the wood as he slammed into me, and I cried out into his mind as my climax *finally* hit. He drenched my channel with his release—and then pulled out quickly, yanked my dress back down, and tucked his cock back into his shorts.

"We're leaving," he told me, grabbing our plate and leading me toward the door. My body was positioned in front of his to hide his erection. He pulled the ice down from the doors with a glance at them, opening everything back up.

A big group of people stepped in just as we stepped out, and Kierden grunted a greeting at them as we passed.

He led me into the room nearest to the dining hall. The door shut behind us—and then our plate clattered to the ground as Kierden pinned me to the wall. He kissed me, his mouth brutal on mine.

"That was so damn sexy, little human," he growled into my mind. *"You were perfect."*

He released my mouth, then dragged me to the ground. *"You're going to sit on my face now. I need to hear you scream."*

My face flushed. "I—" I began, but he cut me off with his tongue and teeth on my clit as he held me against his face. A cry escaped me at the first sensation, and then I was lost to the pleasure.

He definitely got what he wanted—but honestly, so did I.

EPILOGUE

"Swords out, swords out, swords out," I bellowed at the hoard of small, yelling warriors who sprinted through the castle's hallway. Our children loved running around like wild animals—and we loved watching them grin like madmen.

The violent events we held to keep the peace every year were going on in the stadium, but Nissa, Kaelle, and Laeli had convinced the other kings and I to spend the day watching our children run around together instead.

It hadn't taken much convincing at all.

"The gourd king has risen!" Ravv barked, as we jogged behind the kids. "Go, go, go!"

We came around the corner, and found Nissa's forehead wrinkled furiously. Her hands were held out toward the massive yellow gourd as she focused her magic on it. Control was still a struggle at times, but she had figured it out for the most part.

All of the kids started hacking at the large, squishy vegetable with their dull icy swords, shouting insults at the *"smelly, rabid beast"*.

I pushed my magic toward Nissa, and she flashed me a quick smile as she took a hold of it. The gourd king swelled even larger, growing just as lopsided as I knew she was hoping it would.

The kids yelled with renewed fury and swung harder and faster, throwing in some punches and kicks too.

"He's falling!" one of my boys hollered. "Harder!"

I tugged Nissa away from the massive vegetable, pulling her back flush against my front just in time for our little warriors to defeat their monster.

Cheers of victory erupted from them, and they started jumping, dancing, and laughing about the king they had slain.

"You're so damn perfect," I murmured to Nissa, brushing a kiss to her cheek.

"I know, I know," she teased me.

I squeezed her tightly, thanking the veil that the Beast had sent me running toward the little human who had brought me more happiness than I could've ever imagined.

THE END

AFTERTHOUGHTS

When I sat down to write this book, I sat down to write something that would challenge me. That's probably a terrible thing to admit, but here I am, admitting it.

I wanted to see if I could create my current personal idea of a perfect book—a medium-length standalone fantasy romance, with plenty of steam but also real relationship building. I wanted the characters to start at zero, at neutrality and maybe even a little hatred, and become not just lovers, but friends. I wanted to see if I could balance the feelings of healing and hope I love, with the larger plots and deeper emotions of my favorite high fantasy books.

Despite my intentions, the book did not turn out perfect. I don't think I'll ever write a perfect book, honestly. I spent nearly as much time editing this one as I did writing it, which never happens. But that's what I love about being an indie author—that I get to learn and grow constantly as I write. And despite this book's many imperfections, I love the way Kierden and Nissa's story turned out. I love the dynamics of their relationship, and I love that as I wrote and edited it, I got myself that much closer to the ever-elusive "perfect" book. Anyway, I have so much planned for the world of Evare, and I can't wait to see where Laeli's story takes me next. The elves' assassins will also be getting their own series after I'm finished with our trio of fae kings, and I am SO excited to see what happens with the Beast and his future woman.

As always, thank you so much for reading!

All the love,

Lola Glass <3

P.S. thank you to the wonderful ladies in my Facebook group who won my giveaway and helped me create a few of the side characters for this series! Emily and Alison, I hope you love how Eisley and Alida turned out! Maybe we'll see them again in future series... only time will tell ;)

ALL SERIES BY LOLA GLASS

Fantasy Romance-

Forbidden Mates

Wild Hunt

Kings of Disaster

Night's Curse

Burning Kingdom

Sacrificed to the Fae King

Shifter Queen

Supernatural Underworld

Paranormal Romance-

Feral Pack

Mate Hunt

Wolfsbane

Shifter City

Moon of the Monsters

Rejected Mate Refuge

Outcast Pack

ABOUT THE AUTHOR

Lola is a book-lover with a *slight* romance obsession and a passion for love—real love. Not the flowers-and-chocolates kind of love, but the kind where two people build a relationship strong enough to last. That's the kind of relationship she loves to read about, and the kind she tries to portray in her books.

Even if they're about shifters :)